The Faerie Guild Trials

Earth & Shadows
Book One

G. L. PRESTON
FANTASY AUTHOR

Cover art copyright © 2024 by Gem. L. Preston
www.glpreston.com

Line and Copy Edit by Brittany Corley
www.thisbitchreads.com

ISBN: 978-1-7393193-8-0

This book is a work of pure fiction created from the
author's imagination.

To those who have spent most of their lives living in survival mode, and the ones who can spot the predators around them.

If you cannot find revenge, then I hope you find peace.

Content warning

The Faerie Guild Trials is an adult romantasy between a morally grey dark elf with childhood trauma, and a charming but secretive male. While fun, the story includes elements that might not be suitable for some readers. Graphic violence, death, mental health, sexual content, and alcohol consumption are all depicted. Readers who may be sensitive to these elements, please take note.

The Guilds

Seelie Court:

The Luz Guild – Light fae
The Mona Guild – Lunar faeries, Werewolves
The Kora Guild – Dryads, Woodland Nymph
The Aigua Guild – Water nymph, Siren, Selkie

Unseelie Court:

The Umbra Guild – Dark fae
Asgell Guild – Harpy, Griffin
The Daeva Guild – Vampires, Kappa, Lamia
The Voda Guild – Hydra, Afanc

The High King is dead.
With no known heir to
take his place.
Let the games begin...

Of all the Unseelie Generals that have lived, none have ever been as feared as Lord Bron Mathonwy, brother of High King Gwydion. His cold and efficient methods are notorious, and weakness met with disdain.
Rumours state this even applies to his own family…
UNSEELIE FAMILIES OF THE AGES BY KAEL ARTURIAN

CHAPTER ONE

For three days, she had hunted him.
Not someone of great significance, merely a petty thief. But he had dared to steal from Lord Bron Mathonwy, General of the Unseelie King. And in the faerie courts, they did not take such transgressions lightly. Efia knew this all too well; after all, she was Bron's daughter, and the consequences of her transgressions were carved upon her back.

Efia navigated the bustling night of the Unseelie court, her cloak draping around her like a veil of pure darkness. Though her prey was skilled at evading capture, he couldn't outwit her for long.

Having uncovered his usual haunts and hiding spots, Efia was prepared to end her hunt tonight. She tracked him through the crowded alleyways, Efia observed his hurried steps, leading her to a secluded area. With the cover of darkness and the revelry of the night providing a distraction, she closed in on him.

He turned into a dimly lit alley, bumping his should on the corner as he did so. Efia descended from the rooftops, dropping herself directly in his path. Startled, the fae froze, his eyes widening as he realized his predicament.

Realised who exactly stood in front of him.

Efia saw the fear flicker in his gaze, mirrored by the turmoil within her heart. Was this truly justice?

With a wave of her hand, the shadows peeled away from their surroundings, taking shape and forming ominous figures behind him. A dark stain started to form on the front of the male's breeches, knowing what was coming.

"Bron sends his regards," Efia said coldly. Her hand flexed and her shade lunged forward. Without mercy, it impaled through the fae's chest with a shard of solid blackness.

The fae choked, a drop of blood falling from the corner of his mouth before the shadow receded, and his body crumpled to the ground.

Efia crouched over his body and claimed a trophy—a finger—as proof of her accomplishment. She retreated into the night, leaving behind no trace of her presence.

But all would know who had committed such an act.

That Bron had sent his Nüwch to dole out what punishment he'd seen fit.

And all would learn from the fae's mistake.

"Marin Velarde," Efia extended the severed finger as evidence of a completed task, announcing the name of the thief. Her father made a disgusted noise in his throat, the dimly lit study revealing the sharp contours of his face.

"That back-alley thief stole from *me*? I'll have the guards on duty strung from the gates. How will this look to the other guilds?" Bron scrutinised the finger with a calculated gaze. "Well." He picked up the digit, turning it around in his hand. "At least *you* proved useful to me, Efia."

His praise was as cold as his demeanour, and she nodded in acknowledgement.

"Any update from that lunar faerie you keep?" he asked.

Efia bit back her frustration. He always referred to Wen as if she were some kind of pet. But she needed him to think that of her.

"There was a disagreement between the siren elders. Almoira is dead."

Bron grinned. Almoira was allegedly a close friend of the Seelie queen. Any loss for her was a plus for the Unseelie court.

"Good. Tomorrow," he put the finger down and turned his attention to Efia, "there will be an announcement from King Lew and Queen Lilah."

Efia's curiosity was piqued. The King and Queen couldn't stand each other. Hardly ever graced each other's presence. Whatever it was must be important.

"What kind of news?"

Bron's teeth flashed in a wicked smile. "News that is going to change everything for us, Efia. Be ready."

That could only mean one thing—a decision on how the new High King or Queen would be chosen. High King Gwydion passed away six moons ago, leaving no children to take his place. Seelie Queen Lilah and Unseelie King Lew jointly managed the realm. But now everything was about to shift. A sliver of dread crept through Efia's bones as she contemplated what lied ahead…

Should the High Ruler meet their demise without a known heir, a tournament shall unfold to unveil the worthy candidate for the throne. The rulers of both the Seelie and Unseelie courts, while barred from direct participation, will orchestrate the necessary arrangements with a watchful eye over the proceedings.
THE CYTUNDEB, AS DICTATED BY HIGH KING GWYDION

CHAPTER TWO

There's nothing like the sound of tearing flesh in the morning.

Fresh dew still clings to the oak leaves and blades of grass, and the scent of iron now mingles with it.

I lean back against the trunk of a thick oak tree, staying away from the melodramatics and hoping the fractured peace between the courts will hold out until this meeting is over.

So many faerie folk from the Seelie and Unseelie courts in all gather in the Betwixt. The sole passage between realms—aside from portalling. A sacred space, where conflict between the Seelie and Unseelie courts is forbidden. This day will bring about a change in that dynamic.

It's already made for a deadly mix.

Already, a vampire had been torn apart by a manticore—the latter incapacitating the vamp with its lesser magic, then tearing his heart through his chest… and they're from the same court. Yet we all know, that if a conflict erupts between a Seelie and Unseelie, the royal guards will inevitably intervene.

Gwydion help us when the games begin.

Hundreds await the entrance of Seelie Queen Lilah and Unseelie King Lew, who will make a declaration on how our next high ruler will be determined.

The demise of High King Gwydion left no living heir. And according to a centuries-old treaty between Gwydion and the courts, in the absence of a successor, the throne will pass to the individual who prevails in a series of trials. This pact, established long before my birth, now will shape the destiny of the faerie realm.

Queen Lilah and King Lew themselves cannot ascend; they're poised to involve their offspring in the contention.

The specific trials awaiting us remained shrouded in mystery, although it's reasonable to assume they encompass elements of magic, guile, combat, and any challenges that would pit contestants against each other in a tournament to the death.

This meeting is the first opportunity to size up the competition.

Which is why I couldn't miss it.

Though both courts seem to be staying well clear of each other, an obvious divide down the clearing which has me rolling my eyes.

The whole idea seems like a farce. I remember the way my uncle, King Gwydion, spoke of a vision that seemed impossible to many but was, to him, the ultimate dream—peace between both courts and among all faeries.

He wasn't naive; he knew the challenges that lay ahead. He was unyielding in his conviction that our combined strength could forge a future where faeries of all kinds coexisted in harmony. It was a vision that stirred hearts and minds, sparking conversations and planting seeds of possibility.

Whilst he was alive…

Those conversations almost extinguished since his death.

An old heart, they said. Not that any faerie in existence ever died from such a thing.

But, from all appearances, that is what my beloved uncle passed from, still sitting at his breakfast table at Castell Narbeth. There was no sign of poison, wound or anything to suggest some faerie dared to take his life… not that his shades would have allowed anyone to get close enough for that.

I had to accept his passing.

Now, there shall be a fight to the death, or the throne. The prospect of which had never held an allure for me. Nevertheless, my father, Bron Mathonwy, meticulously groomed me for this very situation since my early years, shaping me into a dark fae warrior. Regrettably, I am nothing more than a means to an end in his eyes.

Despite being centuries too old to partake himself, he has no qualms about sacrificing his only daughter—at only twenty-eight cycles of the sun—to the whims of fate and the enemies of our guild.

In the event of my demise? One less mouth to feed.

So, following my father's orders and entering the competition is my best way forward. Gods, if being a queen means some sort of freedom from his grasp, then I'd take it.

The old fae hadn't even bothered to show up today, but from the long, thick brown curls I can see bouncing through the crowds, Branwen has.

She scrunches up her button nose and comes to stand beside me. My back straightens as she approaches and a smile tugs at the corner of my mouth.

"I can't believe you're doing this," Branwen mutters under her breath.

"Hey, Wen," I nod with a small smile.

Her large silver eyes scan the area, and she baulks at the faeries walking past us, their disdain and malice evident in their eyes—both Seelie and Unseelie alike. She childishly pokes her tongue out at a nymph who gives us a peculiar look as he walks past.

Branwen belongs to the lunar faeries of the Mona Guild. Her pure aura follows her around, like a cloudless night with starry skies. Her skin has always been a deep reddish brown, only broken up by the fawn-coloured freckles that scatter her shoulders and cheeks. She's short. But short enough to make a grown fae cry by tearing him down with how sharp her tongue can get when she's angry. Whilst physically she may not be the most intimidating, I'd hate to be on the wrong side of one of her tirades.

She's someone I am very lucky to call a friend.

Notably, she's a member of the Seelie court. Given her affiliation, it's unsurprising that we attract curious gazes from other faeries. What motivates a Seelie faerie to associate with an Unseelie dark fae like myself? Our intrinsic natures should inherently render our connection repugnant to each other.

However, Wen and I have shared a deep friendship since our young years.

Her full lips raise into a wry smile. "You do realise you're essentially at the top of their 'to eliminate' list, right?"

"I greatly appreciate your unwavering confidence in my capabilities," I reply in jest.

"It's not your competence that concerns me." A massive ogre that saunters by, each of its strides causing the ground to quiver. Wen's eyes widen. "It's the size of your competition."

I let out a dismissive snort. Leave it to Wen, who stands nearly a foot shorter than me, to emphasise the significance of size in combat.

"I believe these trials will be about intellect as well as strength, my dear Wen."

"No hope for you then, Efia," a deep voice breaks through the cacophony of the crowd. Emerging from behind a tree, a tall figure steps forward, his bright blue eyes locking onto mine. He positions himself beside me, leaning his shoulder against the tree.

Arms crossed, I offer a grin to our newfound companion, who exchanges greetings with Wen.

"Beinon," I say, "I was wondering when your *displeasing* presence would grace us."

Although, in truth, his presence is far from displeasing... that's a sentiment I'd never openly share for fear of inflating his ego.

A hint of a smirk pulls at his lips, sharp teeth teasing his lower lip. "You know I couldn't afford to miss out on this, especially with my mother's wrath in mind."

Indeed, his mother's intentions to seize the throne hinge on him, quite literally. He shifts his attention to survey the assembly of faeries.

"I'm surprised your father isn't here, Efia," Beinon says. He tucks his windblown blonde hair behind a pointed ear and my stomach dips at the sight. Beinon grins wider, rubbing the light scruff along the edge of his strong jawline as if realising where my thoughts went.

Beinon could easily win this contest and be a great king. He has the look for it. Fine muscles created from years of training. A beautiful smile that could charm the wings of many a faerie. Most importantly, the correct bloodline...

"Are you? Really?" I arch a brow.

He laughs, and his eyes soften, like the gentle waves of sea waters. "No." He elbows my ribs gently.

"At least you have us."

"Oh, yes." I laugh. "Mighty prince of the *Luz* Guild. You say that as if you won't be one of the faeries I'll be up against," I fire at him, only a hint of jest in my tone.

Each court holds several guilds, to which faerie races belong, and so far, almost every guild in both courts has submitted many faeries as entrants. Prominently featured are the vampires affiliated with the Daeva guild and the prolific nymphs and dryads hailing from the Kora guild. Their rapid reproduction rate ensures a surplus of candidates for sacrifice. Whatever group the winner belongs to would rise to rule, bringing notoriety and prosperity to their guild and their court.

Which is precisely both Beinon and I are competing, despite whether we want to or not.

"So, Beinon, are you going to kill me?" I tip my chin up in defiance and suppress my smile.

Beinon's eyes never leave mine, an expression I can't interpret on his face before he leans down. "You know I could never hurt you, Efia," he whispers, his warm breath brushing against the shell of my ear.

My head turns a fraction, and I hold out my hand. "Fancy making a bargain on it?"

He rolls his eyes.

"I don't need a magical bargain to know it would *never* happen."

"Ahhh," I say. "But you know your mother would never forgive you if you allowed me to live."

"Accurate." He leans back. "But since when do I do anything my mother wants?"

It was true, Beinon wasn't one to follow the rules. But in this case, it meant ruling over the realm or not. And his mother, Queen Lilah, would do anything to rule over the realm—even order her son to murder his best friend.

Beinon's entry is a result of his mother's insistence, as the queen's favourite. Yet, this competition sets the stage for our rivalry. I only hope that someone else takes care of Beinon before I'm forced to do it myself.

A low growl emanates from a passing brownie, its gaze filled with suspicion as it regards the three of us. Catching Wen's eye, I receive a shrug in response, her lavender flower-adorned sleeves fluttering with the motion.

I'm accustomed to the disdainful stares typically directed at us by fellow faeries. My friendship with two Seelies isn't the sole reason for the overt contempt we receive. It's my lineage that fuels the desire in many to slit my throat then and there.

The blood of Gwydion.

Gwydion's brother, Bron—my father—leads the Umbra Guild. As the late king's niece, the throne is out of my reach due to a rule that only faerie descendants can claim it. Despite this, I can win it from this contest. And all the faeries know about my magical abilities which were inherited from Gwydion and skipped my father to come to me.

A Nüwch—shade-wielder.

Over nine hundred years, only two individuals wielding the power of shadows have been born: Gwydion and myself. The source of this power remains enigmatic, a fact that fuels fear and trepidation among many faeries. During daylight hours, my manipulation of shadows is confined to its literal meaning—shadows. I can summon them forth like a dusky mist in the air, temporarily blinding people's sight. They often whisper in my ear. While their mutterings are often incomprehensible, I have grown adept at deciphering their urgency. These whispers can alert me to an approaching ally... or adversary.

It is at night when they are at their most powerful. When I can summon forth the darkness, turning them into more corporeal forms. Forms that can touch, forms that can kill.

This makes the faeries nervous.

It makes me a threat.

This potential danger is the reason my father had raised me to be like a dutiful soldier. He has meticulously cultivated my magical prowess and honed my abilities, ensuring that I can be unforgiving when time demands it. Even though I do not want the throne, my upbringing has been geared towards readiness. And any opportunity to escape that environment is an opportunity seized—a prospect for tranquillity, a shot at reprieve if my abilities are as feared as Gwydion's had been.

I propel myself onward; the bark grazing my back. Mindful of the impassive guards dispersed throughout the trees, who have started their approach toward the raised wooden platform at the heart of a sizable clearing.

Beinon noticed as well. "I'll see you later." He nods without a word before skulking off.

A large raven lands on a branch above our heads.

"Come on, Wen," I call over my shoulder. "They are arriving."

The anticipation in the air grows tense, and I make my way across the clearing towards the platform, pushing past the small pockets of faerie.

A light dusting of my shades rises around me, stroking like soft fingers over the skin of my cheek. Many around me take a step back, scared of the sentient-like energy. No one truly knows the extent of my powers, and I'm happy to keep it that way.

Gwydion could form corporeal shades in the middle of the day, having spent centuries training his abilities. It's something I hope to learn one day. But now with him gone… I'm unsure if it's something I'll ever attain.

A guard raises his staff, then strikes the ground once. The surge of magic is instantaneous, producing a piercing, high-pitched ring that resonates throughout the clearing. Many squint their eyes at the discomfort caused by the sound. A hush falls over the assembly as they converge before the dais, eagerly awaiting the court's sovereigns.

Two portals of magic manifest side by side on the platform, and through them emerge the king and queen.

While I've encountered King Lew many times due to my membership in his court, his appearance still leaves an impression. His lengthy dark braids now bear traces of silver, a testament to his advanced age. The corners of his eyes are lined with fine lines, and though he wears a perpetual broad smile, it exudes an unsettling aura rather than warmth.

What captures the eyes of many, are the brilliant wings attached to his back. Speckled grey feathered wings that ruffle as he tucks them in tight. His silver claws flex, and he glances over the crowd. Claws the same colour but smaller than those on his feet. King Lew is a harpy of the Asgell Guild.

But it is Queen Lilah who continues to seize my breath every time I lay eyes on her. Despite her outward light fae appearance, her identity as a shifter is common knowledge—though the specific creature she transforms into remains a closely guarded secret. The discretion is likely her desire to keep this information hidden from King Lew.

Even though she is the same age as my king, she doesn't look a day over thirty sun cycles. Her golden hair is almost obscured by the floral embellishments that adorn it, the vibrant blooms swaying as she advances. Her blush-pink gown fits impeccably, accentuating her ample, pale-skinned cleavage. Most don't catch the instant when King Lew turns to face her and discreetly rolls his silver eyes, but I do.

A faint grin creeps onto my lips, and I brace for the imminent display of dominance.

King Lew's lips tighten, and he gestures with a dark-brown hand, prompting Queen Lilah to take the lead in addressing the crowd. She demurely shakes her head, then inclines it in his direction. Neither will expose their back to the other—a wise choice.

"Welcome, one and all," Queen Lilah's melodious voice sweeps through the assembly like the harmonious trill of songbirds. A wide smile graces her features, revealing her small fangs. Her gaze briefly flicks to a point beside the dais, where Beinon stands, then returns to face the crowd.

"Yes, welcome indeed," King Lew interjects, his tone teetering on boredom. His eyes also flit in the direction that Queen Lilah's had, then scan across the assembly. My gaze follows suit, aware that the king is seeking out his child, Aisling. I haven't spotted them, but it's hardly surprising that the Unseelie heir remains absent. Aisling is renowned for their disdain toward lesser faeries and considers this competition beneath them. However, their participation is unquestionable, given that Aisling's father would not hesitate to claim their head otherwise.

"As you're all well aware, our esteemed High King Gwydion has departed from this realm," Queen Lilah proceeds, her words carrying over the crowd. "With no heir left behind, King Lew and I have consulted the pact and have decided how to proceed."

I almost let out an audible scoff, the urge just barely suppressed. *Just.*

Their decree was not a result of their choice; they were backed into a corner. Yet, they always present themselves as magnanimous rulers. As if leaving the fate of the throne to a lethal contest is an act of benevolence, rather than a guise for one of them to seize the throne. It's not benevolence they seek; it's bloodshed.

Their intent is clear: to eliminate the strong contenders through these brutal trials, ensuring only the weaker ones remain to rule.

To eliminate contenders like *me.*

It's a strategic move to minimise any potential challenges to their own rule. Weaker faeries can be controlled.

"A tournament shall commence," King Lew's voice resonates over the gathering. "Three trials to sift the worthy from the *un*worthy. Only one shall emerge victorious to ascend the throne. So, enter at your peril."

"These trials will demand your utmost skill and mettle." Queen Lilah takes up the mantle. "Only the formidable shall triumph." Her gaze flashes in Beinon's direction, and his pleasant expression falls. "The rules are, once the trial starts… there are no rules."

An uncomfortable silence sweeps through the clearing. They're inviting chaos by saying this. Many of these faeries would relish the opportunity for a free-for-all. A chance to help destroy rival guilds.

Not that I care about that.

This contest is going to have consequences further reaching than who just wins the crown.

"The contest shall commence on the forthcoming full moon," the king continues, "and between the trials, those taking part... shall dwell in a camp in the Betwixt."

Fury erupts at this announcement. Outrage reverberates throughout the clearing as none are pleased about the decision to confine us together in an interim camp straddling both courts.

I'm sure many were already plotting how to kill their competition back home in their respective courts. Accusatory fingers from both Seelie and Unseelie are pointed amidst the crowd. Amidst the turmoil, a lone pixie, consumed by their anger, dares to approach the dais.

A royal guard from Lilah's court strides forward. With a swift movement of their glaive, it cleaves through the air and the pixie's neck, severing it cleanly.

The pixie's head tumbles to the ground with a sickening thud, its azure blood forming a pool around the severed stump. A hush falls over the gathered multitude; the sole sound is a faint clinking of the royal guard's armoured attire as he resumes his position.

The queen sighs, an expression of disappointment gracing her features. King Lew clears his throat.

"We enact this protocol for the safety and well-being of all. Inhabiting the Betwixt during intermissions ensures contenders cannot eliminate their competition before the next trial. Any individual found guilty of disrupting the tranquillity of the Betwixt forfeits their position and, consequently, their life."

Silence remains throughout the assembly in pronouncements wake—no one else wants to lose their head.

In truth, the king and queen's concern revolves around shielding their cherished offspring from pretrial assassination attempts. Beyond myself, their children will undoubtedly be the primary targets.

"What's the first trial?" a gruff ogre boldly interjects.

A momentary flicker of irritation passes across Queen Lilah's eyes before a saccharine smile adorns her features. "The first trial," she calls out, "is a race."

"A race?" Murmurs ripple through the crowd.

"A race," King Lew repeats, "through the Ravine of Despair."

Only a handful react with shocked gasps; the rest respond with a rumbling of vexed exhalations. The Ravine of Despair lives up to its ominous name—a vast trench gouged through the southeastern boundary of the Betwixt, concealing treacherous sinkholes, jagged rocks, and feral beasts. Those who venture in seldom emerge alive. When also populated by hundreds of bloodthirsty faeries competing for a royal throne? It will be primed for a massacre.

"Make it through one night in the ravine and reach the end, and you will live to see another day. Fall prey to the landscape, or those around you… Well. I don't think I need to finish that sentence." The queen laughs.

My gaze locks on Beinon, who sports a smirking grin and rolls his eyes. The perils of the ravine hardly deter him.

And they don't deter me either. After over two decades of enduring my father's rigorous *training*, I possess the endurance and speed to outmanoeuvre any of these faeries—including Beinon.

King Lew raises his hand, and the hubbub dwindles to a muted hum.

"Anyone wishing to enter will sign a blood contract."

That isn't surprising, despite some of the nervous mutters from those around me.

A blood contract ensures that once someone enters, the only way out is to reach the end. Anyone who fails to show up for a trial, or tries to run, will die.

The faeries scuffle forward, heading for the faerie who holds a long scroll, taking a prick of blood from each entering.

"A camp has been established in the Eryri valley," the king continues, "serving as your dwelling for the following months. I advise you to make the most of this reprieve." King Lew's astute gaze sweeps over all, then he turns to Queen Lilah.

But I don't move yet.

I can't move my gaze as a sinister smile appears at the corners of Queen Lilah's lips, her gaze roaming across the assembled faerie until she locks eyes with me.

"You're going to need it," she states, a determined gleam in her eye.

Whispers tell of the lunar faeries harbouring a trove of mysterious abilities hidden to most of faerie kind. Lumina, once the Queen of the Seelie realm, boasted the gift of precognition, granting her glimpses into the unfolding tapestry of fate. Unfortunately, even with this ability, her sight did not reveal to her the poison in her evening wine.

PAGE 167, THE BOOK OF FAIR FAMILIES

CHAPTER THREE

C amp has been erected already, and despite the tentative truce, the faeries have segregated the two courts. The Seelie faction occupies most tents on the left side of the clearing, while the Unseelie cluster is on the right. Suspicious glances and mounting frustrations are exchanged across the grassy path that cuts a clear division down the centre of the valley, broad enough for ten individuals to walk abreast.

The Eryri Valley has always held a special place in my heart within the Betwixt. An expanse of verdant grass and captivating wildflowers nestled at the confluence of a stream tinted with the most enchanting azure hue. Willow trees trace the clearing's perimeter, and rising hills stand sentinel-like beyond them, akin to vigilant guardians.

Yet now, the wildflowers are heedlessly trampled by hordes of oblivious faeries. I can vividly envision the woodland nymphs and flower faeries shedding tears over the desecration. The valley will require an extensive period to recuperate once these next few months conclude.

Wen strolls alongside me, her vibrant eyes flitting between the divided factions as I navigate to the rear of the field.

"Are you sure you'll be all right here, Ef?" she asks.

I offer her a smile. "I'll be fine, Wen. And if not, my father will be more than willing to execute anyone who dares *disturb* the peace of the Betwixt."

"That's hardly reassuring," she mutters.

I reach out and gently clasp her hand, giving it a reassuring squeeze.

Together, we locate Beinon, who leans nonchalantly against a tent post at the field's back. The tent itself is reasonably sized and as I approach, his gaze sweeps over me.

He nods toward the canvas abode. "Kept this one for you, Efia."

"Is it so you can keep an eye on her, Beinon?" Wen says, a sly tone colouring her words.

Beinon rolls his eyes, and I pass by him, laughingly brushing his face with the canvas flap. He's saved me a generously proportioned shelter. The green-grey canvas contrasts against the lush grass outside, fashioned from a summer mesh that permits a gentle breeze to filter through. Inhaling deeply, I survey the expanse—a pallet adorned with furs laid out on the floor, accompanied by a diminutive lantern. A small table against the far side, by the side of a wooden tub.

This will be my home for the next few moons… if I don't die first.

The notion occurred to me on several occasions that I could flee via the Betwixt and find refuge in the mortal realm. However, mortals could be just as ruthless as the faeries surrounding me. They're just as likely to resort to violence, perhaps even severing my fae ears to keep as a prize token, rather than welcoming me to establish a peaceful existence.

Beinon enters, followed by Wen. The tent is tall enough for the three of us to stand comfortably.

"My tent is three over," Beinon says.

"I could always stay with you?" Wen flicks a dark curl over her shoulder. She walks over, lighting the small lamp with her lesser fire magic—an inherent trait connected to the natural energies of our world.

Aside from lesser magic, there are faeries with abilities specific to their kind. Vampires feed on blood, water nymphs control larger bodies of water, and so on.

I shake my head. "I will not let you linger too long around all these cutthroats, Wen. Trust me, it won't be long until someone is stupid enough to make an attempt on my life, even here."

Beinon's brow furrows at this.

"You go home," I say.

"Yes, Wen. You go back to your little house in the trees. Leave the fighting to us warriors," Beinon teases, and leans down to smirk at Wen.

Wen responds with a rude gesture.

"The full moon and first trial are in three turns of the sun," Wen says with a smile in my direction, and I nod. "I shall come watch."

A vexed sigh escapes me.

"No, you will not, Wen," I shake my head. "You will worship your moon goddess as you usually do on the full moon. I'll see you after the trial."

Wen's smile fades. "But—"

"She's right, Wen," Beinon's blue eyes soften. "It'll be a bloodbath, and her focus will be compromised knowing you're nearby. You could get hurt, even if you're not participating."

It's not that I think Wen couldn't look after herself. Not even *I* know the true extent of Wen's powers. But any affiliation with me puts a target on her back. If I can play off our friendship as a minor acquaintance—like I have for years—and not have anyone believe she means that much to me. That she could be used… I'd rather she stay away for the next few months. Wen's presence would indeed be a distraction. I can't bear the thought of her getting hurt, and I silently vow that I won't let that happen.

Wen crosses her arms with a hint of a pout. "All right."

I won't admit to such vulnerability when it comes

to her, but both are well aware it exists.

My father would kill me for it.

Efia, the joy that courses through me upon discovering your manifestation as a Nüwch is indescribable. Come to me this coming full moon and I shall teach you all I know about shade-wielding. I understand you may be scared child, but there is more power than you know running through your veins. Remember, run with the shadows. They will protect you.

PERSONAL CORRESPONDENCE FROM HIGH KING GWYDION TO EFIA MATHONWY

CHAPTER FOUR

A murmuring whisper brushes against my ears, like a gentle caress; the lantern's small flame wavers, casting dancing light over my half-closed eyelids. Gradually, the murmurs intensify—a warning.

Amid the dimmed light, there's a rustling and shifting of fabric. Swiftly, I sit up, blowing forcefully across the palm of my hand. My shadows unravel from around me, coalescing into a dense form to immobilise the intruder. A cloud of pink-tinged mist swirls from my skin, wafting over the trow faeric's face. His hand is raised, clutching a crudely whittled wooden knife, but the shades constrict around him, and he staggers backwards with a strangled sound. The knife slips from his grasp, and he clutches his throat.

"The first night? *Really*?" I tilt my head and laugh

as I stand.

The trows eyes widen and fill with tears, struggling to shuffle back and breathe as the poison makes its way through his system.

Footsteps grow louder, moving closer to my tent.

The canvas flap is shoved, and I unsheathe my short sword and place it against the throat of my new visitor. A shade hovers between us, preventing him from fully entering.

Beinon freezes and raises both hands. He takes in the scene before him, his gaze darkening toward the faerie creature below me.

His eyes travel over my body, as if trying to catalogue injuries that aren't there. "Are you all right?"

I nod, relaxing my hold on my blade. My shade takes a moment longer to allow him to enter. I release the other shadows from my control, allowing the trow to collapse to the ground.

Beinon's eyes remain fixed on my retreating shades, as he has never quite mastered concealing the wariness that flickers across his countenance when he witnesses me wield my abilities. Every faerie possesses a trace of magic, though the extent varies. Some exhibit a stronger affinity toward elemental magic, their capabilities aligned with their faerie lineage—Beinon possesses some minor control of water. Others possess healing abilities— typically these are earthen faeries.

But no one else possesses my power.

Beinon's unease isn't entirely unfounded; my

shadows can be as capricious as the moon, both a shield and a weapon, a force that can both conceal and consume.

The trow's choking gasps continue, and Beinon's lips part, as if he's on the verge of asking a question. But then he merely shakes his head, his eyes containing a mixture of curiosity, apprehension, and something else I can't decipher.

I crouch down before the poisoned faerie, my gaze levelled with his. "So, would you prefer I put an end to your suffering right here?" I grin wide, revealing my teeth. "Or shall I keep you alive until Bron can have his way with you?"

If I hand him over to my father, his fate would be one of agonising torment. Death would not be swift, but rather a protracted ordeal my father would thoroughly relish.

His head shakes vigorously, a hand scrambling along the ground, his fingers groping for the fallen knife while unintelligible utterances spill from his constricted throat.

"Here," I extend my hand and retrieve the knife. "Allow me."

The wooden blade impales the flesh beneath his chin, and a nauseating squelch permeates the air. The trow's eyes widen in shock, his cerulean blood staining my hand. Soon enough, his struggle ceases, his limp hand thudding against the ground as it falls from his throat.

I rise to my feet, casually wiping my blood-smeared hand on his grimy trousers.

Beinon's face twists in a repulsed expression. Turning his attention away, he lifts his fingers to his lips and emits a sharp whistle. Within moments, two guards appear, peering into the tent through its entrance.

"Any witnesses?" One of the queen's guards asks. No doubt the queen stationed near Beinon's tent, ensuring his protection. My father wouldn't dare suggest such a thing for me, nor would I ask. He would see it as a weakness.

"Me," Beinon replies with confidence. "The trow snuck in whilst she slept."

The guard grunts, then bends and takes a firm hold of the trow's lifeless arm, dragging him out and leaving a trail of blood behind him. I wander to the side of the tent, to the small wash basin placed on a small table. Dipping my hands into the cool water, I wash the blood off.

"I'll ask one of the earth pixies to get rid of that," Beinon gestures towards the blue spilt upon the ground. He exhales, and I turn to face him. "I despise this."

"It's likely only going to get worse once the trials start." I shake off the water then rise to my feet and approach him.

A muscle twitches in his jaw. There's a fervour in his eyes that I've never seen before.

"Maybe—"

I place my finger over his lips, forestalling the words before they can be spoken. My pulse quickens at the softness of his mouth beneath my touch. For a fleeting second, his eyes widen in astonishment, then kindle with intensity. I can't allow him to continue, to suggest we work together. Collaborating as allies would only complicate matters when we inevitably face each other in a trial.

And would only ensure my punishment if my father found out.

"No." I retract my hand.

He lets out a resigned sigh, his demeanour shifting briefly before a playful glint enters his eyes. "I was merely going to suggest sharing a tent for the night. Unless other faeries dare to test their luck with you."

"You'd enjoy that." I roll my eyes. "But I can deal with them the same way I handled the trow."

"By the way… where did you acquire that?" He changes the subject and nods toward my pack and the small brown bag of dust nestled within it.

"Bought it from Jill. She's made a place for herself in the camp. Thought it wise to have some herbs on hand."

"Ah." A smile tugs on his lips. "And some poisons as well, perhaps?"

"Well, you know me," I grin, relishing the easy banter between us. "I believe in being thorough."

His eyes soften. "Are you certain you won't consider staying with me?"

"Beinon…" I draw out his name, the hesitation evident in my tone. The truth is, I would consider it, more than he might realise. There's always been an attraction between us, a silent understanding that's never pushed into the realm of physical intimacy. Fear has kept me from acting on these feelings, fear that my father would discover any emotional attachment I have for anyone—especially Wen and Beinon. If he even got a whiff, he would have me facing his wrath before I could apologise.

"I can handle myself—"

He shakes his head, his face hardening.

"I know that probably better than anyone."

His gaze studies me intently, a look that sends warmth through my veins, causing me to lean slightly toward him.

But I clear my throat, patting his arm, and I walk past before turning to look at him. "I will be fine. Now get back to your tent before anyone gets the wrong idea."

The warmth in his gaze remains, and he smirks. "That wouldn't be wise."

"Disastrous," I suppress a smile.

"Terrible."

I roll my eyes, stepping forward to lightly push his chest. "Go on, then. Out with you. I'll see you at the first trial."

He allows himself to be pushed back, a mock expression of shock on his face. "You don't want to see me tomorrow, fair maiden?"

"No," I reply promptly, a teasing glint in my eyes. "Otherwise, you might remind me how irritating you are, and I might reconsider sticking my blade into your gut."

He chuckles heartily at the notion, his laughter trailing behind him as he leaves the tent, his eyes nearly closed with amusement, and he waves me a playful good night.

As much as I jest, there's an underlying current between us I can't ignore. A current that makes me wonder if one day my jests might turn into reality.

In the realm of faeries, there exists no graver sin than the murder of one's own kin. The consequence, a sentence to the ruthless human world or the ultimate price—death.
PRIESTESS MWFANWY, 93bcr

CHAPTER FIVE

Heads of various faeries turn to watch me as I laugh, the imp I've subdued struggling against my hold. I twist her arm further up her back, applying just enough pressure to threaten it breaking.

I must look mad, but it amuses me she had the audacity to try and kill me the moment I stepped outside my tent in the early morning. It's before I've even tended to my basic needs. The dimmed version of my shadow abilities had alerted me to her presence as I left the tent.

Like the trow from the early hours, this faerie believes breaking the rules of the Betwixt is worth eliminating competition.

It isn't.

And this is one I won't spare from my father's wrath.

Because, although taking life isn't my favourite thing to do, I feel no remorse for those who threaten to break the rules. Nor for someone who attempts to kill me.

A throat clearing behind me draws my attention…

Ahhh, right on time.

It's my father's second, Arawn, his most loyal guard, accompanied by two of my father's men dressed in the black leathers of the guild, with a grey flame insignia on their right shoulders. Their matching silver blades stay sheathed at their hips. It's a display of my father's authority and a reminder that he expects no faerie in the valley to dare harm him or his soldiers.

"Your father wishes to speak with you," Arawn says, his tone even and controlled.

I grin, unyielding in my amusement even as the struggling imp attempts to escape my grasp. "Tell him he can visit me at my tent." I keep my smile wide and teeth flashing, and I turn my attention back to the squirming imp.

Efia, can we please do this the easy way for once? Arawn's voice enters my mind to save us both from yet another public scene showcasing my defiance. He's exasperated with me, and I relish it.

"Where is he?" I give a dismissive huff as I push the imp toward my father's men, who grab her with firm hands.

"Hold that for me, thanks."

She shakes her head, trembling as she realises who they are.

Arawn runs a hand through his short brown hair, his expression a hint of relief. "He awaits you in the Whispering Woods."

"Give me a minute." I don't listen to his response and slip back into the tree line to address my morning necessities.

Upon my return, his face is tinged with annoyance, evidence of having been forced to wait for me.

"Well then, Arawn, lead the way," I brush my hand in a gesture that invites him to guide me. He hesitates for just a moment, likely torn between not trusting me to run away and not wanting to present his back to me—a gesture that might prove unwise given my history.

In my defence, the incident involving sinking my blade into Arawn's back was during a heated sparring session, and it came right after he had employed a rather underhanded move to unbalance me. My father had been highly pleased with my quick retaliation against his guard, but Arawn had not shared the sentiment—despite his swift recovery. Arawn was a few years older than me, but we both knew who was more accomplished in combat.

"How is the manor?" I ask Arawn, the watchful gazes of passing faeries following our every move. There's a hushed undertone of conversation and whispers that accompany us like a shadow.

"Quieter without you," Arawn replies, and his words carry a sense of relief. I wouldn't be surprised if my absence has brought him a measure of peace. After all, when I misbehaved under Arawn's watch, he bore the spectators' brunt of it too.

"Sounds boring."

He raises a brow, and I smile in response.

The path narrows beneath my feet as we continue through the dense trees, the strip of earth fading into the darkness of the forest.

A raven caws somewhere in the trees.

My fae eyesight allows me to navigate relatively well, but the shadows in this forest are unlike any other. Even at night, when my magic is most potent, I doubt I could dispel all the shadows that linger here.

A break in the trees ahead reveals my father waiting for us. He acknowledges Arawn with a nod, and his eyes narrow when he spots me.

There's little physical resemblance between my father and me, aside from the almost-black eyes that run in our bloodline. His features are sharp, almost angular. My cheeks are rounder, my nose slimmer and straighter, my lips are full and my eyes large. My freckles across the bridge of my nose make him sneer, his skin pale and blemish-free. His long burgundy red hair cascades down to his waist, darker and longer than my own, which rests atop my shoulders.

My mother has remained a mystery to me; I've never met her. Perhaps that's why my father looks at me with such disdain. I've never dared to ask again, as the scars on my back from the first and only time I inquired about her are a vivid reminder of his anger.

My steps halt a few feet away from him, bracing myself for what will undoubtedly be a lecture or reprimand. His first signal of displeasure comes as a prolonged inhale through his flared nostrils.

"I heard you were attacked in your tent?" he inquires, his tone deceptively calm.

I stand tall, my hands clasped firmly behind my back. "An attempt, but not a successful one."

The atmosphere remains tense, but his eyes haven't ignited with anger just yet.

"Why wasn't the perpetrator brought to me?" His tone sharpens instantly, the tension increasing like a taut bowstring.

I choose my words carefully, avoiding revealing my reasons. "I handled the situation myself." A hint of anger seeping into my voice, as if my personal vendetta against the attacker was too strong to let anyone else deal with it. I won't let him know that sparing the faerie from his wrath was due to something else entirely.

Father's lip curls into a sneer, his annoyance evident. But he nods, his gaze lingering on me. He sees in me what he detests—resemblances to Gwydion. Despite my rigorous training and honing of skills, there's a vulnerability within me, an empathy I share with my late uncle. My father resented Gwydion's influence on me, even though Gwydion himself wanted me to have that time with him. My father and I are stark opposites, and he perceives me as his greatest weakness because of it.

"Don't worry, Father," I sigh. "I have another one for you already."

"Oh?" He leans forward, relishing a chance to showcase his authority.

"An imp attacked her as she was leaving her tent," Arawn chimes in, and I shoot him a venomous glare. He has no business revealing such details, but it's done now.

"An imp?" Father's disgust is palpable. "You were nearly overcome by a creature I wouldn't allow to kiss my feet?"

"I was not nearly *overcome*," I reply through clenched teeth. "She didn't even get close.
But *I've* brought her for you, Father." The last word is laced with a bitterness I can't fully suppress.

My teeth shake. The sting to my cheek comes after, my face snapped to the side.

After years of this, it still takes everything in me not to raise a hand to comfort my cheek—the side of my face he has just backhanded.

It still feels unnatural.

But the blood rushes through my body with a heightened sense of doing what I must to survive. To avoid more pain.

Do not dare give him another reason to question my strength.

Face straight once more. Be quiet. Be obedient.
Turn it off.

"Hmm," he sneers at me again. "Are you prepared?" He changes the subject as if he hadn't just harmed his only daughter—his only child. As if discussing a trivial matter rather than my readiness to participate in a potentially lethal series of challenges.

"I am," I reply, my voice firm.

"Good," he continues. "We can't afford to display weakness to the other guilds. I expect you to eliminate your competition swiftly and excel in these tasks. The sooner we seize that throne, the better."

My scoff escapes before I can stifle it, and the glare he sends me almost makes me flinch. I hastily clear my throat, steeling myself to explain.

"Some of the participants might pose a more challenging threat than—"

"You're not referring to the king and queen's offspring, are you?" There's a dangerous edge to his voice, one that matches the glint in his eye.

I offer a nonchalant shrug.

He takes a measured step toward me, his demeanour demanding my full attention. "I've invested too much in your education, training, and *everything* else for you to be defeated by their illegitimate brats."

I hold my ground, refusing to cower beneath his rage.

"You *will* win this competition, Efia. You will restore our guild's reputation and bring honour back, and you will emerge victorious… or you will cease to be useful to me."

It's not a mere threat; it's a chilling promise. I know he's capable of making good on it. And there would be no escape for me. With our shared bloodline, he could employ ancient magic to trace me anywhere. There would be no sanctuary. And with my uncle gone, there's no one left to try to shield me.

Either I die in the trials... Win and take the throne. Or lose and likely die anyways.

I hold his gaze, and he takes a deep breath, the air around us growing colder with his presence.

"I will win, Father," I assert, my words a pledge to placate him and escape further retribution. He sighs, as if my response has exasperated him, and turns away dismissively.

"Go. I'll come to see you again before this contest concludes."

I pivot on my heels, fighting the urge to flee rather than have my back exposed to him. I step into the treeline, ready to disappear.

"And Efia." His voice freezes me in place. My heart pounds in my chest, squeezing tight. "When the opportunity arises, ensure the Seelie prince meets his end."

Swallowing the lump in my throat, I resume walking. Someone has witnessed my interactions with Beinon. And father knows the trials have given me the chance to eliminate him.

"Yes, Father."

By day's end, the imp's lifeless body hangs suspended from a tree on the outskirts of the camp. It serves as a chilling reminder of the consequences awaiting those who dare challenge the might of the Umbra Guild. Whispers spread like wildfire, telling tales of my swift and brutal revenge against the audacious attacker. The imp's fate casts an aura of unease and caution across the encampment, further ostracising me from my kind.

I despise it more than I can say.

In the human world, there's a tendency to misinterpret encounters with faerie creatures, and one of the commonly misunderstood beings is the vampire. Humans depict them with just two sharp canine teeth, overlooking the full set of sharpened fangs they truly possess. There's another deviation from faerie lore—these supernatural beings in their world crumble in sunlight. But we know better.

FAERIE CREATURES AND KNOWN WEAKNESSES BY TOMAS CEREDWEN

CHAPTER SIX

Living in this makeshift camp isn't entirely unbearable, as long as faeries are content within the confines of their tent and avoid the overwhelming presence of hundreds of other faeries. It's in these quiet moments that I find solace in the pages of a good book, an escape from the chaos that surrounds us. But those peaceful intervals are rare and fleeting.

The attempts on my life have ceased, a credit to my father's heavy-handed punishment that rippled through the camp. Whispers of his actions circulate, and I can feel the fear and unease in the way other faeries avert their eyes as I pass by. It's a double-edged sword—frustrating that my reputation is marred by his deeds, but also advantageous in maintaining an aura of intimidation.

I like being alone.

I hate small talk.

Sometimes loneliness can be a blessing, when some faeries offer no stimulating conversation to begin with.

Navigating the stalls scattered across the field for essential supplies has been less troublesome than expected. The camp's inhabitants are wary, and my path is often cleared with hasty deference. The assortment of goods I've acquired includes mouthwatering Seelie fruit loaves and candlewine infused with the essence of Wen's Orbed forest—a piece of comfort amidst this trial's impending challenges. I've secured them in my pack, ready to fuel my body for the trial ahead.

Wen's presence has been scarce since my arrival, a fact for which I'm secretly relieved. News of the attempts on my life has inevitably reached her, transmitted by a glowing firesprite that entered my tent under the cover of night. These lesser faeries possess a magic just potent enough to carry spoken messages, and their timely appearances keep me connected to my friend while she is away.

Wen's fiery words delivered through the firesprite brought a smile to my face, even as the underlying worry tugged at my heart. She promised to visit after the first trial but told me all about her plans for the sprouting grass moon, which added a touch of lightness to her message… but I had sensed the underlying anxiety she tried to conceal.

I awoke at dawn on the morning of the first trial,

choosing to find a small clearing in the woods nearby to stretch out my limbs and train a little.

I returned to my tent when the sounds of the camp grew louder, signalling that faerie folk were on the move.

My pack feels heavier than when I packed it as I hoist it onto my shoulder, the anticipation of the first trial hanging heavily in the air. With a sense of confusion, I delve into my pack, revealing its contents one by one. A chuckle escapes my lips as I uncover a gleaming silver throwing knife and two perfectly wrapped cold meat pies—Beinon's thoughtful offering. Gratitude and a warm sensation spread through me, even though I refuse to let it linger for too long.

The reality of the first trial beckons, and I can't afford to dwell on my emotions.

Not when there will be so much killing on this day.

Exiting my tent, I observe the faeries advancing to the field's end, where fae guards are using their lesser magic to open portals to the ravine's edge.

I join the seemingly never-ending queue behind some vampires. They hiss as they notice me, but no one tries to harm me—not yet anyway.

One vampire stares at me hungrily, his red eyes brightening, and he runs his tongue over his fangs. As soon as the trial starts, they will be out for blood, trying to sink their fangs into anything that comes their way—

including me. It's their opportunity to freely gorge themselves.

My hand tightens on the hilt of one of my silver swords, and I smile at him viciously, imagining my blade embedding itself into his chest cavity to stab his heart. I call forth the shades from around me, allowing them to float delicately around my form. I feel several faeries widen the space between us, but I keep my eyes on the vampire.

Behind the bravado and hunger, I see that sliver of fear spark. That delicious seed of doubt before he spins back around. I doubt the vampires would try to harm me during daylight—their strength is much weaker under the sun. I laugh internally, remembering a book I read in my uncle's library. How humans believe that vampires have two sharp fangs and perish in the sun, and only a wooden stake could kill them.

Silly humans.

They would shit themselves if they came to the faerie realms and met a true vampire. In our world, only pure-born vampires have two fangs, and they rarely leave their realm. Dealing with vampires also requires more than just a simple stake through the heart—silver or decapitation were the surefire ways to end them. Our vampires have upper jaws bristling with jagged teeth meant to rip throats as they feed—it's reminiscent of a picture I once saw of a sea creature from the human realm. Uncle used to call them *sharks*, creatures he had a peculiar fascination with. He often journeyed between our faerie realm and the human world, cloaked in a glamour to gather a treasure trove of knowledge.

"Those who remain ignorant are the most dangerous," he'd tell me. "True power comes from knowledge, Efia."

But his vast knowledge couldn't shield him from his death. Still, his words resonated with me, pushing me to seek every bit of understanding and wisdom I could find. It's a path that has shaped me into who I am today.

The line moved forward.

Royal guards from both courts stand in a disciplined line. Gaps in their formation reveal tall portals, their luminous waves beckoning as faeries stream through. I step into one of these portals. A familiar surge of magic envelopes me, my arm rising to shield my eyes against the dazzling sun that greets me on the other side.

The sun's searing heat and the sensation of sand scraping against my skin remind me why the ravine is infamous for being a nightmarish place. We're at our starting positions, and I'm acutely aware that the next couple of days are going to be an ordeal beyond description. Enduring the scorching heat during the day and bone-chilling cold at night tempts me to question my decision to enter this contest. The ravine holds no comfort, no reprieve—only an unforgiving expanse of desolation.

The thought isn't lost on me as I stand amid the barren landscape. Stretching endlessly, an agonising emptiness interwoven with concealed pitfalls and dying creatures that seem to hold a grudge against the living. Vegetation that survives the relentless sun is armed with thorns and barbs, as if nature itself conspires to impede any traveller and leave them torn until scavenging creatures can finish the task.

The last of the faeries emerge, and the portals seal shut behind them. I scan the faces for any sign of Beinon, or Aisling—the Unseelie king's offspring. Yet, they're nowhere to be seen. Perhaps it's for the best. I brace myself with each inch forward; the crowd forming orderly lines at the entrance of the ravine. Towering reddish rock walls flank us on either side, enclosing the passage and creating a canyon that stretches far beyond my sight, its end curving away into the distant landscape.

I pull up my hood and put on my black mask, a small piece of fabric that covers my nose and mouth—it will not hide me from most faeries, but they may look twice and fail to realise who I am. I push through the crowd, jostling for a spot near the front, and position myself behind a massive ogre. He grunts in response to my presence, his immense frame turned briefly to acknowledge me before he focuses back on the imminent ordeal, flexing his hulking green fists. Tension ripples through the crowd. Hands tighten on weapons, bodies brace themselves, and the air grows thick with anticipation. We all stand on the precipice, awaiting the signal that will unleash chaos, and I know it's time.

Turn it off.

I close my eyes and my mind drifts back to the years of rigorous training under my father. Those memories are etched into my mind, like scars on my soul. He pushed me beyond my limits, demanding perfection with every strike, every stab, every whispered shadow. No room for error, no space for sentiment. Emotions were a weakness, and he drilled that lesson into me with ruthless precision.

A lesson which was carved into my very skin.

I learned to shut down that part of me that felt, that yearned, that questioned. Instead, I became a weapon, an unfeeling assassin, a vessel for his ambition. The years of honing my skills, of becoming the embodiment of his goals, have led me to this moment. And as I stand here, waiting for the trial to begin, I embrace the cold detachment that has become my shield. When this contest starts, sentiment will have no place in the ravine, and we all know it will start bloody.

So, I replay my uncle's motto in my head, just once before I shut it all out.

Run with the shadows.

My gaze is drawn upwards by the fluttering of vibrant fabric in the breeze. Atop one of the towering walls that flank the ravine, the Seelie Queen and Unseelie King stand, overlooking the gathering of contestants—eager, hungry eyes anticipating the violence that is about to unfold.

The guard's staff strikes the ground, and pandemonium erupts. Shrieks of terror and the sickening sound of flesh being torn fill the air. The ogre before me swings around, and his massive arms reach for me. I react instinctively, ducking under one arm and gripping my short swords with a white-knuckled grip. With a swift arc, I cleave off a couple of his fingers from his other hand.

The ogre howls in agony, clutching his injured hand as blue blood spills between his fingers. I can't help but smile with a smug sense of satisfaction. Darting away from him, I distance myself from the immediate chaos, and plunge deeper into the heart of the ravine.

Above, faeries engage in fierce midair battles, their claws, talons, and teeth clashing in a brutal ballet of violence. Wings beat too close to me, and I duck. Sharpened nails graze the back of my neck. A hiss escapes my lips, and I extend my fingers and summon my shadow to rise and obscure my assailant's vision. The faerie crashes into a gnarled tree, the sickening crunch of bone meeting wood. My satisfaction deepens.

I need to find shelter for tonight. The first night will undoubtedly be the most vicious, but whilst a battle continues behind me, I shall head on and find safety— not that much of that can be found around this place.

Many don't realise that dragging themselves into conflicts at the start is to tread a fine line with death. It could be avoided. And so, I spend hours running, hiding, and striking when necessary. I weave my way through the terrain, skirting past danger and dispatching threats only when absolutely required.

Deeper into the canyon I go, and I navigate

through treacherous terrain, my body slick with sweat and my neck slightly sore. I avoid a large group of faeries locked in a ferocious battle, too engrossed in their own struggle to notice my passage. I shake my head at their shortsightedness and rush past them. Some faeries seem to revel in violence, seizing every opportunity to tear others apart, even when it serves no real purpose. But grudges are grudges. So Unseelie and Seelie alike will try to take out their rage on each other.

It was this exact hate that my uncle had tried to get rid of.

Yet, I'm resolute in my commitment to reach the end of the ravine without unnecessary bloodshed, without succumbing to the thrill of killing for sport.

The sun begins to dip below the horizon, casting an eerie twilight glow over the ravine. My urgency to find shelter intensifies. I spot a rocky outcrop ahead, a potential refuge for the night. With each step, the air grows colder, and the shadows deepen, amplifying the dangers that lurk around every corner.

A bone-chilling growl resonates through the air. My heart quickens, and I tense, my hand gripping the hilt of my sword.

A massive manticore emerges from behind the rocks and strides forward, its leonine body bristling with spines and its tail poised to strike. Yellow eyes fixate on me, hunger and aggression gleaming within them.

And with the sun's last rays still lingering in the sky, my shadow magic won't be enough to defeat it.

Legends speak of its guardian role over hidden treasures, but be cautious, for the manticore's roar can paralyze the bravest souls. Navigate these mythical realms with care, as encounters with the Manticore test the mettle of those who dare venture into its domain.

FAERIE CREATURES AND KNOWN WEAKNESSES BY TOMAS CEREDWEN

CHAPTER SEVEN

My grip tightens on one of my swords and I focus on the rhythmic sound of the manticore's breathing, the sound thumping in its chest. Its heart skips a beat just before it lunges at me with a grunt I pivot to the side, narrowly avoiding its deadly tail. The force of its attack propels it past me, momentarily exposing its flank.

I strike, my blade biting into its side. A guttural sound of pain reverberates through the ravine as the manticore stumbles. Its tail whips around, but I anticipate the move and duck under it, avoiding the lethal spines. Adrenaline courses through my veins, and I dance around the creature, my movements fluid and calculated.

The manticore's attempts to strike become increasingly desperate as I continue to evade its attacks, chipping away at its defences. Its hot, acrid breath sends my stomach roiling. I crouch, waiting for the right moment.

The manticore lunges, its jaws unhinging with a horrifying snap—ready to roar.

I spring into action, and I dive beneath the gaping maw, narrowly escaping the razor-sharp teeth that, instead, clamp shut inches from my face. My sword, an extension of my will, finds its mark without hesitation.

The blade slices through the air with a silent, deadly grace, embedding itself deep within the beast's underbelly. A blood-curdling screech erupts from the manticore, piercing the entire canyon. The creature's spines quiver like a final note of defiance.

With a last, ragged breath, the manticore collapses to the ground, life extinguished from its once ferocious form.

I'm slightly out of breath as I stand over the fallen creature, bloodied and victorious. The echoes of battle continue to resound through the ravine, and I take a moment to catch my breath, my heart slowing its frenetic pace.

Darkness fully envelops the ravine. I feel the rush of magic through my veins, and a shiver runs down my spine as the temperature drops—the sweat on my spine now feeling clammy. I listen to the distant sounds of faeries clashing; the night filled with both desperation and determination. The first day of the trials has ended, but now night comes.

Night is much worse.

My skin feels like it has been scraped with sand, but as I move through a rocky outcrop, my shades guide me to a narrow pathway to a cave carved in the rock face, hidden by large boulders. The faint scent of damp earth and the distant echo of dripping water fill the air. Dim light filters through the entrance revealing jagged walls and a smooth stone floor. The cave's chill bites into my skin, but it offers relative safety from the chaos outside. I tense, however, as my shades whisper and I glimpse movement in the shadows.

Emerging from the darkness, a fae female steps into the meagre light filtering in from the rising moon. Her eyes gleam with a mixture of curiosity and wariness. She's unarmed, her attire a mix of earthy colours, blending seamlessly with the cave's natural hues. I grip my sword, ready for whatever might come next.

"It's time for you to leave," I say, breaking the silence.

Without word or warning, she lunges towards me, her expression shifting from vulnerability to aggression.

My training and instincts taking over, and my sword cuts through the air. The light fae's eyes widen in shock as blood stains her attire. She collapses to the ground, her breaths shallow and laboured.

It didn't take much, but as the life fades from her eyes, regret claws at my chest. Another life taken. I wipe the blade clean, the weight of what I've done trying to break through the emotionless mask I've adorned for this trial.

Standing over the fallen faerie, I'm engulfed in a tempest of conflicting emotions. The weight of my duty as my father's Nüwch clashes with the echoes of my conscience, tearing at my soul.

I understand the consequences of disobedience, the punishment awaiting me if I fail to execute my father's orders. My father would say it's Uncle Gwydion's influence that makes me *weak*. Even though I dispatched with the female, my regret at doing so would earn me twenty lashes.

Yet, beneath my unwavering facade, doubt and remorse gnaw at me.

Now, safely alone, I question the morality of my actions, struggling with the senseless violence I'm compelled to commit in the name of *loyalty* and duty. Each life I take leaves behind a trail of guilt and self-doubt.

Who, besides Wen, has ever been loyal to *me*?

Who has ever had the power to stand for me?

What happens to those who do?

My uncle is no longer here. I am only permitted to be around Wen because my father feels it benefits him.

If I win and become queen, the company around me will be monitored even more closely, under my father's control.

I don't realise my shades are violently swirling around me or am I aware of the anger boiling in my veins until the ground seems to shake a little under my feet.

Blinking a few times, I rein them in, easing them with a comforting whisper.

At the end of the day, I gave the female an opportunity to leave. That is what I must tell myself. But despite my attempts to justify my deeds, I can't escape the feeling that I'm straying further and further from righteousness. Further from what my uncle wanted.

Ever since his death, my father used me more and more as an executioner. The internal struggle rages on, tearing me apart as I grapple with the harsh realities of my existence as my father's instrument of death.

I must suppress it now. Now is not the time to lose focus. I decide to sleep early, one of my swords unsheathed and resting in my grip, my sack next to me, trusting that the later hours of darkness will be the best time to move onward.

But it feels like no time has passed when I wake to commotion, instead of silence. Something is happening close to the entrance of the cave, just beyond the boulders. Leaving my bag behind, I sneak out, my grip tight on my sword and I unsheathe its twin. A snarling noise pierces the air like a knife, the sound vicious but pained. I chance a peek around the largest boulder.

It is a group of dryads, woodland nymphs with gnarled sharp fingers and cruel teeth. They have surrounded a Seelie fae—noticeable by his longer ears.

He's alone.

He lit a fire—idiot.

His white shirt is torn and his back is soaked with

blood on one side as the dryads stab at it with crude daggers and sticks. He lashes out with a short sword, wicked growls escaping his mouth.

His bright eyes blink furiously. He is tiring, and soon they will kill him.

I start to return to my cave when a pained groan escapes his mouth.

I try to take another step, try to shut out the noise but something stops me. Perhaps I allowed those doubts to linger in my head a bit too long.

I try to move, but my foot is frozen. My instinct is to turn, and I scold myself for feeling sorry for him, my father's voice echoing in my mind. If the dryads don't kill him, I'll only have to do it myself.

But I am shocked at my decision, and the first dryad doesn't see me coming as I sneak up behind it— but the fae does. A sharp golden gaze watches me. I slice my blades in front of me, crossing over each other, and I remove the dryad's arm. Its companions swivel their faces to me, a scream of pain and fury coming from their kin.

The shadows whisper incoherently in my ear as the dryads charge me, black eyes vicious and mouths wide, ready to take a chunk out of my hide.

But they're not fast enough.

I laugh, because travelling unseen was not the only reason I waited for the true cover of darkness. My abilities are much stronger at night. More corporeal— more lethal.

A smile widens on my face, and I call forth the darkness. The shades become physical shapes that swarm the dryads, causing them to falter in their steps whilst the shadows trap them and give me every opportunity to jump forward, bringing my right sword across the throat of one of them, whilst my shade guts another, a thick blackness impaled through the dryad's chest. It rips its limb out, rejoining the shadows as if there were never a trace of it.

The dryads fall without even seeing me coming, my shadows blinding and crippling them—the last dryad screeches at me. Before it can attack, the fae launches forward, embedding his sword into the faerie's shoulder. He twists the blade sharply and rags it around for a moment. A sickening sound of wood snapping and muscle tearing catches my attention, and the fae kicks him, tearing the dryad's arm from its body before it falls silent.

I stand there, the adrenaline from the fight slowly receding, and I can feel the chill of the night air seeping into my skin. Night has come, and the temperature is dropping rapidly. My attention is fixed on the fae, who now stands panting, amidst the fallen dryads.

The adrenaline is gone, and all that is left is the realisation of what I've done.

I've helped one of the *Seelie* fae.

This contest fortunately has no spectators, no stands for those not competing to watch the slaughter. As if these trials are some petty games for entertainment.

But I'll be incredibly lucky if this doesn't get back to my father.

I should kill him now.

The darkness thickens at my side, ready to enact my will—I'm surprised it hasn't killed him already. But in the blink of an eye, the fae is before me, his teeth bared and sword raised, and my blade is at his throat. A shade had materialised, holding his raised dark-skinned arm in midair. But not harming him. The fae pants, his eyes locked onto mine with suspicion.

"*Why did you help me?*" His deep voice resonates in my mind, and I conceal my surprise as I regard him carefully.

This is what he wants to know. Not, why haven't you killed me?

"It was one against many," I reply tersely, offering nothing more.

Kill him, the echo of my father's voice hisses in the back of my mind, reminding me of my duty. But I shove it aside.

"*I am fae*," he retorts, and I can't help but wonder if his real voice is as smooth as the one in my mind. "*I could have bested them.*"

Scoffing, I shake my head at his arrogance. "Well, from where I stood, it looked like they had the upper hand."

"*That still does not explain why you helped*," he bites back, his eyes flaring.

"Efia."

He blinks. "*What?*"

"My name is Efia."

He looks even more suspicious now, but his arm relaxes. I release my shade and he jerks in surprise, but it allows him to take a step back as I lower my weapon. He is probably wondering why I dare offer up my name informally when most faeries in both courts know it anyway. I take a moment to get a good look at the man I have just saved.

His hair is shaved on the sides, short locs on top that are so white they look like freshly fallen snow, though there are speckles of grey that line the sides of his head. He rubs the back of his neck with a dark-brown hand as a couple fall over his bright golden eyes.

He's eye-catching, and I try to remember if I have ever seen him in the Betwixt.

I huff, holding my blade to my side. "I know this is a kill-or-be-killed contest. But maybe I am slightly traditional when it comes to fairness. Eight on one— even if you are fae—doesn't seem fair to me."

He clenches his fist around the hilt of his sword, knuckles turning white, as if in preparation. "*Or perhaps you wanted to claim the kill for yourself?*"

My eyes roll before I bend, wiping my blades on the filthy shirt of one dryad. When I stand, I sheath them back at my thigh. "If I wanted to kill you, you'd already be dead."

"*Fair point.*" His head tilts to the side. "*So, what now?*"

"What now?" I repeat. "You go on your way, and I'll be on mine."

"*Or.*" He groans, his shoulders sagging as takes a step closer. My brows raise. "*Here's another idea. You helped me, let me help you finish the race.*"

"And why would I do that? If anything, you'll just be a hindrance with that injury." My lips tug up at the corner at the thought. The fae, especially light and dark fae, weren't typically a group that worked together. But my eyes glance over the wound on his side, the blood pouring from it. He is tired. If I leave him out here, he'll likely die or be killed by another.

"*You know what the pack faeries say. Teamwork over talent.*" He stretches out his muscular arms, his injured one dropping as he winces, but the tension in his legs relaxes as he seems to realise, I'll not kill him.

Why haven't I killed him?

Why am I even entertaining this idea?

A sceptical noise escapes from my throat.

"*I give you my word, I won't attempt to take your life. I just… I am weakened.*" He gestures to his back. "*Since you haven't killed me already…*"

"Who's to say I'm not going to?" I smile widely.

"*I think… if you truly wanted me dead, you would have done it already and you wouldn't even have to lift a finger. So maybe I should be the suspicious one. I'm wondering, why* haven't *you killed me?*"

My smile drops.

Because I don't know.

There's no logical reason going through my mind. I don't enjoy taking life. I avoid spilling unnecessary blood. But he is a competitor. An enemy maybe. And I have allowed no one to live after placing a blade to my throat.

So why am I hesitating?

I glance over at him and consider unsheathing my blade again. Ending him now. Or sending one of my shades through his beating chest. But… I don't. I find the idea abhorrent. Perhaps it's because he has lowered his weapon.

But I also don't mind the idea of working together, which shocks me more than my reluctance to kill him—because I wouldn't partner with anyone.

Not even Beinon.

I have allowed my doubts to wander too much this night whilst away from my father's watchful eye.

My gaze skips to the side, my shadows dance upon a non-existent breeze around me. They seem relaxed.

"Perhaps…" I crossed my arms. "We could travel the rest of the way together." There's no way I'm getting into a conversation about my motives for not killing him—not when I don't know them myself.

His eyes narrow, but he doesn't point out I have avoided his question. "*Deal.*"

His eyes drop with the effort of remaining awake. His blood loss must be bad, and I ignore the fact that he agrees so quickly, deciding to watch my back for the

foreseeable future—not wanting to find a knife
embedded into it.

"But you should rest first." I eye the blood on his
shoulder. "That wound looks nasty. There's a cave just a
little way back."

"*I'll manage, vicious on.*" A wry smile pulls at his lips.
"*It'll heal up soon.*"

"Vicious?" I raise an eyebrow, unable to suppress
a chuckle.

He nods. "*I've never seen anyone dispatch so many fellow
faeries before with so little feeling.*"

That, I flinch at.

"*But then,*" he continues, "*I know of your father,
Mathonwy.*"

Who doesn't?

I think with resentment as I hear my last name
enter my mind. My father's reputation is beyond reproach
in the Unseelie court. Apparently, so is the rearing of his
daughter—an unfeeling soldier. If my name hadn't given
me away, the abilities I share with my late uncle Gwydion
would have. No other Nüwch exist within the courts—
my gifts, praised as powerful and beautiful when
Gwydion bore them, are now deemed an abomination
underneath my skin and around me.

"Vicious it is," I mumble, acknowledging his
observation. "And your name?" I ask.

His gaze peruses me for a moment before
answering. "*It's Ansel.*"

"Ansel," I repeat, the name foreign to me in both courts. "Do you speak?"

"*I do not,*" he replies, his answer slightly evasive.

"Well," I continue, "you won't be getting too far until that wound heals, Ansel. I don't feel like drawing any more attention to myself this evening, especially since the air cools. So, if you'd like for us to work together, you'll do as I say."

I won't argue with him. He will only slow me down if we continue to travel until his wound healed.

"*All right. Lead the way,*" he concedes, his hesitation evident in his posture. But we both know, that if I wanted to kill him, I would've done it before now. I unfurl my hands and I turn, allowing the shadows to curl around the edges of my form, ready to alert me if Ansel makes any sudden moves. I can feel his gaze upon me like a burn, his steps almost silent as they pad across the ground.

His eyes widen as he sees the dead faerie once we enter the cave, skipping to me for an explanation.

"She wouldn't leave," is all I offer.

He makes a gruff noise in his throat, almost like a chuckle, and manoeuvres to the back, resting up against the rough stone. "*Just a few hours. I should be healed enough by then.*"

I lean against the stone wall, closing my eyes and pulling the shadows close, letting the darkness provide a protective shield. "Whatever you say."

Learning telepathy isn't mandatory, but fae with a formidable will can connect mentally. Sustaining it requires considerable strength, typically achievable only by those with potent magic.

PAGE 952 OF THE MABIN

CHAPTER EIGHT

*E*ach lash feels like a searing brand, a venomous serpent sinking its fangs into my flesh.

The cruel whip's leather tendrils crack through the air malevolently, biting into my back. With each contact, time seems to slow, and a storm of thoughts and sensations rage within me.

Rage at me to lash out, for my shades to rip them apart. But I cannot, for the sun is high in the sky.

My shades swirl about angrily but are as corpore al as a light fog in the night. And even if they could, they would not intervene. Not unless I order it.

I will not cry out. I will not give him the pleasure.

"You dare question me? Do you dare ask questions you have not earned the right to ask? You are a failure!"

I will never admit it, but my father's words hurt far worse than the bite of the weapon he used against my back.

My muscles clench in protest, desperate to escape the torment; the sting of each blow is a vivid mosaic of agony. The world around me blurs, and my vision sways, distorted by the overwhelming ache that radiates from my lacerated back. My arms are spread, pulled away from my body and tied to the walls on either side of me, held by two guards I could end in a second.

Arawn looks on from the corner in front of me, his face as angry red as he winces through each lash. I wish he would move; I hate seeing the pity there. But Father made him perform the first five, and now he must watch in punishment after my father deemed them too weak.

The insidious voice of doubt whispers in my mind, urging me to surrender, to let the pain consume me. But beneath the torment, a flicker of determination burns. I clench my teeth and focus on the harsh breaths that punctuate the assault, refusing to allow the pain to break my spirit. I allow some of my shades to rise from the weak shadows of the daylight-flooded room to float around me, whispering words I cannot decipher but ones I know are attempts at comfort.

The whip falls once more, and as the pain reaches its crescendo, a strange dissonance creeps into my consciousness. A pitch blackness floods the edges of my vision and a groan of pain that isn't my own has me tumbling into the abyss.

My eyes open. It takes a few precious moments to realise I'm in the cave, the torment a mere haunting memory of a dream. Yet the phantom pain lingers, a cruel reminder of the twisted past that my subconscious likes to remind me of.

It was Ansel's sounds of discomfort that reached me in my nightmare. That woke me.

It only takes him a second to notice I am awake.

"*I apologise,*" he says.

"Not necessary," I tell him, not willing to share that I was grateful he had woken me up. "Would you…" I wince, considering if I have gone mad for the thought that crosses my mind, but it's too late to ignore my words, Ansel is already giving me a suspicious look. "Would you like me to check your wound?"

His bright eyes widen.

"*Um,*" it's the first time I have heard him sound unsure, and he raises a hand to pinch the bridge of his straight nose. "*It's my shoulder. I can't check it properly.*" I take that as confirmation and stand, unsheathing my weapons and placing them on the ground before walking slowly over. He tenses slightly at my approach, and I pause, holding my hands up to show him I don't hold a weapon—it's technically an empty gesture. I don't need weapons to kill him, and he knows this.

Ansel shifts around, leaning sideways against the cave wall, and remains still as I kneel by his side. My hands travel gently over his shoulder, and he takes a breath and holds it. This is a big thing, I remind myself. It is a brave thing—to offer your back to a faerie who does not come from your court.

I tear his white shirt so I can access his skin easier, and a hiss escapes his throat as my fingers trace the edges of the wound. Lower down, covered by the shirt, I can see thin lines of light brown.

Scars.

And there seem to be many of them.

They remind me of my own, my nightmare still fresh in my mind—my eyes dart away.

I don't mention them, but swallow down my shock at the sight. He must have borne such pain, for scars to be left like that and left untreated. It takes a lot to scar a faerie. Leaving wounds to heal with no healing aid at all. No magic.

I would know.

"I'm sorry," I say, though I know not what I am apologising for.

"*It's all right.*" He leans forward with a groan and removes the shirt entirely.

I swallow, my eyes grazing over the strong, defined muscles of his back and shoulders.

His skin is smooth between the lines carved into his back.

There must be at least fifty of them.

But still his skin is soft, as soft as a gentle morning breeze, and russet brown, like the late leaves that grace the forests of the Betwixt in autumn. I ignore the fact my fingers tingle when I first touch his skin, and he lifts his shoulder slightly, allowing me to see the wound.

The fresh wound is not too deep, the jagged edges red but with no sign of poison. The pain is coming from the entry point, right behind the muscle.

"It's not serious. The dryad stabbed you directly

behind your shoulder blade, so it will be sore whilst you move around. A bitch whilst healing really, but it's healing well." I tell him honestly. His injury should be completely gone by tomorrow night if left. I debate my next question for a moment, deciding I've already done so much, so there will be no harm in offering my help once more. "I have some herbs in my sack if you'd like me to apply some. It'll speed up the healing."

He turns and his eyes flick to meet mine, reluctantly revealing a moment of vulnerability. Where he seems to want to say yes but doesn't want to owe anyone for their help.

I shake my head softly. "Honestly, it's nothing."

He nods, saying nothing, and I retrieve the herbs from my sack. For a split second, just a second… my eyes roam over the poisonous herbs packed beside them. And that wicked part of me considers it—the part of me trained by my father. That ruthless, unfeeling monster.

I take out the healing herbs and return to his side.

Ansel is quiet, his fists clenched whilst I chew them up, mashing them up into a paste in my hand until I can apply them to the wound. He stays quiet until I rub them over his shoulder, and he sighs in content at the pain easing.

"*Thank you,*" he whispers into my mind, his head tilting.

I nod. "So." I swallow. "Why have you entered?"

"*You really think I'm going to tell you that?*"

"Well, it only seems fair," I say. "I think everyone

knows why I've entered." An attempt to joke. I'm Bron's daughter. Like I have a choice.

His head falls forward, and he inhales deeply.

"It's complicated."

"I get it." I chuckle. "Family is hard work."

He huffs.

"So, what is it? Not happy with who the light fae nominated? Want to win this thing by yourself?" I push.

"Perhaps I look to forge my fate. To choose my family by ruling over it all."

That takes me by surprise. Fae from the Seelie realm cohabit and work together—are usually pack faeries. He must have had a serious falling out if he wishes to leave it.

"Pushy father?" I ask with a laugh, rubbing my hand gently over the edge of the wound and hearing a hiss leave his mouth.

"Mother," he admits after a silent moment.

"Ah," I reply. We have something in common. That makes me feel better about our current alliance. He doesn't seem too keen on competing in this tourney. The only ambition he's shown for the crown is so he can make decisions for his life… for his own family. I understood that more than most.

But he's wrong.

"Winning won't give you what you want. Rulers don't have a chosen family," I tell him, remembering my uncle and the court around him—the king and queen. "They are surrounded by leeches and liars. Forever watching in the darkness for the inevitable knife in their back."

"Wow" he replies, looking contemplative. *"If that's how you really feel, why are you joining the fight?"*

"I don't have a choice," I admit with unabashed honesty.

"Everyone has a choice." He looks at me as if seeing a complete stranger for the first time—even though I am—but as he blinks, it's gone.

"That's a naive belief," I reply.

"Why?" he asks. *"Because of your father?"*

I bare my teeth slightly. "You know nothing of my father."

His brows raise as he stares at me. *"Perhaps not. But everyone has heard of Bron's temperament. So, I think I'm starting to."*

"Well keep those thoughts to yourself," I spit at him.

An awkward silence falls between us for a moment as he turns away from me before I hear his deep inhale.

"I apologise."

He doesn't see it, but I nod in thanks, standing and returning to my pack. I wipe my hands on a scrap of cloth inside before settling back against the cold stone and avoiding meeting his golden gaze.

"I will say, Mathonwy... However, you've been treated in the past, or how you've been raised doesn't have to have a bearing upon your future. You can make your own path."

I ignore the way my stomach dips at the soft tone when he says my last name, almost like pity.

"Is that what you're doing?" I ask.

For a split second, an expression of guilt passes across his eyes, and I assume it's to do with stepping away from his family.

"*It's what I want to do.*" His tone is sad.

"Well, you're wrong," I say. "Our pasts always linger in the shadows, always just too out of reach to push it away."

The crumpling of his eyes makes me realise he knows that feeling all too well.

The title "Ravine of Despair" isn't given lightly; it has earned its ominous reputation. While some might venture in to sharpen their skills, the wise understand it's a journey with no return for the living.
THE REALM OF FAERIE BY SCHOLAR LOREN

CHAPTER NINE

The ravine stretches before us like a jagged scar on the earth's skin, its walls rising high, casting shadows that dance eerily in the moonlight. I suppress a shudder as we wander through it, pulling my cloak tighter around me as the cold seeps into my bones. The air is heavy with the hushed tension of the dead of night. Moonbeams cut through the darkness, revealing the uneven terrain beneath our feet, a mix of loose gravel and patches of frost-kissed gnarled bushes.

I lead the way, the hem of my dark cloak brushing against the rocky ground.

Ansel follows close behind, his steps silent but deliberate.

My shades are always aware of his presence, pulling from the deepest black darkness around me and reaching towards me like an old friend. I know he is aware of them. How his steps falter every now and again when one brushes too close to him.

But he hasn't gained their distrust yet. He has done nothing to make me believe he will reach for the short sword at his side.

The narrow ravine amplifies every footfall, creating muted echoes that resonate in the night air. Our breaths hang like mist, vanishing into the cold abyss. We've rarely spoken since we left the cave, besides me sharing some of the pie I carried—even if he sniffed it first to check for poison. We tread carefully through the rocky canyon, and every now and then the air is pierced by a scream or cry of pain somewhere deeper in the darkness.

"This place is more treacherous than I imagined." Ansel breaks the quiet with a hushed voice that brushes against my mind.

I glance back at him, his features partially obscured by the play of shadows. "It's the quickest route," I reply in a tone just above a whisper. "We can't afford to be out in the open for long."

His golden eyes flicker, catching the moonlight. *"I'm not complaining. Just an observation."*

I offer a tight smile and continue forward. The ravine narrows further, and the tension thickens with each step. Ansel matches my pace, braving my shades to walk by my side, his movements fluid despite the cold.

The silver strands in his locs gleam as he tilts his head. *"I didn't expect you to be so skilled with a blade. Assumed you'd just use your Nüwch abilities."*

I scoff. "Adaptation is survival."

I don't offer information freely; don't tell him that my shades are weaker in the day, so I have had to learn to be a weapon myself. Though if some were to pay attention—and some most definitely have—they'd notice that my shades were stronger at night.

Ansel seems to accept the response, and we fall into a contemplative silence.

The ravine winds on, its icy breath clinging to our every step.

I feel Ansel's eyes on me, the weight of his unspoken thoughts echoing in the quiet.

"What really made you help me back there?"

I glance at him, my expression guarded. "Sometimes survival requires unexpected alliances. I'm not one to let someone die needlessly. Not unless provoked."

His brow quirks because we both know I'm not someone who would accept allies. My father works with no one, and his daughter is expected to do the same. Judging from Ansel's own scars, I think he knows what would happen if my father found out I had an *ally*.

But I still don't know *why* I helped him.

The conversation doesn't continue, and for that I am grateful.

After a few hours, when the moon still casts its silvery glow on our path, but has dipped in the sky, Ansel points to the northeast.

"There."

I follow the direction of his hand, spotting a rising slope in the distance which reveals our path to the exit.

I almost sigh in relief, but I don't want him to

know that I can't wait to exit this cursed place… but the ground beneath us shudders, sending tremors through the cold sand. My instincts kick in, and I drop to one knee, placing my hand on the quivering surface. A low growl escapes my lips, and I mutter a curse under my breath.

Ansel mirrors my movements, his eyes narrowing in question.

I draw my swords with swift precision. "A seitaad,"

The grains of sand seem to ripple in response, as if the creature senses our readiness.

Ansel's eyes flicker with understanding and we space ourselves apart several feet, scanning the shifting dunes ahead.

The sand ahead of us explodes in a swirl of motion, revealing the sinuous form of the seitaad. A serpentine creature whose scales glint in the moonlight. Its elongated body undulates with predatory grace and Ansel and I move in unison, blades at the ready.

The seitaad lunges with blinding speed, its fanged maw open wide. Ansel blocks the attack with his sword, the clash of metal against scales ringing in the night.

But he winces.

His shoulder is too injured, and he can't use it to the best of his ability. I move to flank, my swords cutting through the air with lethal precision. The seitaad is swift, but we are faster. Our movements become a seamless collaboration, and as the creature recoils from a well-aimed strike from Ansel. But he groans and his arm drops, his shoulder hurting.

The seitaad sees this opportunity and swings to face Ansel, but I seize the moment. Ripping the silver knife Beinon left me from a sheath hidden in my leather armour, I take a steadying breath and allow the shadows to coil around the blade, enhancing their deadly edge. I throw it and it stabs through the hard scales of its tail, causing it to falter.

Its cry pierces the sky, and I need to end this quickly before other faeries hear the commotion. With one smooth motion, I slide away from its lunging fangs and strike at the seitaad's underbelly, slicing through scales and drawing blood.

Ansel follows up with a decisive blow, his blade finding its mark. The seitaad thrashes in agony, its movements slowing. We press the advantage, our strikes coordinated and relentless.

Finally, with a last assault, Ansel and I bring down the creature. It convulses in its death throes, the sand around it stained crimson. We stand, breathless, our swords still raised in readiness.

Ansel looks in my direction, his golden eyes reflecting the moonlight. "*Well fought*," he says, a genuine note of appreciation in his voice.

I nod in acknowledgement. "You're not bad yourself, for a Seelie."

He grins, a flash of white. "*I'll take that as a compliment, vicious one.*"

As the echoes of the battle subside, we lower our swords, the moonlight casting long shadows around us.

The ravine remains silent; the sand settling as if it too acknowledges our triumph.

My shades relax once more, dancing around me in lively energy.

And as we turn to leave behind the body of the desert creature, I swear I see a small flicker of blue in the far-off darkness, but with a blink it's gone.

Legend has it that a nocturnal call of 'dewch' signals Corph's arrival for your soul. No survivor's account exists, except one elusive tale. Whispers speak of the death god manifesting as a wingless, featherless bird, a haunting harbinger of one's final departure from the realm.
DARK FAE AND DEATH GODS, BY UNSEELIE KING BENEDICT

CHAPTER TEN

The vampire doesn't let up, and neither does the light fae fighting Ansel.

Two of their friends are already scattered across the ground, Ansel and I having eliminated them.

Yet, my focus on my fight with the vampire wavers as we engage in a back-and-forth clash—though he's not much of a challenge. My attention keeps flitting towards Ansel as his sword meets the strikes of the female fae.

His style resembles a dance, infused with raw power. I realise that dispatching him would have proven more difficult than I initially assumed had we not formed an alliance. He raises his blade, his well-built arms straining, and he counters each swipe with fluid precision.

The vampire hisses, seizing an opportunity to lunge at my throat while I'm momentarily distracted. Swiftly sidestepping, I slash across his arm and deliver a forceful kick, causing him to kneel. Without hesitation, I advance, crossing my blades behind his neck and pulling them forward, cleanly severing his head from his body. It topples forward, thudding as it hits the ground, sending a smattering of sand into the air.

A sliver of regret blanches through me at killing another one of my Unseelie kin. Then again, the vampires have never held any love for the fae.

Soon after, Ansel concludes his skirmish with the fae with a sword through her chest.

The journey since the seitaad remained rather uneventful until we reached the ascent. A lengthy and rugged sloped path that stretches from the floor of the ravine to the cliffs high above—our intended route. Several faeries have already surged ahead, sprinting towards the slope's summit. Atop the cliffs, the king and queen observe the survivors. While her facial features are not discernible from this distance, I sense the queen's gaze as she notices my presence on the slope.

We had only a few hundred feet remaining before our progress was disrupted by the sudden appearance of four faeries springing forth from behind a cluster of boulders.

Ansel frowns up at the cliff edge before his gaze meets mine, his eyes vivid and intense, his breath slightly laboured from the skirmish.

"You holding up, vicious one?"

I offer a nod.

His lips curl into a lopsided grin as he gestures

toward me with his sword. "*Blood suits you.*"

I glance at the crimson droplets speckling my leather attire, and shrug. "Not my preferred style."

"*No? Red is definitely your colour,*" he teases, in a much better mood than the night before.

It unnerves me. Why offer relatively kind words at the *end* of the trial?

Is this, perhaps, where he will try to kill me?

It seems he has come to the same thought.

Because it takes less than a second for his blade to rest near my throat, one of my own placed precariously against his thigh, right where I know the fat, juicy vein to be.

He grins, and I can't help but chuckle.

"I prefer pink," I tell him with a tilt of my head. Not really. I despise the colour.

"*Really?*" He grimaces, his sword lowering an inch.

"It reminds me of brain matter."

His laughter follows, our swords falling as we step back, and the timbre of the sound catching me off guard. Deeper and smokier than his internal voice.

So how is he unable to speak?

I shift my focus away, dismissing the flutter in my stomach, and instead direct my attention to the cliff's edge.

The end of the ravine looms into view, and I seize the moment to inhale deeply, a smile tugging at my lips. My blades still find refuge in my grasp, a testament to my lingering distrust, not entirely convinced that Ansel wouldn't turn on me at any instant. However, his widened eyes draw my attention, and the ground trembles beneath my feet, compelling me to pivot.

Countless faeries—dozens of them—emerge, as though they've recollected the trial's objective and are now desperate to escape the chaos.

I spot Beinon at the forefront of the rushing faeries, my hand involuntarily reaching out as if drawn toward Ansel, gripping his forearm. His head turns the corners of his mouth falling agape, forming a perfect "o" of disbelief.

"Run." I take a few steps back, for the horde of faeries is closing in fast. I know none of them would hesitate to eliminate me—an obstacle standing in their way to freedom.

I turn, locking eyes with Ansel. He jerks back as I reach out for him, his sword arm raising a little.

But there's no time for him to be suspicious of me,

"Run!" I demand, pivoting and channelling every ounce of strength into my legs. My fatigued limbs protest, but I grit my teeth and push. Push, push, relentlessly toward the path's end.

The sound of scrambling feet informs me that Ansel is nearby, running with the same fervour as I. The ground's vibrations intensify, resonating with the frantic flapping of wings above.

Pixies and harpies soar overhead, utterly disregarding us, fixated solely on reaching the exit.

Tired of the night's bloodshed and chaos. I lift my gaze, witnessing the radiant magic of portals transporting them away from the ravine's clutches.

"*We're almost there, Mathonwy,*" Ansel says clearly in my mind but pants.

My hand reaches out, fingers gripping his wrist tightly, and I yank him forward as the noise behind us escalates to an ear-splitting volume.

A brilliant light blinds me, the sensation of magic brushing against my skin as the portal envelops us. In an instant, we're hurtling through the air, the ground rudely greeting us before we can brace ourselves.

Ansel twists me in midair, and a loud grunt escapes me as I collide with his chest, and I struggle to breathe for a moment before I promptly sit up. Ansel is below me, having turned us, so he took the brunt of the fall.

With heat filling my cheeks, I realise I am practically sat on his lap. I almost fall on my arse in a bid to stand, and I look around to hide my embarrassment.

The valley stretches before us, and we've been portalled back to the edge of camp—multiple shimmering gateways punctuating the expanse, disgorging faeries who have triumphed in the trial. Jubilant cheers and applause ripple through the valley, the faeries celebrating their survival with exuberance.

A huff escapes my nostrils, and Ansel rises beside me, so I bend and brush the sand from my leathers. A weighty hand lands on my shoulder and, oddly enough, I can discern that it's Ansel's touch.

"*Thanks, Mathonwy,*" he murmurs, a faint smile tugging at his lips. "*See you next time?*"

"Sure thing," I reply.

I don't know what else to say. But the smile falls from my face. We both know that next time might not be so pleasant. He turns, wandering to wherever it is he is staying. Just as I'm about to head back to my tent, a collision knocks the air from my lungs, and a cascade of brown curls tickles my nose, Wen wrapping me in a near-painful hug.

"Hey, Wen," I grunt out amidst my breathlessness.

"I worried when others came through, but you still hadn't," she remarks, her voice muffled by my chest.

I chuckle. "Your *unwavering* confidence in me is starting to hurt."

"Oh, come on." Wen disentangles herself, her silver eyes sparkling in the sunlight as she sniffs lightly. She smooths the skirts of her exquisite periwinkle dress, fussing over the long sleeves despite the complete absence of dirt. "So." A sly grin graces her face. "Who was the mystery fae?"

My eyes roll, entirely unsurprised that Wen spotted Ansel. I can't help but think back to the definition of his back muscles, the brilliance of his golden eyes... He wasn't someone easily overlooked.

My gaze flicks around the growing crowd of faeries populating the field. "I'll fill you in once we're back in my tent."

She nods and clasps my hand. We amble through the camp. An electrifying buzz fills the air, surviving fae mingling with their court compatriots, all celebrating the conclusion of the initial trial.

It still doesn't stop the suspicious looks I get as I pass them.

But a faint smile tugs at the corners of my lips, the jubilant atmosphere proving contagious. My lungs fill with a complete breath as I step into my tent and remove my pack and blades. Wen draws the canvas closed behind us.

Wen twirls in a flourish of her skirts. "Well?"

"He was just a fae who had a run-in with dryads," I respond, my words succinct.

"And you stepped in to *help* him?" Her inquiry isn't fuelled by any doubt in assisting another faerie, but rather an awareness of the repercussions my father might impose if he found out. Her brow is crumpled with concern.

I falter for a moment, because I haven't fully grasped the reasons behind my choice to aid Ansel. Maybe there's a grander scheme in play, perhaps I might require his assistance in the future—a good deed repaid in kind. All I can do is remain patient and observe how events unfold.

Wen's twinkling gaze catches the hesitation in my response, allowing her to deduce her own interpretations. Her lips part, likely ready to voice her thoughts, when the tent flap is kicked open.

"Efia!" Beinon's smile is wide, his breath still a bit uneven, and he pauses, his gaze sweeping over me before he charges forward, enfolding me in a tight hug and lifting me off the ground.

"Why does everyone seem to think I was headed for Corph?" I inquire, referring to the faerie god of death. The silent conductor of the inevitable, the keeper of the delicate balance between life and its inevitable end.

Wen's laughter rings out as Beinon releases me from his embrace. "Well, we were pretty sure many would have their sights set on you. But it seems like you had it relatively easy. Maybe thanks to your companion?" Her sly smirk betrays her intentions.

Beinon's grin falters, his eyebrows knitting together. "You had someone with you? *You*?" His expression shifts to one of disbelief. "Was it the fae I saw running alongside you? I thought you were being chased."

"No," I begin, a peculiar intuition guiding me to withhold the full truth from him. So, I opt for vagueness. "I helped him out of a tricky situation with some dryads, and we sort of… teamed up after that. He went his own way as soon as we got through the portal."

Beinon emits a surprised noise, his hands landing on his hips.

I tilt my head. "What?"

"Nothing, nothing," he quickly responds, raising his hands in a placating gesture. "Just a bit unexpected."

"That's exactly what I thought," Wen interjects.

"Is today tease Efia day?" I chuckle, wagging a finger at them. "All right, you two, out you go. I'm in dire need of a bath."

Wen nudges Beinon towards the exit, and he glances over her head, wiggling his eyebrows playfully.

"Want me to stay? I could do with a bath myself."

"Only if you want me to remove your favourite appendage." I smile and smile wider when he covers his crotch and winces.

Wen laughs brightly.

"Maybe next time, then," he calls back, his voice fading as they exit the tent.

I sink onto my sleeping mat, forgetting the bath for now altogether, welcoming the calming hush that's descended. My head sinks into the soft furs, eyes closing. The first trial had proven relatively manageable, but as I lie there, the faces of those I'd dispatched flicker behind my closed eyelids. I pull my dimmed shades towards me, allowing them to comfort me, and I pray to the faerie god's that I'll find sleep, but knowing I'll never forget the faces.

Sage, renowned for treating skin maladies, wounds, and bites, extends beyond its healing prowess. Beyond medicinal benefits, it tastes really nice with chestnuts.
HEALING THE FAERIE REALM BY JILL HOLDER

CHAPTER ELEVEN

"Evening, Jill," I greet the diminutive pixie with a smile and extract a few chunks of chrysolite. She eyes the gems with a covetous gleam, her sharp teeth flashing. Jill is an earth pixie, her talents lying in healing, herbs, and natural gemstones.

She's also something of an adventurer, often glamouring herself to sneak into the human realm. There, she typically collects odd trinkets and jewels from their world, though she has a penchant for swiping their clothing more often than not. Today, she sports a short, sleek coat crafted from smooth black leather, its shoulders adorned with tiny silver spikes and its pockets lined with curious silver metal teeth.

The thing looks terrifying.

Her bright eyes dart between my hand and my face. "Mathonwy."

I suppress a smirk. "Do you have more sage? Maybe some yarrow?"

Her eyes narrow. "You're not saying you used up all those herbs in the last trial, are you?"

"I have a bit left," I reply. But then I pause, debating whether to divulge about Ansel.

She rolls her eyes. "Don't tell me you gave some to that fancy princeling?"

I seize upon Beinon as a cover for my near slip. "I did," I confess quickly. "Sorry, Jill."

Jill mutters something under her breath, pivoting to retrieve a bundle of herbs wrapped in a small cloth. She extends her hand, and I drop a handful of chrysolite onto her open palm and add a few more as a token of appreciation before accepting the package.

"Only because you bring me my favourites," she remarks, her smile hidden behind her words.

"Thanks, Jill." I grin, then turn to make my way back to my tent.

Camp life has grown relatively comfortable in the two weeks that have passed since the inaugural trial— especially with the fewer faeries around due to the losses incurred. I haven't seen Ansel since; our brief alliance ended with the conclusion of the first trial. Yet, I can't help but occasionally wonder if my intervention spared him another scar.

Word spread that a messenger is due to arrive tomorrow, bearing information about the second contest scheduled for the hare moon in two weeks' time.

Wen has been a frequent visitor, often bringing homemade wine and apples gathered from her forest.

Her visits break up the camp's monotony, with Beinon and her joining me every other night. We usually share a goatskin of wine, becoming merry, singing songs well into the early hours, much to the chagrin of the faeries who call out for us to quiet down—though none dare venture in.

Tonight, the tent is cosily lit by the gentle glow of the suspended moonstones I had placed earlier through the wooden beams, casting soft shadows on the fabric walls. The three of us sit in a semicircle, our laughter mingling with the rolling of wine bottles that are scattered haphazardly, serving as testament to the revelry that had already begun.

Wen leans back, her silvery laughter ringing out as she raises her goblet high. The little lunar faerie has drunk enough for a whole burrow of trows. "To Beinon," she toasts, her voice dripping with theatricality, "whose good looks can blind the beautiful moon herself."

She is making fun of him, one of her favourite things to do when feeling merry—because she knows he can take it.

Beinon grins, his cheeks taking on a charming flush as he places a hand against his cheek. "It's a burden I've grown to bear."

I can't help but snicker, my goblet of wine held in midair. "Yes, the moon weeps in envy every time you grace her with your presence."

Wen's laughter grows, the sound as musical as the tinkling of wind chimes. "I've heard faeries swoon in your wake, Beinon. Careful where you step—you might cause their hearts to stop."

Beinon pretends to preen, brushing a hand through his tousled hair. "Well, it's important to keep the realm's healers employed, isn't it?"

Wen rolls her eyes. "Oh, don't be so *humble*. We all know you've struck a deal with the mirror—it cracks a little every time you wink at yourself."

Beinon mock sighs, his hand clutching dramatically over his heart.

I burst into laughter; my goblet dangerously close to spilling. My shades still float protectively around me, even as I relax and try to allow myself to be just *me*.

"I'll have you know I only wink at myself on full moons." He sniffs.

Wen snorts, her laughter infectious. "Good thing it's not for another two weeks then."

The tent echoes with our laughter, the sound bouncing off the canvas walls and into the night. As we share stories and exchange playful jabs.

But there has been a shift.

These nights are not so unusual. I have shared many times with Beinon and Wen. But now it appears to be a bit of a facade. Because an unspoken tension simmers underneath. As the days pass and the contest continues, the shadow of our potential confrontation looms larger. Beinon and I often exchange subtle glances, unspoken questions lingering in the air. We know that with each trial, the likelihood of our paths crossing in a deadly encounter grows.

Wen's bright eyes don't miss much, and I can tell she senses the undercurrents as well. Her laughter still rings true, but there's a depth in her gaze that betrays her awareness. This looming possibility casts a sombre note over our usual lightheartedness.

Late into the night, after the wine has mellowed our spirits and the stars are fully on display beyond the walls of my tent, we sit in a contemplative silence. Each of us lost in our own thoughts, grappling with the unspoken question that hangs in the air like a heavy fog. When the time comes, will one of us be able to raise our weapons against a friend? What will it mean for our friendship with Wen if we do?

I steal a glance at Beinon, his features softened by the dim lighting, and then at Wen, her usually playful demeanour tinged with a touch of sadness. We've formed a bond stronger than many, considering we come from different realms.

Considering my background. And Beinon's.

But for now, we push those thoughts aside, drowning them in the remnants of faerie wine and the warmth of the late spring evening. The future may be filled with uncertainties, but in this moment, we find solace in each other's company… however long that may last.

Perhaps unwisely, I choose to use some of the healing herbs I bought from Jill to ease the dreadful ache in my head from the previous night's drinking. Maybe I allowed myself to relax a little *too* much.

The sun is painful to my eyes when I step out from my tent, but the temperature is welcome. Each passing day brings with it a surge of warmth, as if each sunrise is determined to outshine the one before, propelling us towards the zenith of summer. The wood faeries, like sunflowers, turn their faces to the daytime warmth, while the lunar faeries dance beneath the stars' silver glow, revelling in the crystal-clear nights. Our camp thrives with bustling interaction, faeries from various courts mingling and bonding, even as they gravitate towards the familiarity of their own kin.

Complacency is a silent killer, Efia.

My father would tell me. Which is why I don't even attempt to branch out and speak to other faeries. Many of these creatures will break bread together tonight but kill each other in the morning.

Despite being alone most of the time, I don't dare take risks by trusting anyone else.

I don't take the risk that my father may hear of me conversing with anyone outside my court besides Beinon and Wen.

He has already ordered me to end Beinon's life. But, due to the rules of the Betwixt, I fortunately will have to wait for a trial to do so.

Father's absence continues to be a resounding

blessing, his enigmatic demeanour most likely keeping him away from the camp. The lack of any displeased missives or stern appearances hints at his silent approval of my performance in the opening trial. Had he heard about Ansel or had his sentiment been different, I'm certain words would have reached my ears. In his stead, his adviser, Arawn, has become a frequent visitor, his presence often gracing the outskirts of my tent, flanked by my father's guards.

This morning, as the dawn paints the sky with hues of gold and pink, Arawn is already waiting for me outside my tent, his lips quirked up in a barely noticeable smile—a rare sight indeed.

He can tell I am suffering from the wine.

"Morning, Efia. You need to train for the next trial."

I can't help but groan, wondering if I could put him off for an hour or two. "Do you have doubts about my abilities, Arawn?"

His eyes flicker, a moment of amusement dancing within them. "I think your ego is much stronger than your skills."

Before I can retort, he diverts my attention to the matter at hand. "The king and queen will unveil details of the next trial this afternoon."

A sense of apprehension ripples through me. "Any hints about what it might entail?"

Arawn's grin widens, mischief dancing in his eyes as he pretends to brush off imaginary lint from his

Umbra Guild badge. "Oh, my dear Efia, you know I won't spoil the surprise."

My eyes narrow at him. He knows more than just the second trial. And he knows well that I'm onto his little game, his deliberate withholding of information. But what he doesn't realise is that I see it as a strategy, not just secrecy. Why not gather all the pieces of the puzzle before plunging into the fray? Knowledge is power, especially in these trials. Gwydion understood that. It wasn't just his abilities that allowed him to surpass my father. My father lacks vision, but that's where I excel.

I fix Arawn with a sly smile, a glint of mischief in my eyes. "You know, Arawn, I've always admired your ability to keep secrets. Almost as much as I admire your impeccable fashion sense."

I eye him up and down, knowing he despises the almost-suffocating uniform of the guild. He chuckles, a genuine warmth in his eyes as he plays along. "Faux flattery won't get you any closer to answers, Efia."

I sigh in mock disappointment, then straighten up, feigning seriousness. "Very well, Arawn. Keep your secrets, for now."

Arawn huffs playfully. "Free for a session?"

"With you?" I say. "Any opportunity to knock you on your arse, of course."

Training will certainly take my mind off everything. I can't deny that my mind has been swirling with ideas for the next trial, and the worry that I will finally face Beinon. Do I follow my father's command

and kill my friend? Do I potentially cause a rift between Wen and me if I do so?

Arawn's steps wrench me from that downhill thought process as the early morning sun filters through the dense canopy, and I follow him to a small clearing. It's a serene spot, tucked away just a short walk from camp, shielded from prying eyes by towering trees and lush ferns.

I stand with my back straight. In my hand, I hold one of my slender, gleaming blades, the metal catching the sunlight. My eyes, however, remain locked onto my opponent. Arawn, a lithe and agile figure, holds a slender sword of his own, its blade humming with latent energy. He ties his red hair at the back of his head before tipping it in my direction.

We circle each other, the tension in the air palpable. The forest seems to hold its breath, as if anticipating the clash of our blades. With a sudden, fluid movement, Arawn lunges forward, his sword slashing through the air. I deftly sidestep and our blades meet with a resounding clash, sending sparks dancing into the air.

We're usually evenly matched, our movements graceful and precise. But for once I am... finding this harder.

I don't understand it as we exchange blows, our swords blurring in the morning light, each strike met with a parry. I can't help but frown faintly as I block one of Arawn's strikes.

"You've improved," I remark, my voice calm and

composed despite the intensity of our spar. I can feel my chest rising and falling quicker with each breath.

Arawn smiles and his eyes gleam with determination as he pushes against me, his strength evident. "As have you," he replies, a hint of admiration in his voice.

But I don't feel like it.

Why does this feel difficult?

I have allowed my brain to wander, because despite what I felt was my best efforts, Arawn gains the upper hand. With a swift move, he disarms me, leaving my sword on the ground.

Panic.

Panic is what I feel.

He has disarmed me.

It's a rare occurrence for me to lose—and years since I last did—and the shock of it lingers. Arawn looks just as taken aback, his eyes wide and unsure as if it really happened.

I can barely catch my breath, the taste of defeat bitter on my tongue. Losing is never an option, not for someone like me, not under my father's relentless training. But here I am, defeated, feeling humiliated, and panic claws at the edges of my consciousness like sharp talons.

My chest tightens, suffocating me, as if the weight of my failure is pressing down on me, crushing me under its merciless grip. My father's voice echoes in my mind, relentless and unforgiving, reminding me of the consequences of failure, of the shame it brings upon our name.

It takes everything in me not to show this to Arawn. Not to gasp for air under this unfamiliar feeling, desperate to escape the suffocating grip of my inadequacy, but there is no reprieve, no escape from the relentless expectations that bind me.

Turn it off.

Every beat of my heart feels like a drumroll of impending doom, each slow inhale a struggle against the weight of my father's disappointment. Wisps of shadow rise around me delicately, as if they know to keep calm.

Arawn recovers from his surprise, standing quickly and looking around the edges of the clearing before he picks up and hands me my sword.

I'm not even sure what the consequences would be for what just happened. Probably bad for Arawn as well as for myself.

"You okay, Efia?" he asks quietly, concern flickering in his eyes.

Turn it off.

I shove the panic down, down, down, until it is locked away behind an almost impenetrable wall of solid oak trees in my mind. I nod, taking my blade and swallowing down my shame.

Why do I feel shame?

"Just caught off guard. It's obviously the wine still going to my head. Best two out of three?"

My voice only wavered once. He looks uncertain

for a moment, before he agrees, and we resume our spar.

Focus.

My eyes close and I take a deep breath, focusing on the present. Telling myself that in this moment, nothing else matters.

It may just be a training session, but if word of this got back to my father, I would be punished. I push aside the doubts that threaten to cloud my focus. Instead of letting my mind drift to worries and distractions, I channel all my energy into the fight.

My eyes open, homing in on Arawn. He must see the change in my stance as he smiles and nods, and we continue our spar.

Once more, we are mostly equal in ability, but it is no longer a struggle for me. With a sudden burst of energy, I disengage, twirling away from Arawn's reach. I lunge forward, my blade aimed at his side. Arawn counters with a swift parry, our swords clashing once more.

"Any estimates on how many faeries remain for the next trial?" I breathe out, stepping back.

"Enough to cause you issue should you not *focus*," he jabs, and I roll my eyes.

Arawn would never be this relaxed or friendly if my father were watching. I enjoy our sparring sessions when Father is unavailable. It gives me a glimpse of who Arawn truly is, behind the duty.

The world around us seems to fade away as we focus on each other. The only sounds are the rustling of leaves and the ringing of steel.

"Are you going to come watch me in the next trial?" I ask with heavy breaths.

His blade slips against mine a sliver.

"Your father hasn't instructed me. Why, would you want me there?"

"I mean, it would be nice to have a supporter." I smile as we circle each other.

His jaw clenches, holding back something he wants to say.

"Will father be watching?" I ask quickly whilst he is distracted. If I can get him to answer that, I'll know the trial is taking place somewhere where an audience can watch.

"He will not." He shakes his head. "He's been instructed by King Lew to create a portal in the centre, but it won't be possible for him to watch."

"In the centre, huh?"

Not possible to watch. Meaning it will be similar to the ravine. Likely just as vicious and deadly as the first trial. Not a trial of strategy, but strength—something faeries revere more than almost anything else.

Arawn's eyes widen as they snap to meet mine. He presses his tongue against his cheek, shaking his head in frustration at himself.

"Don't worry." I laugh. "I won't tell father you slipped up."

He points his sword at me. "You are sly, Efia."

"Wouldn't Father be *proud*?" I say with as much

sarcasm as I can muster.

Arawn lunges towards me.

As the sun climbs higher in the sky, our movements grow more fluid, our strikes more precise. It's a test of endurance now, a battle of wills as much as skill.

With an unexpected manoeuvre, I disarm him.

His sword goes flying, and I catch it effortlessly in my free hand.

Arawn blinks in surprise, his eyes wide. He hadn't seen that move coming, and neither had I until that very moment.

I offer him a triumphant grin as I hold both swords, one in each hand. "Seems like I've still got a few surprises up my sleeve," I tease, my voice filled with playful satisfaction.

Arawn chuckles, a mixture of shock and amusement in his expression. "Very funny. Good spar."

I nod, a sense of satisfaction washing over me. "Indeed."

With that, we sheathe our swords. We make our way back to camp, and my breath gradually steadies, the comforting weight of my blade against my side.

A slight mental struggle washes over me as I think about losing the first round. I can't help but wonder if I'm becoming soft, losing my edge. My father's expectations weigh heavily on my shoulders, and I can't help but feel a nagging sense of curiosity about my father's thoughts on my performance in the first trial.

Father's expectations have always been high. And his silence so far is both a blessing and a curse.

"Arawn, has my father mentioned about how I fared in the first trial?" I ask, my tone laced with uncertainty.

Arawn's eyes meet mine, and he shakes his head slowly. "No, Efia. He hasn't said a word."

I can't help but feel a mixture of relief and frustration. Relief that there have been no criticisms or reprimands, but frustration at the silence that hangs in the absence of his praise or encouragement.

I don't know why I expect any. I've never had it before.

Arawn seems to sense my conflicting emotions and offers a reassuring smile. "Sometimes, no comment is better than any comment, you know that."

I nod, appreciating his attempt to ease my concerns. Arawn has always been my father's man. He is his second in command. He will always take my father's side and will always do as commanded. But when we are alone, he offers support and advice. I can't resent him for the times he has been present during my punishments. Father would harm him far worse than he does to me if Arawn were to speak up. I have some value. Father would count Arawn as expendable and exchange him for a more loyal fae if he were to stand up for me.

Even I can see the conflict in Arawn's eyes when he has to watch. When he must deal out a punishment.

It is something we do not talk about.

But it is there.

We continue walking toward camp, the conversation about my father and the trials lingering in the air.

"Efia," Arawn says. As if he were fighting to keep the words behind his teeth. "It... it won't always be this bad."

My head tilts in confusion as he runs a hand through his brown hair, his dark brows furrowed over concerned eyes.

"What do you mean?" I ask with an unsure smile.

"I just... never mind."

I don't press. I don't want to get into the conversation about my punishments. Bringing it up would just make it awkward between us. I know Arawn's duty is important. I know that if he were to stand up for me, he would be punished—likely killed. So I do not blame him.

But I don't want to talk about it either.

"I suppose I shall see you after the second trial?" I change the subject and ask him when we reach the border of the trees.

"No doubt." With a simple nod, he looks at me with an unfamiliar expression for a split second, before he turns and leaves, and I wonder if the next time I see him will be as pleasant.

I take a deep breath, casually walking through the tents when my shades rise and whisper affectionately and the sight of white catches my eye. Pulling back a step, I glance through the open canvas of a tent.

I—perhaps stupidly—take a step in.

He is sat cross legged on the furs of his bed. He has a bottle filled with what looks like oil in his hand, the fingers of his free one slick with it as he rubs it into his scalp. I inhale, smelling something sweet with a hint of nuttiness. It smells delicious.

"Ansel?"

Forged metal screeches, my ears ringing as I bring my blade up in time to meet Ansel's.

His face is inches from mine, his teeth bared.

I grin. "Nice to see you too."

Golden eyes jerk and meet mine, blinking a few times as he realizes who has entered his tent. There's a wariness to his gaze… but it soon fades to a warmth. He lowers his arm.

"*Vicious one?*"

I smile and step into the shelter of his tent without thinking.

"How are you?" I ask, tilting my head up as I face him.

I forgot how tall he is. He stretches his shoulders and I suddenly realise he is shirtless. Turning, he shows me his back as he places his sword on a small table.

"*Good as new, and no scar.*" He faces me, ignoring my astonishment that he so easily turned his back on me. "*I must thank you again.*"

"It was nothing." I wave a hand. He looks down, eyeing my swords and flushed face.

"*Training?*"

A noise of confirmation leaves me. "Perhaps we could spar one day?" I ask without thought, mentally slapping myself. Although, it would be a great opportunity to learn his fighting technique.

He narrows his eyes as if he heard where my thoughts went. But the corners of his lips rise. "*Sure. Why not?*" His golden eyes glinting mischievously. "*I suppose we'll have to see if your skills match your confidence in a spar, won't we?*"

I feel a playful challenge in his words and decide to meet it head-on. "Oh, you might be surprised."

He takes a step closer, his presence filling the small space between us. "*I feel like I find myself constantly surprised by you, Mathonwy.*"

My heart quickens, and I can't help but return his smile. "Well, Ansel, I think you and I are going to get along just fine."

He chuckles. "*I'm counting on it. Are you going to the announcement?*"

"Of course," I reply. "I need all the information I can get. Are you?"

His gaze holds mine. "*Absolutely.*"

My cheeks flush, and I'm glad for the dim lighting in the tent. "Well, I'll see you there, Ansel."

He nods, an unreadable look in his eyes. "*I'll look forward to it.*"

As I leave his tent, the smile drops from my face as my chest tightens.

What the hell was that? Was I *flirting* with my competition? Someone I barely knew?

What was my brain and mouth doing?

What unnerved me was that it felt completely natural to speak with him like that. But the thing that took me most by surprise was I think he flirted back.

This is a sickness of the mind I cannot heal, though I have tried. It is as if her spirit is determined to reunite with this spectre she believes she has seen. I would dare not say this to your brother for fear of being killed, but I'm afraid, Your Majesty, there is nothing more I can do for her... Other than pray that Corph takes her swiftly before she becomes a danger to herself, or you.

PERSONAL CORRESPONDENCE TO HIGH KING GWYDION FROM HIGH PRIEST CAELON

CHAPTER TWELVE

I don't see Ansel in the gathered crowd. But I do see Beinon.

The whole crowd is buzzing with the thought of seeing the king and queen together again so soon, not used to having the leaders in the same air so often.

But I can see through their facade. This isn't just about relaying information—it's an opportunity for them to assess the remaining contenders, to gauge the extent of the threat each faerie poses. They're strategists, just like me, and every move they make is calculated.

Beinon's gaze briefly meets mine, and I see the knowing look in his eyes. He understands the significance of my presence here, as does his mother. I scan the crowd, my senses sharp, searching for any signs of Aisling. I did not see them during the first trial, and their absence weighs heavily on my mind. Aisling is a force to be reckoned with, a fierce and agile warrior—the fastest harpy ever known, even surpassing their father's speed.

With any luck, they were taken out in the first trial—but if they were I have not heard about it.

The royal voices cut through the murmurs.

"Welcome, everyone." Queen Lilah's tone like a soft bell, brings everyone's attention to her. The queen's eyes shimmer with hidden knowledge as she surveys the assembly.

King Lew continues, his voice confident and commanding, not waiting for her to continue. "We won't beat around the bush. The second trial will take place in the Gwenhwyvar fields."

Confusion ripples through the crowd, and I feel a knot forming in my stomach. The Gwenhwyvar fields, named after Gwydion and Bron's mother, stretches with endless beauty—rolling meadows adorned with vibrant green grass and wild yellow spring flowers that bloom perpetually. My heart aches at the idea of the king and queen's actions tainting yet another corner of the Betwixt, but I'm powerless to stop it.

If Uncle Gwydion was here…

A subtle exchange passes between the monarchs—a brief, imperceptible glare from the queen towards King Lew. Her expression shifts into an eerie smile, her delicate features framed by her pale skin. She lifts her chin. "Your objective is simple: survive and reach the centre."

The centre?

Arawn's words from our spar filter through my mind once more as it races, contemplating the implications of their words. The Gwenhwyvar fields aren't just a picturesque landscape, they're home to secrets, perhaps even ancient magic. The king and queen's choice of location isn't arbitrary; it's loaded with meaning. As the noise of the crowd rises, abuzz with speculation and whispered conversations, I remain rooted to the spot. My instincts are screaming, and a disappointing realisation seeps into my bones.

I spot Beinon, his blonde hair tied back, standing close to the dais.

"Once you reach the centre," the king continues, "you will be portalled back to camp, having survived the second trial. You have less than two weeks to prepare."

The portals open behind the rulers, and they step away, leaving us all to digest the information.

Well... That was as useful as a wishing well with a hole in the bottom.

Beinon navigates his way through the shifting crowd, reaching my side. "So, what's your guess on the trial?" I pivot toward him, curious if he has come to the same thinking as me.

He hums thoughtfully. "Well, I'm not sure you're going to be thrilled with my answer."

I groan in anticipation, and he chuckles.

"A labyrinth," we both say simultaneously.

"I despise puzzle mazes," I remind him, a shudder running down my spine.

Uncle Gwydion was known for crafting intricate mazes using the large hedges in the castle gardens. Every year, he would challenge me to navigate them. But it wasn't the physical challenge that unsettled me; it was the thought of unseen dangers lurking in those leafy corridors. The trap hedges that could ensnare you, the sand pits that could swallow you whole, and even a time when he transformed one of his guards into something monstrous to chase me along the narrow pathways.

It wasn't a matter of whether I could complete the maze—I did so every time. It was the psychological torment, the fear of the unknown, the risk that I couldn't fully see. Uncle Gwydion had always ensured my abilities couldn't be used to their full potential within the maze, suppressing my command over shadows.

It was a different type of training to what my father did… but it was torment all the same.

The only difference was, Uncle Gwydion would never allow me to be truly harmed, but this trial feels different. I wonder if the king and queen are aware of Gwydion's fascination with mazes and if they drew inspiration from his creations.

The challenge ahead will test not only my skills but also my courage to confront the darkness within those winding passages.

Beinon nods, his blue eyes glinting with a mixture of amusement and concern. "I know, but I'm betting this maze won't be as straightforward as those you've faced before."

Straightforward?!

I roll my eyes, half in jest. "Thanks for the reassurance."

He grins, a hint of mischief in his expression. "You'll do just fine, Efia. You always do. Fancy a spar?"

My eyes roll. He asks me this all the time, knowing I will say no. I do not spar with Beinon, not giving him an opportunity to learn how I move.

I also know that I would monitor his own skills. See him as someone to eliminate.

He laughs without waiting for an answer, walking off between the faerie folk as we make our way to my tent to hopefully find Wen. Sure enough, when we step inside, Wen is already there, perched on my pallet with a bottle of faerie wine in hand.

"Ready for the second trial, Efia?" Wen teases, her dark eyes dancing with mirth, knowing how many mazes I have conquered over the years. "Or are you already planning your escape?"

I chuckle and flop down beside her. "Oh, you know me, Wen. Always plotting."

Beinon settles on the other side of me, a thoughtful expression on his face. "Seriously, though, we need to think about our approach. If it's a labyrinth, there could be traps, dead ends, and who knows what else."

"Uh, since when is this a group project?" I raise a brow at him.

Wen takes a sip of wine.

I'll never understand how the little faerie has such

a high tolerance for the drink.

"Forget all the blood, guts and glory," she tells me. "Remember, the aim is to reach the centre. You'll need to stay focused on that goal."

As the conversation continues, ideas and strategies bouncing around, I can't help but feel grateful for these two by my side. The uncertainty of the trials, the looming possibility of facing each other, it's all easier to bear when we're together.

The atmosphere within the tent eases the weight of the impending trial, but my thoughts drift back to Ansel. I wonder where he is, how he's preparing, and if he's facing the same unease that's gnawing at me. It's been hours since we spoke, our alliance forged in the heat of the first trial, now just a memory—would we see each other again as enemies?

I catch myself wondering if he's skilled in mazes, if he's used to the disorienting feeling of being trapped in twists and turns. The image of his confident smile flashes before my eyes, and I can't help but admit that part of me hopes he'll be all right.

But as the moments tick by and the conversation in the tent continues, I push those thoughts to the back of my mind. Right now, I need to focus on the present and the challenges ahead. I need to be ready for whatever awaits in the Gwenhwyvar fields and make sure I come out of it unscathed.

As Beinon and Wen eventually step out of the tent, the sun is beginning to set, and I lay awake for a while, surrounded by the dim noise of camp, and the loudness of my own thoughts.

"Oh," I say. "Hello."

Ansel has taken me by surprise, my shades not alerting me to his presence in my training section of the clearing beyond the woods.

"*Mathonwy*," he acknowledges with a nod.

I watch as he swings his sword for a few moments, so effortlessly trained in using it.

"Shall we have our session now?" I ask him, thinking it would be a good opportunity to learn how he fights. If I come up against him in one of the other trials, I'll need every advantage I can.

Wait… do I really feel comfortable revealing my skills to this faerie? This stranger?

His dark chest rises and falls with his heavy breathing. But he smiles in a way that tells me he knows exactly what I'm thinking.

Just a small smile, but it is beautiful, nevertheless.

"*I'd like that. Let's see how good you really are*," he teases.

I brush aside my thoughts and laugh softly, catching the way his eyes widen slightly, as if surprised to hear it leave my mouth.

I unsheathe one blade, swinging it around with my wrist to warm it up.

Ansel stands tall. He remains that way as I lower myself slightly into a fighting stance.

"Ready—"

He whips forward with an incredible speed, causing me to bring up my sword at the last moment, blocking his strike. I grit my teeth, pushing with my strength against his.

He grins, inches from my face, satisfied he has taken me by surprise.

And he has. Again. My shades are remarkably quiet, as if they have taken a step back to watch.

I shove him away, straightening my spine as we circle each other.

Now we are alone, maybe I can learn more about my *ally*. "So, Ansel. You're far too mysterious for my liking. Care to share a little about yourself, considering I saved your life?"

I lunge forward, one blade in hand.

He parries my strike effortlessly, a smirk playing on his lips.

"And you think that allows you to know anything about me? Why ruin the mystery, vicious one? Keeps things interesting."

I sidestep a swipe from his blade, my eyes narrowing playfully at the name he calls me.

"Interesting, huh? I was hoping for a bit more substance than that."

Ansel brushes a snow-white loc out of his eyes,

grinning wickedly. "*Substance is overrated. Leaves little room for surprise.*"

And he is a surprise.

But our conversation dies off for a minute, our skills interestingly on equal footing as our swords gleam in the mid-morning sun.

Turn it off.

"You're quick on your feet," I tell him after avoiding another one of his sweeps of his sword. "Must have a few tricks up your sleeve."

"*Wouldn't you like to find out?*" He grunts as he goes for me again.

With a swift move, I jump to avoid his arm, leaping over him and bringing my elbow against his arm, disarming him, holding my sword at his throat.

"Perhaps I would," I tease through heavy breathing.

I would like to know them all.

Know what I am truly up against when he inevitably turns on me.

Ansel's laughter fills the air as he concedes defeat, and there's a different kind of tension in the air.

I blink a few times, stepping back and bringing my sword down.

"*Well played, Mathonwy.*"

He stretches his arms out, catching his breath, and a question comes out before I can stop it.

"You're good. Where did you learn to fight like that?"

All at once, the playful atmosphere gutters. His eyes darken for a moment as he looks towards me, before he shakes his head, looking away.

"Survival tends to be a great teacher."

My curiosity deepens, but I do not question him further. I know more than most, the lessons of a strict teacher. Ansel feels like a kindred spirit in that regard. Everyone may know the brutality of my father, but there are many other faeries in the realm that can commit cruel acts in the name of family.

Blood and family don't mean everything. To faeries, sometimes all that matters is strength, no matter the cost.

Charging crystals beneath the full moon is believed to not only enhance their mystical properties, but also infuse them with the ethereal energy of the lunar cycle. Whether used for divination, energy work, or spiritual balance, a crystal charged under the full moon is thought to carry a touch of lunar magic.
HEALING, CRYSTALS & FAERIE MAGIC BY JESIBA LUNASTRA

CHAPTER THIRTEEN

The air in the marketplace within the depths of the Betwixt is alive with the vibrant hum of magical energy. It's possibly one of the few places I enjoy when it's busy…

Or maybe that's due to the lack of bloodshed.

Fighting is banned in the Fujin Market—a market led by one of the most renowned Seelie fae families. And they're almost as vicious as my father, so no one dares break their laws.

There's a kaleidoscope of colours and scents that can overwhelm the senses. Enchanting melodies, stalls adorned with sparkling crystals, glowing herbs, and ethereal artefacts beckoning curious onlookers.

It's where Jill usually sells her human wares when she isn't at camp.

It's where Wen sells her crystals charged by the moon.

"How many have you got to sell today?"

"Six full crystals!" She beams. "It was a good full moon."

Wen loves the summer months. The skies are clearer, the moon is more visible, and it gives her more opportunity to bask in its bright glow.

"I just need to drop these in to Magdala, and we can go."

She wanders towards a medium sized tent, draped in bright coloured fabrics, and I follow.

"Mathonwy, fancy seeing you here."

I turn on instinct, spotting Ansel as he approaches, a smile on his face as he packs away his purchases into a leather satchel at his waist.

"Ansel," I exclaim, my voice unintentionally rising, while Wen barely conceals a smirk.

"And who might this enchanting faerie be?" he inquires, extending his hand to gently clasp Wen's.

Smooth.

I roll my eyes, and predictably, Wen's cheeks flush, accompanied by a giggle.

A giggle.

What the fuck?

"This is Wen. Wen, meet Ansel."

"It's a pleasure to finally meet you, Ansel." She grins at me with a mischievous glint. "Efia's shared all sorts of tales about you."

I might just strangle her.

"Oh, has she?" Ansel raises an eyebrow.

Wen's sly grin widens. "Oh, just the usual sisterly banter. You know how it is."

Ansel chuckles, looking between Wen and me. "*I'm sure it's all in good fun.*"

Wen nods enthusiastically. "Absolutely. So, Ansel, how do you find having to deal with our Ef?"

Ansel's gaze shifts to me, and I fight the urge to squirm under his scrutiny. "*It's... interesting. Full of surprises.*"

"Well, Ansel." I force a smile. "I'm sure you're *very* busy. We'll just be heading off."

As we retreat, I shoot Wen another menacing glance, silently warning her of the impending retribution for her antics. Ansel's lingering smirk suggests he's caught on to the unspoken tension between us.

Turning Wen around, I guide her away, determined to put some distance between us and Ansel's amused gaze.

"*Of course, pleasure to meet you, Wen.*"

"You too!" Wen calls out cheerfully after him.

The moment we're out of earshot, I can't resist muttering to Wen, "You enjoy making my life difficult, don't you?"

Wen chuckles, unrepentant. "Oh, come on, Efia. A little fun never hurt anyone. And Ansel definitely looks like *fun.*"

She waggles her eyebrows at me, and I decide to let it slide for now. I'll find a way to get her back.

My current priority is to bring these crystals to Magdala and then return to camp. But thoughts of

Ansel's intentions linger in my mind as we make our way through the market. Why do our paths keep crossing? Is he deliberately seeking me out? I push away these unsettling thoughts as we enter a tent.

Magdala is one of the oldest living lunar faeries in our living memory. She's a bit... odd, but harmless.

Magdala's tent hums with an energy. Crystals of all shapes and sizes, aged scrolls, and vibrant fabrics create, what appears to be, a cosy and mysterious atmosphere that draws people in. The scent of exotic herbs lingers, and the tent seems alive with pulsating mystique.

When we enter, Mags is nowhere to be seen. Wen wonders out loud about where she is, but she heads to the back to stow away the crystals, and my gaze wanders over the array of arcane artefacts. My fingers trace the edges of a peculiar talisman, the shadows whispering in a rush when a gnarled hand clasps my arm. I turn to find Magdala, her wrinkled face tense and eyes unseeing.

"Mags?" I go to pull my arm away, but she holds on tightly.

"A rare gift. To run among the shadows."

I stop my movements, eyes roaming over her face as a shiver runs up my spine. She doesn't blink. She doesn't bear any expression. "But beware, child of death, for the threads of fate are ever-changing."

"What... What do you mean, Mags?"

Wen enters the main area of the tent, her brow falling once she sees Magdala.

"Mags? Everything all right?" Magdala's gaze shifts to

her. "And you, moon child. Your part is yet to be revealed. But bigger than all of us know. A powerful connection, indeed."

With a cryptic nod, Magdala releases my arm. "Be mindful of the turns, for destinies are woven in ways we cannot always foresee."

Wen laughs awkwardly, taking a hold of the old faerie's arm.

"Come on, let's get you back to your tea leaves."

Magdala blinks a few times, as if clearing the tiredness from her eyes.

"Wen dear, when did you get here?" she asks with surprise.

Wen's eyes widen a little.

"Are you feeling all right, Mags?" she asks her.

"Course I am." She waves a dismissive hand at her and starts wandering to the back of her tent.

"Morning, Efia," she calls back without a glance back. I wave pathetically, still stunned from what just happened.

As Magdala returns to her mystical artefacts, Wen and I exchange glances, both feeling a little discomfort.

"What did she say to you?" Wen whispers, taking a step closer to me.

"She mentioned my shadows… called me a child of death."

Wen scoffed. "Probably one of the more *flattering* names I've heard you called."

I huffed. "You're telling me… What do you think it

means?"

"I have no idea. There's seer blood in Mag's bloodline. But I've never seen her do that before, and look, she doesn't even remember."

It was true. Magdala had returned to pottering about with her belongings in the back.

Wen's gaze returns to me, assessing me from head to toe.

"You're spooked. *You*. Scared of a little old lunar faerie," she remarks.

"I am not *scared*," I deny, though it's a blatant lie. Anything involving fate or destiny fills me with dread. The idea of being controlled by unseen forces terrifies me, especially considering the lifetime of manipulation I've endured at my father's hands. To acknowledge that there might be something larger at play, orchestrating every action and situation, is deeply unsettling.

Wen brushes off my concerns with a wave of her hand. "Mags is old. Her mind is muddled now. Pay her no mind."

I force a tight smile and nod as we exit the tent and step back into the bustling market. But as we emerge, we're confronted by the last person I want to see—aside from my father.

"Efia," they greet with a grin, their dark red eyes brightening.

"Aisling," I reply through gritted teeth, my smile strained.

Aisling is the child of King Lew.

Whilst they carry the typical harpy traits of their father—large wings pulled in tightly right now to protect them, blackened claws ending each finger and taloned feet—they have the noticeable dark red colouring of their infamous mother. A vicious harpy that died in a previous battle between the Seelie and Unseelie courts.

Aisling's gaze drifts over my shoulder towards Mags' tent, and a smirk plays on their lips. "Still consorting with the lunar faeries, I see," they taunt, their tone dripping with mockery. "Tell me, Efia, have they given you any prophecies lately? Seen any visions of your impending doom?"

I clench my jaw, resisting the urge to snap back at them. Instead, I force a tight smile. "They have their uses," I reply curtly, trying to maintain my composure despite the barb. Wen doesn't react. She knows I can't let on how close we actually are. Best let my enemies believe I use her for information and nothing else.

Their laughter rings out, sharp and grating, echoing through the market. "Oh, I'm sure they do," they retort, their tone filled with thinly veiled disdain as her gaze drifts over to Wen. It takes everything in me not to step in front of her, to block their view. "I'll be seeing you in the next trial, Efia."

With that parting shot, Aisling turns on their heel and disappears into the crowd, leaving me to stew in their words as I watch their retreating form, a knot of unease tightening in my chest.

Aisling is likely my biggest competition, other than

Beinon. I know it will be a difficult challenge if I were to come up against them. I have no idea of their abilities outside of their harpy nature—and that's deadly enough.

All I can do is hope I am ready when the time comes.

"You wanted to see me, Father?" It had been a surprise to receive a firesprite from Arawn, informing me that my father requested my presence at home.

I thought I wouldn't hear from him again until after the second trial. Calling me back to the Unseelie court was dangerous. If any of the Unseelie Guilds learned of my return to the Unseelie court, they would no doubt be lying in wait as soon as I portalled in. They can try to kill me without consequence here... well, without consequence if my father did not catch them. Fortunately, my father must have been feeling generous, allowing me to portal in directly outside the manor gates.

Home is Du Manor, which lies directly in the centre of the Unseelie court. It has belonged to my family for almost a millennium... so I'm told.

It had never felt like home to me.

There is no warmth there.

Only painful memories.

My father's guards nod their heads respectfully as I pass, and I adjust my leather vest, afraid that Father would spot even the tiniest bit of dust from camp. Pick me up on it.

Any reflection on the guild is a reflection on him.

And his daughter is held mostly to his standards.

I enter the main hall, where my father stood at the bottom of the stairs, Arawn at his side with a subtle frown on his face.

That doesn't bode well.

I come to stand a few feet in front of him with my head held high. "Father."

Perhaps he is to commend me on my performance so far.

Father sneers at me.

Perhaps not.

"I have a job for you."

My spine stiffens. Perhaps I could say no, use the trials as an excuse.

"Father." My gaze meets his cold, calculating eyes. "Is it wise for me to be carrying out these tasks during the trials?"

Father scoffs. "Wisdom is for the cautious, Efia. Power is for the bold. You want the throne, don't you?"

His tone is challenging. Daring me to say I don't. Daring me to decline this task. I want to.

I don't want to take a life when I don't have to.

I should argue. I should say no. I should run…

"What is it?" is all I say.

"Celeste is being… a nuisance. She has become a thorn in our side. Her *ambition* threatens our guild. I want you to send her a warning."

Dread causes my stomach to gutter.

Celeste is one of the most well-known elders in the vampire clans. There weren't many clans in the faerie realm, the majority lived in their own. But those who did reside here were powerful... and often liked to push the boundaries of my father's patience.

It must be serious if father is considering this. But in all honesty, it could be as simple as her threatening my life within the contest. Father just likes to exercise his power every now and again. Remind everyone who is the brother of Gwydion. Who is most powerful in the Unseelie court besides King Lew.

"Her nephew, Darick. He runs The Cob Web in the Ogwr district," I tell him. "He retires to his home above it after close, he'll be a strong enough message for Celeste."

He leans forward, his eyes narrowing. "Make sure it's done discreetly. We don't need unnecessary attention."

I nod, my expression unwavering as I pull up my mask. "Consider it done."

Without another word from him, I head to my room, where I can prepare for yet another one of my father's orders.

"Failure is not an option, Efia." His ominous voice follows me as I stride away.

I don't break my pace as my shadows intensify around me, but the weight of his threat lingers in the air. I know the consequences of failure in my father's world.

But I have never failed at a mission yet.

Once a Nüwch has you in their sights, the only way to escape is to offer yourself up to Corph before they find you…
DARK FAE AND DEATH GODS, BY UNSEELIE KING BENEDICT

CHAPTER FOURTEEN

The darkened lower floor of the inn still lingers with the odours of stale beer and sweat, remnants of Darick's revelry that persists until the early hours. The music has been turned down, a slower beat than what played earlier, enticing locals to lose themselves in its rhythms. A few faeries lie passed out in corners, remnants of those Darick permits to drink recklessly.

The inn is mostly silent, save for the hushed murmurs of my shades echoing in my ears and the music, allowing me to pass through the darkened inn easily.

No one stirs at my almost silent movements as I ascend the wooden staircase.

No one stirs as I enter his room, the door groaning, the wind outside blowing and covering any noise my boots make.

It feels wrong, sneaking up on someone when they are as vulnerable as Darick is right now. The vampire is sprawled half-naked on his bed, accompanied by a *fae* woman, her short ears and exposed breasts visible.

Turn it off.

Like a silent wraith, I approach and kneel beside the bed, retrieving a small blade from my thigh sheath.

I gaze at Darick's slumbering face, a flicker of gratitude surfacing—thankful that the life I'm about to end is not an innocent one.

My choice of victim was a careful one. Celeste has a large family. By giving my father a name, I eliminated the possibility of him choosing someone—likely a youngling. Someone whose death will be far more painful than Darick's, who is becoming a bit of an outsider to his clan.

Darick is notorious for dealing Rixin, a rampant drug among some of the Unseelie. I cling to my rationalisation as I inhale deeply, tightening my grip on the blade's handle.

Darick's eyes snap open just as I draw the blade across his throat.

The manor echoes with silence as I glide down its cold halls. My cloak billows with each step, and servants cower behind corners at the mere sight of me dressed in my mask. The guards offer no interference, wisely keeping silent after a mission.

In the grand hall, Father and Arawn await once more. Father is perched upon his imposing black stone chair, a semblance of a throne he wishes he had. A mockery of the throne his own brother once held.

"Is it done?" he asks, devoid of concern. No inquiries about my well-being—such courtesy is a foreign concept.

Yet, I feel Arawn's gaze sweep over me, checking me for any injuries.

I lower my mask, presenting the small sack in my hand. The sickening squelch as it hits the floor is stomach churning, and I suppress the rising nausea.

"One hand of Darick Davena. Family ring intact. Sufficient to quell any rebellion from Celeste," I state.

"Any issues?" Father probes.

I shake my head. "There was a fae in his bed."

"Who?" Father's head snaps up, and the consequences for our guild members flash in his eyes if it is someone known.

"No one of note. She remained asleep until I removed the hand."

"What of her now?"

"My shades left little to identify," I report.

I don't tell him that I would've left her alive if she stayed asleep. If she hadn't woken and lunged for me. I don't tell him that what I did makes me feel sick.

A cruel smile curls Father's lips. "Very well. Return to the Betwixt. I shall summon you if needed."

Arawn conjures a portal at his side. Suppressing the urge to demand gratitude for my grim task, I resist the temptation to say, 'you're welcome.' Instead, I offer a perfunctory, "Thank you, Father," as if gratitude is warranted for executing his gruesome orders. Leaving the sack on the floor, I cast a brief look at Arawn before striding toward the portal.

I walk calmly through camp and return to my tent, a surprisingly chilly breeze in the night's air seeping through the fabric.

I'm not shocked when I enter to find Beinon is there, waiting, as my shades continue to hiss in my ear. His eyes, usually warm and inquisitive, darken at the sight of me in my mask and cloak. One look, and he knows.

He knows me and my father enough to realise what I've been doing.

Silence hangs in the air, heavy and suffocating as he watches me remove my mask and cloak, eyeing the small drops of blood on my boots. Beinon's expression twists, torn between understanding and fury.

He steps closer, but it is a mistake.

It is too soon.

A shade forms before he can blink, gripping him by the throat and lifting him from his feet.

He doesn't fight it but grips the humanoid arm firmly. "Who was it? What did he make you do?"

He knows without me telling him it takes a little piece of me every time.

That each time it takes longer and longer to pull back.

What he doesn't know is that it scares me how easy I find it to do the things my father commands. But it is so difficult at the same time. To take a step out of myself, become something I believe I'm not. Even if it feels like a part of me.

To turn it off.

I turn away, my fingers tracing the hilt of one of my swords. The weight of the sack's contents back in the manor lingers in my mind. "It doesn't matter, Beinon."

I hear his feet touch the ground as my shade releases him.

"It matters, Efia," he insists.

I refuse to meet his gaze, unable to face the judgment in his eyes. "I can't tell you. It's done."

His hand tentatively grips my shoulder. "You shouldn't have to bear this alone."

I shake my head, a bitter smile playing on my lips. "We all bear our burdens, Beinon. This one is mine."

I face him, and he searches my eyes, seeking answers I won't give. "I wish you wouldn't shut me out."

"It's better this way," I murmur. "For all of us."

Beinon's grip tightens, as if he can anchor me to reality. "You don't have to do as he says."

I laugh. Because he doesn't know. He doesn't know the horrors my father has woven into my existence. He guesses. But he doesn't know the true extent of my father's cruelty.

Wen has been there many times, but Beinon has never seen me after.

I gently pry his hand from my shoulder, a silent plea for him to let it go.

"What if he ordered you to kill *me*, Efia? Would you do it?" There's an edge to his voice, his frustration boiling over.

The blackness coalesces either side of me, like two steadfast sentries. But they are cautious. I believe Beinon isn't a threat.

I don't tell him I've had those orders. So I avoid the truth.

I meet his gaze, the intensity of his question slicing through the air. "He can't do that."

Not whilst I am in the Betwixt. But there is nothing to stop me from doing so in the trials.

Beinon knows that outside of this contest, I couldn't kill him. Father has me deal with his enemies in the Unseelie court. I've never journeyed to the other court to do his bidding. He wouldn't dare give Queen Lilah reason to cause trouble for King Lew or the Unseelie court.

I don't tell him anything more. The sliver of fear is there, deep in my gut, that I don't know if Beinon will hold back at the final trial.

"You can't keep doing his bidding without question. What if one day he asks the unthinkable of you?"

The room tightens around us, the walls echoing the gravity of his words. I know what he means.

Wen.

I choose my words carefully, each syllable heavy. "If that day comes, I'll find a way out."

It's a dangerous admission. But one I make none the less. Because it almost kills me believing he thinks I could ever do that.

"Then find a way out now," he says desperately, as if it could change his life if I did.

I can't. And he knows this. Because that would be the end for me. As soon as I openly choose Wen, a *Seelie* faerie, over my family. Father would kill me. I would save Wen, I would protect her. But I would die because of it. The only thing that currently protects her is the fact she doesn't live in our court, and that my father believes I can get information about the Seelie court from her.

"I want to be alone, Beinon. Please."

A mix of concern and frustration etches on his face. With a final, longing look, he steps back, leaving me alone in the icy embrace of my tent.

The shadows, both literal and metaphorical, cling to me, and I'm left with the haunting echoes of the choices I make for the sake of my father's will.

Life, like a maze, can take you down many paths, my dear. It's easy to lose yourself in there, Efia.
Don't.
PERSONAL CORRESPONDENCE FROM HIGH KING GWYDION TO EFIA MATHONWY

CHAPTER FIFTEEN

Beinon and I are correct in our prediction, and my frustration is audible as I step through the portal, greeted by the sight before me.

What once sprawled as an endless expanse of lush green grass and vibrant yellow trumpet flowers has been altered. A colossal chunk at the heart of the field has been carved out, replaced by an intricate network of towering hedges that form a labyrinth so expansive it seems to stretch beyond the limits of sight. The hedges rise like giants, creating a mesmerising pattern of rows and columns, concealing secrets within their leafy walls.

There are gaps along each side of the maze—the entry points. Faerie folk flow toward these openings, a crowd gathering around each entrance as anticipation hangs heavy in the air. The challenge has changed, but the competitive spirit remains strong. Paths are chosen at random, each faerie looking for the opportunity to outwit their competitors and reach the coveted centre.

In contrast to the first trial, the atmosphere

buzzes with excitement rather than apprehension. A hunger for action and triumph has replaced the initial nerves. The bell's impending toll marks the transition from eager anticipation to bloodthirsty competition.

Positioning myself strategically, I opt for the entrance with the most activity, shouldering my way through the crowd until I stand near the front. While most faeries gravitate toward the paths with fewer participants, I know that visibility—or lack of it—can work to my advantage. Chaos is bound to erupt the moment the bell rings, and amid the frenzy, I can slip away from the main fray when my abilities are at their weakest. My eyes quickly scan the throngs, looking for Beinon, before I remember to ground myself.

There's no time for sentiment now.

My chest shudders with the breath I inhale, my chest tightening with the expanding of my lungs as I force myself into that unfeeling place needed to survive another trial like this. I pull up my hood and put on my black mask. My blades are drawn, held ready at my sides as I await the signal.

Then, with a sharp, resonating 'ding,' the trial begins.

Instinct propels me forward, a quick, fluid motion allowing me to evade a troll's sweeping axe that has beheaded and ripped through those unfortunate enough to be in its path. The carnage begins before we even step into the maze, as kin of the fallen launch a counterattack on the enraged troll. The resulting skirmish is nothing short of bloody, but I refuse to get caught in the spectacle.

Several faeries surge ahead of me, driven by their eagerness to distance themselves from the violence behind. They dart off in different paths, their focus on escaping the impending battle and not sparing me a second glance.

As I venture further into the maze, the verdant walls enclose around me, and the real trial begins. It's a test of wit, agility, and the ability to adapt on the fly. Paths twist and fork, each turn leading me deeper into the labyrinth's heart.

Adrenaline surges through my veins as I navigate the maze's pathways, a mix of competition and survival guiding my every move.

Flashes of memory fight to the forefront of my brain but I shove them aside. Love and sentiment of my late uncle is not a useful emotion at this moment.

Emotion will only hinder you, Efia. It will only make you weak.

There he is. I wondered when my father's words would pop into my brain.

My footsteps quicken and I veer sharply to the left, seeking refuge from the chaos and bloodshed that swirls around me. Yet, in my desperate bid to escape the harrowing screams and pained cries, I unwittingly plunge headfirst into another encounter.

Two vampires, their malevolent eyes aflame with bloodlust, are viciously assaulting a water nymph—a delicate creature with flowing teal hair now tainted by the bright blue of her own life essence. The scene is grim; one vampire sinking his teeth into her arm while the other tears at her throat.

Her anguished screams pierce the air, causing my heart to clench.

Turn it off.

I go to step away onto a different path, but something makes me stop.

I should leave.

But he isn't watching.

I growl at myself as, without hesitation, I surge forward, every fibre of my being consumed by the need to intervene. My silver sword cleaves through the air, driven by raw strength and unyielding purpose. With a ferocious thrust, I plunge my sword into the vampire's back; the blade punching through his chest until it meets his heart. As I wrench it out, crimson stains my hand.

Hopefully, they weren't part of Celeste's clan.

The water nymph's captor crumbles to the ground, releasing her from his grip. The second vampire whirls around, hissing in a grotesque display of fangs and fury. Before he can react, my blade slices through the air once more, severing his head from his body with a swift, decisive strike. The threat is vanquished, but the weight of the moment lingers heavily in the air.

The weight of what I've done.

Gaze locked on the water nymph, I extend a cautious hand toward her. Her wary, yellow-tinged eyes flit between me and the fallen foes, uncertainty clouding her expression. My silence speaks to my intentions, a silent reassurance that I mean her no harm. With a hesitant movement, her cold and clammy fingers touch mine as she accepts my hand, using it to steady herself as she rises from the ground.

"It's all right," I reassure her, my voice a soothing murmur as I offer her a small, empathetic smile.

Her wariness doesn't waver, a reminder of who I am.

"You should go." A jerk of my head points in the direction they had come from. "More are on their way once they're done back there."

A raven landing on the hedge above us catches her eye for a second, before she looks back to me and nods, a mixture of relief and apprehension in her gaze as she retreats down one of the branching pathways. She glances back once, her yellow eyes briefly meeting mine before she disappears, fading into the labyrinth.

Alone once more, I'm left to grapple with the reality of the situation, praying to all the Gods that my father will not hear of it.

The sounds of battle still echo through the maze, a reminder that this trial is far from over. As the cries of the wounded and the clashing of weapons fill the air, the weight of the challenge ahead settles upon my shoulders.

The Gwenhwyvar fields have transformed into a battlefield of survival, and every choice I make will shape the outcome of this day—and what happens after.

Any silence in the maze is palpable.

Despite my steady steps, an unsettling feeling crawls up my spine, a sense that I'm being watched from the shadows.

I navigate the maze's twisting paths, and the sun's descent paints the tops of the hedges with a warm, golden hue. The pathways darken, lit only by a bracketed torch every now and again. I can't help feeling the anxious anticipation of obtaining my shades full powers. Like waiting for the calm *after* a storm, my senses tingle with hypervigilance. My shades give me an added comfort when I have full use of them, like a shield.

With each passing step, I remain alert, searching for any sign of an opponent worth remembering. So far, the encounters have been unremarkable, minor skirmishes against lesser faerie creatures that scarcely warrant my attention. The absence of stronger adversaries leaves me on edge, the quietude unnerving.

Amid my unease, a whisper of wind carries a distant cry to my ears. Swift as a shadow, I spin around, twin swords at the ready. Metal clashes as my blades intercept a long, metal spear aimed for my back. I lock eyes with my foe, anger and determination flickering in their furious gaze—Aisling.

Aisling's dark wings flare behind them, a

manifestation of their harpy heritage.

My heart races, adrenaline pumping through my veins, and I maintain my defensive stance.

My lips curl into a sardonic grin, laced with defiance. "Aisling. Nice of you to finally join the competition." I twist my blades, pushing against their weapon before stepping back. Aisling's harsh laughter, dripping with malice, sends a shiver down my spine. This fight isn't just about survival—it's about proving myself against one of my biggest threats.

"Efia." They grin wickedly, red eyes narrowing. "I wondered when I'd have the pleasure of taking your life."

I laugh, my palms sweating as I grip my swords tighter. "Not today."

They launch toward me with startling speed, their harpy-like agility making them an elusive target as their long maroon hair flows behind them. I narrowly avoid their attack, sidestepping their outstretched claws by a hairsbreadth. My muscles tighten, my focus unwavering as I launch into a counterattack. My blades dance through the air, attempting to breach their defences and find an opening.

Aisling has the benefit of speed, so I need to finish this skirmish before they can have time to tire me out.

My blades continue to meet their staff, and I'm all too aware that the remaining daylight hampers the full extent of my shadow abilities. What shades I can muster just annoy Aisling more than anything, trying to obscure their view.

A movement catches my eye—a large owl swoops down and lands on a hedge further down the path. Aisling takes advantage of it.

Their spear darts forward, slicing through the muscle and tissue of my arm as they stab forward before ripping it up and out. I can't help the loud cry that escapes me. The warm blood runs down my arm, soaking it immediately—they've hit something vital. I will not die, but it will take longer to heal if I don't pack it with herbs now.

I need this fight to end.

Their laugh fills the air between us, and I bare my lengthening fangs at them, hissing. Movement behind them catches my eye and I grin through my heavy breaths.

We clash again, the force of their attack pushing me back. Their spear darts toward me. I deflect it with my uninjured arm, narrowly avoiding a fatal strike. Adrenaline courses through me, lending me a burst of energy and focus. My swift retaliation catches them off guard, my blade slicing across their heels.

Aisling falls to their knees, momentarily incapacitated.

Seizing the opportunity, I rush forward. The surrounding hedges shift, revealing their true nature as animated barriers. With a surge of determination, I dart past Aisling, allowing the hedges to close behind me, effectively imprisoning them in the maze's heart.

Their enraged scream echoes in my ears.

The sound fades, and I take a deep breath, my heartbeat slowing as I regain my composure. The path ahead remains uncertain, but for now, I've emerged victorious from a battle that could have turned fatal. With my wound open and my resolve unshaken, I steel myself to move on.

The throbbing pulse of my vein, expending blood too quickly from my arm, roars over the beat of my heart. I grab a wrap from my bag and tear a bit off, then bind it. It's not a cure, but hopefully it'll be enough until I can find shelter for the night.

The owl's piercing eyes are fixed on me, a curious observer. The owl rests on a wooden perch before a dense hedge, as if anticipating my approach—something that I proceed with cautiously.

"Salutations," the owl's coo breaks the silence, and my steps falter. Its intense blue eyes hold my gaze. "To move ahead, answer my riddles three. But beware, false answers could spell your end, you see."

That's not creepy at all. I suppress a shiver.

Before I can inquire about the bird's cryptic message, its talons morph slowly into menacing, razor-sharp points, surrounded by an ominous aura. So, that's how failing the test ends—painfully.

There is the alternative path to the left, but that would take me towards the outer wall—likely a much longer path to the middle. The quickest path would likely take me closer to danger, meaning this owl. Despite the sun setting, this is the only way to move forward without running into more faeries than needed, and my wound means I need to get to the centre as soon as possible. If I continue to lose blood, my abilities will be weakened.

It won't matter if I have my shades if I am too dizzy to use them.

No turning back now.

"All right." I exhale, loosening the tension in my shoulders. "Hit me with the first one."

The owl's oversized sapphire eyes appear eager, as though anticipating my success... or failure.

"Voiceless, it cries and wingless it flutters." The creature's melodic tone bears an undercurrent of excitement. "Toothless it bites and mouth-less it mutters. What is it?"

The riddle hangs in the air, challenging my mind to decipher its meaning.

What cries without a voice? The answer comes to me with ease, and I can almost sense a hint of satisfaction in the curve of the owl's beak—a satisfaction that fades as I smile. I won't let on that the first riddle was relatively straightforward.

"The wind," I respond confidently.

The suggested smile seems to vanish from the owl's face. Its wings subtly flare, feathers rustling as it shakes its head.

This is more my kind of game.

Although my early life was marred by my father's cruelty, I fondly remember the hours spent in his library between training sessions, soaking in knowledge about the realms. It was during these times that I immersed myself in the riddles my uncle Gwydion would send me—riddles that he adored crafting.

"Riddle two," the owl hoots, shifting my attention to the next challenge. "Though I live beneath a roof, I never seem to dry. If you will only hold me, I swear I will not lie. What am I?"

"Tongue," I answer almost instantly.

It shrieks in irritation for a moment before settling. If you're going to give me a riddle, at least make it somewhat challenging—unless it says something for the intelligence of the other faeries involved in the competition.

"Riddle three," it hisses, and I wonder why it is getting so irate. "Only one colour, but not one size. Stuck at the bottom, yet I easily fly. Present in sun, but not in rain. Doing no harm and feeling no pain. What. Am. I?"

Only one colour but not one size?

I pace along the ground before the owl sits on its pedestal, as I analyse the final riddle. If I answer wrong, it'll have its claws on my neck before I can draw my blade.

The bird's gaze skips past my shoulder, a glimmer of mischief dancing in its eyes. A grin seems to curl its beak, a silent proclamation of a victory already claimed. A whispered murmur drifts into my ear, growing in intensity as the sun's glow surrenders to the encroaching horizon, and shadows begin their dance toward me along the edges of the pathway. As the final rays of sunshine fade from the sky, my pacing comes to an abrupt halt.

A warmth spreads through me, my hand lowering from my face.

"A shadow," I say to the bird with a wicked grin, my fingers beckoning as darkness responds to my call, swirling into a shroud of inky blackness. My sword is unsheathed, my body spinning just in time for the clash of metal meeting metal—stopping a glinting silver blade before it could find its place in my back.

My gaze locks onto a pair of vibrant blue eyes as I draw back the shadows as quick as they appeared. "Beinon?"

My arm quivers just slightly under the strength he exudes. A corona of my darkness holds his wrist, my shades whispering with urgency, his blade suspended a breath's width above my left shoulder.

His eyes widen, and he relaxes his arm. His free fingers grip my mask, pulling it down to reveal my face. *"Efia?"*

My shades have changed. Before I was limited by the daylight, but it seems after his visit, there has been a change to my Nüwch powers. I will not complain, it means they can protect me in the daylight. And I can feel a change coming… I'll need all the protection I can get.

PERSONAL JOURNAL OF HIGH KING GWYDION

CHAPTER SIXTEEN

The shadows recede, returning to their natural abode. Behind me, the owl lets loose a piercing cry, its wings flapping vehemently before it takes flight. The hedge it perched before retreats, unveiling a new pathway, an alternative route.

Beinon sheathes his dagger and I pull down my hood. He shakes his head, releasing a rough sigh. "Efia, I could've killed you."

A sly smile curves my lips as I tuck away my blade. "Isn't that the point?"

An impatient huff escapes him, his gaze flickering between the path behind me before he enfolds me in an embrace. The scent of his masculine blend—floral notes entwined with the earthy warmth of oak—drifts to my senses, blanching through my surprise.

This feels more intimate than how Beinon has embraced me in the past, the unfamiliar kind touch causing me to melt into his arms, encircling his form with my own.

He draws back, his eyes searching mine, a world of unspoken words contained within them.

"You're injured?" his voice rises as he looks at my wrapped arm.

"I'm fine." I wave a hand; despite the odd spells of dizziness I'm having. A streak of red shows on the wrap, the blood now leaking through.

"I can't believe I nearly killed you," he says to himself more than me, with some frantic undertone to his voice.

"I think you're seriously overestimating your skills, Beinon. I knew you were there," I hold my hand out and smile as the shadows flutter towards me just a smidge.

He rolls his eyes at my casual dismissal, not fully convinced. "You could've been faster." He grins. "I thought *I* was the one with the element of surprise."

I can't help but chuckle, a mixture of relief and amusement bubbling up within me. "Well, next time I'll kill you first."

"Please do," he retorts, the tension from earlier dissipating like morning mist. Our banter feels comforting, a welcome distraction from the intensity of the trial. He looks at me again as I smile at him, and he looks in pain. He looks terrified.

"Efia…" He breathes, his hands cupping my cheeks and an odd expression passing over his features. I pull back my head a little, but he holds me steady.

My stomach dips, and my eyes narrow. "Beinon, I'm *fine*. "We're both all right—"

He pulls me towards him, and it takes a second for me to process that his lips are against mine.

My body is frozen, surprise erasing the words from my mind as it catches up with what my body is doing. Because I am returning his kiss. And before I can contemplate how bad this could be, I indulge myself, because this touch is soft. This touch is nice.

He tastes like faerie wine on a summer's eve and smells like morning dew on the grass. My hands find themselves resting against his leather vest as he pulls me closer with desperation, as if he's been waiting his whole life to kiss me.

We are not entirely gentle. We have never known gentleness in our lives and don't start now.

Too soon, and too early for me to process what we've just done, he pulls away.

"We need to stop." He pants and pulls back.

We should. But the way his slight hardness presses against my stomach between us proves that his body doesn't really feel the same way, and I wonder at the lack of heat that would usually settle within me.

I may never have ventured into this kind of intimacy with Beinon. But I have shared my bed within my court. Nameless, forgetful faces of Unseelie faerie folk that helped me fulfil an urge for a night, nevermore.

"Yes." I laugh awkwardly, the sound breathless. "Well, that was a fucking surprise."

He rolls his eyes before his teeth flash in a wide, happy smile. "Future Queens shouldn't curse."

"Fuck you." I laugh in response, my face heating at the unexpected moment we just shared.

He groans. "Believe me, if I'd let you continue for one more minute, you would be."

My teeth tease the skin of my bottom lip. "Presumptuous of you. Personally, I don't think being outdoors in the middle of a trial would be the best place for *that*."

"Not unless you enjoy voyeurism?" He runs his thumb over my cheek and asks with a wicked grin, his eyes skipping over my shoulders.

My nose scrunches up in distaste as I pull away slightly from his touch, realising he is becoming too bold. "Not my favourite kink, I will admit."

"Good." His eyes darken. "Because we have a guest."

I turn, surprised the shadows did not alert me to our companion. Beyond the owl's pedestal is Ansel, stood proudly in the centre of the path with his hands tucked into the pockets of his breeches—his golden gaze fixed on us.

"*Hello, vicious one,*" he says into my mind.

I smile in his direction and my cheeks heat a little that he saw or overheard us. As I step out of Beinon's arms, his hand stops me from taking a step forward, his other on the hilt of his sword.

"Hi," I reply shyly.

"You know him?" Beinon asks, his expression alarmed.

"I do." I nod. "We worked together in the ravine."

"You… worked with *him*." Beinon's tone is shocked.

I elbow him out of the way. "I am capable."

"*Surprisingly,*" Ansel comments before I send him a rude gesture.

Beinon clears his throat, eyeing Ansel. "So, what are your plans?" he asks him with such familiarity, and I try not to furrow my brow—this is their first meeting. *Right?* "To lure her into a false sense of security before stabbing her in the back?"

"Beinon," I scold him.

"*My plans are no concern of yours, princeling.*" Ansel teeth bare slightly in a soft snarl. "*But if you must know, harming Mathonwy has never crossed* my *mind.*"

I catch Beinon's surprised expression for a second before I turn to Ansel. Like a rope being stretched, the air fills with tension and I can practically see the magic in the air around us.

"All right, all right boys." I take a step away from Beinon and towards Ansel. "Remember, we still have to make it out of here. *Alive.*"

Ansel's eyes are still intense, and Beinon is the first to look away.

"Shall we go?" I ask them both.

Beinon rubs the back of his neck, his eyes veering

off to the path that heads left, where the owl flew.

"You go on," he says. "I'm going to check out this path."

"Are you sure?" A crease forms between my brows, knowing he must have come from that direction but actually slightly relieved he will take his leave, preventing any further tension rising between the two males.

I need space to think about what just happened between us. Although I am surprised Beinon will leave me alone with a stranger.

"I'm sure." He nods and sends me a small smile before glancing at Ansel. "If anything happens to her, you'll have to answer to me."

Ansel scoffs loudly, giving Beinon an indignant expression.

"She needs no champion princeling. She can take care of herself."

I suppress a smile at his words. But before this reaches an ugly climax, I stroll towards Ansel, trying my hardest to turn him.

"Come on," I say, "let's go."

He shakes his head, turning and walking along the path as I fire Beinon a salute.

Ansel is silent as we walk for a few moments, away from that damned owl's perch and away from Beinon. When we take a right turn, coming to another empty pathway, I decide the silence is too much.

"So… how did you find me?" I ask him,

wondering how he came upon me of all faeries.

"*I heard a scream. I couldn't be sure, but I had a feeling it was you,*" he says.

My feet stall.

Scream? When did I—

Oh. When Aisling had injured me.

"I didn't mean to alarm you, it wasn't really anything—"

He stops, turning to face me fully now with an unreadable expression.

"*Do you always do that?*"

"Do what?"

"*Trivialise your own pain.*"

I suck in a breath.

"*You* were *in pain.*" His eyes dip to my wrapped arm briefly before returning to my face, scanning my features for something. "*It is not a sound I will likely forget soon.*"

I roll my eyes, brushing past him as we approach another fork in the maze.

"Don't be so dramatic," I say, masking the deep appreciation I surprisingly feel inside that someone else other than Wen and Beinon cares about my safety. "Don't act like you've never let out a yelp of surprise."

He chuckles, a low and smooth sound that sends a shiver down my spine. "*Perhaps, but I'm not the one who sounded like a wounded animal.*"

I narrow my eyes at him. "Wounded animal? Really?"

He smirks, a glint of mischief in his gaze. "*Come, Mathonwy, let's go before your loudness draws all the remaining competitors to our location.*"

I huff, unable to suppress the smile tugging at the corners of my lips. "As if you wouldn't throw out a curse or two if you were stabbed."

He takes a step closer, his presence suddenly more intense as he points to his throat. "*True, but no one would hear me calling it out.*"

I meet his gaze, my heartbeat quickening. "Oh, very funny."

He tilts his head, his lips quirking into a half-smile. "*I am, aren't I?*"

I scoff, despite the flutter in my stomach, feigning annoyance. "If that's what you need to tell yourself."

"*I was hoping you would tell me.*" His lips curl in amusement.

"You'll be waiting a long time."

"*You wound me.*" A hand over his heart.

"Must hurt."

"*Dreadfully.*"

"What a shame."

He is grinning widely now, and I realise I am too. Coughing to clear my throat, I finally look away from his bright gaze. We continue walking around a bend, but that smile is still on his face, and I shake my head at him.

We soon arrive at a fork in the path. Two different routes stretch before us, shrouded in the same eerie darkness. Ansel glances at me, a mischievous glimmer in his eyes.

"*Well, it seems we have a choice to make,*" he muses. "*Shall we split up and see who reaches the centre first?*"

I cross my arms, raising an eyebrow. "Trying to get rid of me already?"

He chuckles. "*Never. Just adding a bit of friendly competition to the mix.*"

I smirk, unable to resist the challenge. "Fine then. You take the left path, and I'll take the right. Let's see who can navigate this maze faster."

His grin widens, his eyes gleaming with excitement. "*You're on, Mathonwy.*"

With a playful wave, I turn and head down the right path, the echoes of our flirtatious banter lingering in the air. As I walk, I can't help but wonder what surprises this new path holds and whether our paths will cross again before we reach the centre.

The path I follow eventually leads me to a clearing, and my breath catches as I take in the sight before me. A deep pit stretches across the ground, its gaping maw filled with darkness and uncertainty. Tall stone columns rise from the pit, forming a perilous path to the other side. My heart sinks as I realise the challenge—the need to hop from column to column, each step a potential leap into the unknown.

I take a deep breath, trying to steady my nerves. But as I stand on the edge of the pit, I know I can't afford to falter. I shake out my limbs before I jump and place my foot onto the first stone column, just as I hear someone come swooping around the corner I had left behind.

"Don't step on the stones!" His voice reverberates in my mind, a rush of urgency tightening my chest as my head snaps around.

Ansel's steps churn up dust as he skids into view, but it's too late. My weight has already landed on the stone, sending a tremor up through my legs.

The pedestal rumbles beneath me; the stone giving way and plummeting too fast for me to jump to the next one.

No, this can't be happening. I can't die falling into a pit like this.

My body pivots, propelling myself forward as the stone collapses beneath me. A cry escapes my lips, and my hand stretches out, straining to grasp the edge of the pit. I reach out with everything I have, desperation gripping me to escape this impending fall.

In the fraction of a second, time stretches into eternity, my breath catching.

Ansel's eyes widen. His hand lunges out as if he can somehow halt my descent.

My fingertips brush the precipice and slip away, the pit's darkness beckoning me to its deadly embrace. My stomach lurches, and I brace for impact, expecting the jarring collision against jagged rocks.

But a vice-like grip closes around my wrist.

I clamp my eyes shut, ready for the impact against the hard cliff side. My body slams against the rough stone, sending debris scattering into the air. My eyes flicker open to take in my precarious position as the mist of the pit fades away, leaving me dangling over a sea of sharp spikes.

My gaze locks onto the hand that anchors me. Ansel's firm grasp holds my wrist, the strength of his black clawed fingers and feathered arms giving me hope.

My brain stops working for a second.

Claws.

I continue to look up, meeting his wide golden eyes that hold an intensity I've never witnessed before. Beyond his gaze, I see a breathtaking sight—massive wings spread out, their black feathers shimmering with a slight golden hue.

"An… Ansel?" I gasp, my voice a mixture of disbelief and astonishment.

He heaves a breath, relief washing over him, his eyes shutting for a fleeting moment before reopening.

"*Hold on, Mathonwy.*" His words reach me through our mind-link, his breathlessness evident.

His other hand stretches out, offering me his clawed grip.

I reach out quickly yet cautiously, my fingers curling around his hand with determination. I hesitate for just a second, my fingers grazing the rough edges of his claws, and then I pull myself up, not willing to stay suspended over the threat of impaling rocks.

His colossal wings beat the air powerfully, the wind brushing against my skin, and he lifts us back toward the safety of the cliff edge. Once we're hovering over solid ground, I tighten my hold on his muscular arm, my relief palpable as I slowly lower myself onto the ledge. Collapsing onto the ground, I heave, taking deep breaths to steady myself, and roll onto my back.

I almost died.

As easy as that.

No fight, no chance to stop it. Just a simple fall.

The realisation hits me, and I feel nauseous. But I focus on another emotion, forcing it to hit me more potently. I wrench to my feet, my fists clenching with the burden of suppressing my anger, and I turn in Ansel's direction.

"You fucking—oh." I pause, my brain stuttering at the very shirtless man before me, loose, black tatters of fabric hanging from his arms. It takes a second for my thoughts to begin again and I look away, up to the darkening sky. I have seen him without a shirt before, but Gods above, he has been chiselled by a master sculptor. Smooth, dark skin pulls over the most deliciously defined muscles, a small scattering of hair travelling from his navel to his breeches. A few silver scars can be seen on his chest and stomach.

The sound of his footsteps as he approaches draws my attention, and a warm sensation coils low in my abdomen. *Mathonwy, I'm sorry I—*"

"What happened to your shirt?" I blurt out, not wanting to have this discussion with him until he is clothed. To save any distractions.

"*Um.*" He laughs, shrugging out of what remains. "*My wings tore through it.*"

"That, uh, that makes sense." I nod, realising he has no replacement, and I am staring.

This is Ansel, an ally—supposedly, though I reconsider that after this discovery—and yet my gaze betrays me, lingering on his bare torso and the lines of the V that disappear into his breeches for a moment longer than necessary.

Gods, I am no better than a male.

I tear my eyes away, stealing a glance at the black wings that pull in tight and start to gradually retract. The feathers and claws disappearing, leaving smooth skin in their wake. He runs a hand through his hair, causing a few locks to fall over his bright eyes.

"So, you're a… shifter?" I inquire, trying to piece together the puzzle. Shifter fae usually transform into smaller beasts, but Ansel's current appearance bears a striking resemblance to a harpy—an Unseelie faerie I hadn't expected to coexist within the Seelie shifter realm. But there are no clawed feet, his boots still intact.

"*Half-shifter.*" His voice washes over me like warm honey, capturing my attention once again. "*My father is a harpy.*"

My eyes widen in astonishment. "I… never knew that was possible." It was unheard of for faeries to inherit both lineages when their parents hailed from different folk. The typical outcome was that one lineage would prevail. What was even stranger was that his parents were from different courts. It was unheard of, in fact. What kind of magic would have allowed this to happen?

"Does King Lew know?" My question carries a knowing tone, the answer already clear in my mind, evidenced by the wince that briefly contorts Ansel's features.

"*I tend to keep one form or the other, depending on which court I am in. There aren't many who know,*" he admits, his expression heavy with a mix of apprehension and vulnerability. He seems to fear that this revelation might be the beginning of his secret's unravelling, that others would soon discover his duality.

That *I* would be the one to use the information.

"No, I imagine not," I mutter, sensing the discomfort in his demeanour. But I am surprised he has divulged this to me. He could navigate from court to court—the ultimate spy, if he so wished. He has made himself vulnerable by exposing himself to me.

"How did you know about the pillars?"

He looks at me for a moment, his gaze inscrutable. "*It should have been obvious that there was more to it than hopping across the pit.*"

My brows furrow, and I chastise myself silently for missing such a clear point.

"Why reveal yourself to me?" I shift the conversation, feeling his discomfort and deciding to steer away from my moment of weakness. "Why risk exposure?"

His eyes widen a fraction, taken aback by my

question. His throat bobs slightly as he swallows, his hand nervously raking through his hair. It's a tell—his nervousness—and I make a mental note of it.

"*I couldn't let you die,*" he answers, his voice carrying a weight of sincerity that's hard to ignore.

"Why?" I press.

"*I owe you. And... we are allies.*" His tone is simple and matter-of-fact, yet there's an underlying layer of something more, something he doesn't fully articulate.

"That was only a matter of convenience in the first trial," I point out, challenging his answer. "You could've let me fall and have rid yourself of potential competition. So, why?"

"*It will be neither my intention nor desire now, or in the future, vicious one. I simply could not watch you die,*" he retorts, his irritation now showing, a hint of vulnerability in his eyes as well. My suspicion lingers, but I find no signs of deceit in his expression. "*Will you expose my secret?*" he asks, the vulnerability deepening in his voice.

I take a moment to consider my response, though I already know the answer. "I won't," I state firmly, watching with a mixture of amusement and satisfaction as his golden eyes widen in surprise.

Once he recovers from his astonishment, he nods at me, a small smile playing on his lips. "*Thank you, vicious one.*"

"You're welcome," I reply.

A faint smile tugs at Ansel's lips, the corners of his mouth curling up, though the happiness behind his smile seems tinged with something deeper. *"Shall we get out of here?"*

"Most definitely," I reply, my laughter intermingling with the relief that we're finally moving away from the treacherous pillars.

I turn and stumble slightly. Ansel is quick to steady me, his warm hand wrapping around my wrist.

"Mathonwy, what is it?" His gaze drops to inspect me for any further injuries, lingering momentarily on my arm.

My shades rise, brushing soft kisses against my skin.

"I'll be fine." Though an unsettling sense gnaws at me as I notice the increasing waves of dizziness. "Maybe *you're* the one I should worry about," I quip, half-serious, half-teasing. An instinctual feeling, more than any logical reasoning, tells me I'm safe in his presence.

"Oh, I'm definitely the one you should worry about," he responds with a playfully wicked grin, his eyes dancing with a mischievous glint, even as they continue checking over me. His words send a shiver down my spine, and I'm not sure whether it's from the humour or the underlying intensity of his gaze.

Heat rises to my cheeks as I feel his eyes on me, and my mind races to formulate a witty response, but nothing seems adequate. Instead, I'm left dizzy, flustered and speechless, a rarity for me. His lips curve into a smirk, obviously enjoying the effect he has on me.

"Do you ever switch off that mind of yours, vicious one?"

he teases, the words a playful jab, and I'm reminded of our earlier banter. The blush in my cheeks now spreads to my neck. I can't deny the fact that he's unraveled me in ways I didn't anticipate.

"Some of us like to *think*, Ansel. Not all of us can get ahead with our good looks," I retort, irritation and embarrassment mingling. The words come out slightly slurred, and I regret them, my cheeks burning even hotter.

He chuckles softly, a pleased expression crossing his face. "*So, you find me pleasing to look at?*"

My jaw drops in disbelief. I hadn't meant to imply that, and my initial intention was to redirect the conversation away from his flirtatious banter. Mortified panic surges through me as his grin widens, revealing a row of perfect white teeth.

"That's not what I said—"

He takes a step closer, his heated gaze holding mine. My heart skips a beat, and I turn my head away, unable to withstand the intensity of his stare as I try to understand the feelings swirling through me.

"*But that's what you think?*" he challenges, and I can practically hear the smugness in his voice. I struggle to form a coherent response. This isn't a game I'm accustomed to playing.

"I—I am not having this conversation!" I exclaim, my voice pitched slightly higher than normal. His laughter rings in my ears again, sending a delicious shiver down my spine. But then the laughter fades, and his demeanour changes abruptly. He reaches out, his hand gripping my injured arm.

A cry escapes my lips, pain flaring from the movement, and he looks horrified at the sight of the bloodied wrap around my bicep, crimson staining it almost completely.

"*This is more than a flesh wound!*" he exclaims, outrage lacing his voice.

"I'll be fine," I repeat, the words heavier now as I recognise the truth they hold. Aisling's strike was accurate, striking something important. I need to treat it with herbs to stem the blood loss and fend off the encroaching exhaustion.

Ansel releases my arm, his eyes searching the surroundings before he approaches a hedge. My mumbled protests go unnoticed, and the snapping of twigs fills the air. He stretches his hand toward the hedge, and as if he's commanding the earth itself, the twigs and brambles retract, creating a passage.

"You... You have earthen magic?" I murmur, swaying slightly on my feet.

"*I do,*" he replies simply, offering no further explanation.

He walks toward me, snatches my bag from my good shoulder, and takes my hand in his. He guides me toward the opening in the hedge, then ducks under the thicket, pulling me along with him until we are stood inside. I go willingly, too weak to resist, feeling a strange sense of safety in his presence.

Ansel settles on the ground, and I'm gently manoeuvred to sit between his legs, my back resting against his chest as the hedge opening closes. He rummages through my bag, swatting my hand away when I try to retrieve it. From it, he extracts some wrapped cheese, pressing it into my good hand. *"Eat, Mathonwy,"* he commands softly.

I comply, awkwardly unwrapping the cheese and taking a bite as he extracts herbs and a clean cloth. My attention is drawn to my arm, and he begins to unwind the bloody binding. He grips my arm just above the wound, and I hiss at the sudden pain.

"Sorry," he murmurs, his eyes intense and touch gentler as he continues to apply pressure to my arm.

I'm silent as he chews the herbs into a paste, his actions methodical and efficient. He then packs the herbs into the wound, and I suppress a whimper.

His touch is surprisingly gentle as he wraps my arm in a clean binding, securing the herbs in place. The weight of exhaustion tugs at me, and I release a heavy sigh as my head falls back onto his shoulder. He freezes for a moment, but the warmth of his body is comforting, and it's a struggle to keep my eyes open.

"Sleep, Mathonwy," Ansel whispers softly into my mind, his voice sounding more raspy than usual. The temptation to give in to the pull of sleep is strong, my eyelids growing heavy. I turn slightly, my forehead coming to rest against the smooth skin of his neck, finding solace in its softness and warmth.

Perhaps I can allow myself this comfort, even though I know it is due to the blood loss and I will regret it in the morning.

"Maybe." My voice sleepy as I fight to keep my eyes open. "Just for a few minutes. I-I can't hear my shades whisper." My words slur together as fatigue wraps around me like a comforting blanket. "Will you watch me?" I mumble, almost unaware that I've spoken aloud.

His body rumbles with a soothing sound, like a cat's purr, and his arms tighten around me. "*Always, vicious one. You're safe.*" The words drift into my mind as I surrender to the pull of sleep, his presence a steady anchor in the darkness that surrounds me.

In the tales of humans, harpies were often depicted as repulsive beings. However, the reality is quite different. Harpies are faerie creatures, graced with exceptional beauty. Their expansive feathered wings bestow them with remarkable strength, capable of carrying other faeries. Additionally, their sharp claws possess the ability to cut through even leather armour.

PAGE 295, THE BOOK OF FAIR FAMILIES

CHAPTER SEVENTEEN

I have no idea what time it is when I wake, only that I assume it is still dark, judging by the lack of light fighting its way through the thicket. I try to summon the shadows to me, my shoulders sagging in relief once I hear them whisper lovingly in my ear, as if stroking my hair with affection.

A deep sigh sounds from behind me, and I freeze, releasing them immediately. Oh, no. I wriggle slightly, my breath hitching, when two muscular arms tighten around my waist, pulling me closer against a hard chest.

A rush of memories hits me as I remember what happened before I fell asleep. The blood loss. Ansel's nature and earthen magic. Him protecting and healing me.

I press a finger to the wrap, hissing when the area throbs with tenderness. It is healing, thankfully, but it won't completely seal for several hours.

Ansel stirs behind me. "*What's wrong?*" he asks, his inner voice clear and missing the hoarseness I would expect from his actual voice.

"I'm all right. I didn't mean to wake you." I turn my head slightly to see him. "How long were we out?"

"*At least a few hours, I think. It's still dark.*" He squints in the dim light filtering through the foliage. "*We should move soon. The exit must be near.*"

Right. The trial. We're still in the middle of it. I shift uncomfortably in Ansel's grasp, and heat creeps up my neck. This situation is more intimate than I'd like to admit.

"Thanks for helping me," I mumble, my voice soft with gratitude.

His arms around me loosen, and I can almost feel his shrug. "*No need to thank me. It was the least I could do after you helped me.*"

"Well… thank you anyway." I turn slightly.

Ansel's hand comes up to tuck a strand of hair behind my ear, his touch gentle. "*You're welcome, Mathonwy.*"

I meet his gaze, and the air surrounding us feels heavy. There's a tension that seems to pull us closer, and for a moment, it feels as if everything else fades away. The trial, the pain, all of it.

A rustling sound from outside the hedge breaks the spell. Ansel's hand drops away, and a guilty expression rests on his face. He clears his throat and shifts, untangling himself from me and rising to his feet. *"We should start moving. Let's get out of this trial."*

I nod, pushing aside the unexpected swirl of emotions that had overtaken me. I pick up my bag and take his offered hand as he helps me take to my feet.

"Right," I say, just because of the need to say something. "Let's find the exit."

Ansel uses his powers and I go to take a step out, but his hand stops me, pulling my sack from my shoulder until he has placed it over his own. His lips turn up at my bewildered expression, before he steps in front of me, sticking his head out of the safety of the hedge.

"It's clear, let's go."

The atmosphere is charged as we make our way through the intricate pathways of the maze. Ansel and I move in tandem, our senses on high alert, each step taking us closer to our goal. As we walk, I steal glances at Ansel from time to time, his profile illuminated by the torches and faint moonlight that filters from above the hedges. There's a whole side of him I don't understand, and it's like peeling back layers of a complicated puzzle.

And I wonder… why do I feel the need to know more?

"So, Ansel," I begin, breaking the silence between us, "tell me something about yourself."

He tenses and looks at me, his gaze steady. *"You've not learned enough this evening?"*

My eyes narrow.

"What do you want to know?" he asks.

I consider my question carefully, trying to choose something that might reveal a bit more about him. "What's your favourite memory? A moment from your past that brings a smile to your face."

His eyes widen just a little.

I imagine he was expecting me to ask more about his powers, or his harpy nature—perhaps his parents. Maybe that was why he became guarded. But I would not ask him about them. I would not want to talk about my father, so it would be rude of me to ask about his.

His surprise fades, his lips quirk into a half-smile, and for a moment, he seems lost in his thoughts. *"I remember this one summer evening,"* he begins, his voice soft and almost wistful. *"I was just a child, and my mother took me to the edge of the woods near our home. The sky was painted in shades of pink and gold as the sun set, and I watched as fireflies danced among the trees. My mother told me stories about our people, about the magic that runs through our veins. It was the first time I felt a connection to something greater than myself."*

I listen to his words, captivated by the way he speaks about that moment. It's as if I can see the memory playing out in his eyes, the warmth and nostalgia radiating from him. "It sounds beautiful," I reply, genuinely touched by his story.

"*It was.*" His gaze locks with mine. "*Life was simpler back then. Before the burdens of our roles took over.*"

I sense an unspoken weight in his words, a depth of feeling that he's not quite revealing. There's pain in his eyes, and I feel that.

I know that.

What it's like to have your innocence stripped away at a very young age. To have to grow up too quickly, to not get time to discover who you are before you must carry the burden of responsibilities.

His eyes soften as he looks at me. As if he can see the bitterness behind my expression. But his gaze holds a spark of genuine interest. "*What about you? I'd like to hear about a moment that brought you joy.*"

I pause, only for a moment, and then speak the first memory that comes to mind. "I remember visiting my uncle Gwydion's castle when I was young," I say with a soft smile. "He had this library filled with books from all across the realms—the faerie realm, the veiled realm. Even the human one! I would spend hours reading and getting lost in the stories. The air was always filled with the scent of old parchment and ink. It was a place where I felt safe and free, away from the expectations that awaited me back home."

Ansel's gaze brightens, and there's a shared understanding between us. We've both been shaped by our roles, by the expectations placed upon us, by the struggles we've endured.

"*How old were you when Bron started training you?*"

It's a loaded question. Most know of my father's brutality. I know what he is really asking—when did I learn of his cruelty? Start to experience it firsthand.

"I was six."

He doesn't respond, but he also doesn't look at me with pity.

"It—"

My shades suddenly spread and start to form a black wall by my side.

Fuck, I've been complacent and distracted.

A vampire dives through my shadows before they can solidify. He's hardly stopped, and he wraps his arms around my waist, taking me to the ground.

"Efia!"

My shades recover quick, a smoky tendril wrapping around his ankle and dragging him off me as I recover. I'm still slightly dizzy from the blood loss but I get to my feet quickly, about to attack and I feel for a blade at my side.

But Ansel stands before me, claws on display and wide wings blocking me from sight as he faces the vampire down. The vampire that is struggling. That my shadows are holding still… for *Ansel.*

I cannot see Ansel's face. Cannot see the rage in his expression, even though I can see it in the lines of his defined back.

He points his sword out, and I realise I didn't even see him unsheathe it.

"*If I had the time*," Ansel uses his lesser magic so we can all hear him. "*I would end you so fucking slowly for laying a finger on her.*"

My breath hitches as he takes a step forward, and the vampire's eyes widen in fear as he still fights my shades.

"*As it is, we're in a bit of a rush, so fortunately for you, I'll make this quick.*"

I barely see him as he darts forward, his claws embedding into the vampire's throat to hold him up. He shoves his sword through the vampire's chest.

It's incredibly vicious.

It's incredibly attractive.

I consider reflecting on that last thought before I try to think of the last time someone stood up to protect me… and I draw a blank.

Brushing those issues aside for a moment, my shades retreat and slither around me, helping me up as Ansel removes his claws from the creature's throat. The noise makes my stomach turn, and he wipes his hand on the vampire that is now crumpled on the ground.

Ansel takes a breath before turning. His eyes are closed, but I watch closely as he concentrates, and the feathers start to leave his skin. His wings pull in tight and retract. It's fascinating to see as Ansel returns to looking like a Seelie fae.

But when he opens his golden eyes, they are filled with concern. His gaze dips for a second to peruse over my body.

"*Are you all right?*"

I nod with a small smile, quashing the questions I have. The confusing emotions I feel. I'll deal with them later, on my own.

"No harm. Thank you… for that."

It feels odd. Thanking someone for saving my life… again.

"*Shall we finally get out of this place?*" He smiles, sheathing his sword.

"*Please*," I laugh, tired of fighting for the night.

After what feels like days of navigating the labyrinth, I am ready for the furs of my tent. We talk, we stroll through the paths, and I learn more about Ansel.

His quiet calm seems to soothe me and my shades, who float about us serenely.

Considering we are in a trial; I feel more relaxed than I have in a while.

It only takes another uneventful hour to reach the centre of the maze. A circular clearing lies before us, bathed in an eerie blue glow that emanates from the ground. In the centre of the clearing stands a portal, a swirling vortex of energy that seems to pulse with a life of its own.

Ansel and I exchange a look, a mixture of trepidation and determination in our eyes. This is it—the end of the trial, the moment we've been working towards. The portal beckons, promising a way out of this maze.

"*We've come this far,*" Ansel says, his voice steady.

A sigh leaves me. I close my eyes and take a few steps past him, reaching out to touch the portal.

A loud screech has my head spinning.

And all I see before the portal sucks me in, is the long claws of the huge maze owl embedding in Ansel's shoulder and wrenching him backwards. His golden eyes wide with pain and fear capture mine as his voice yells in my mind at me to run and his fingers reach out.

"Ansel!" I cry, my hand reaching out in front of me as I fall through the portal.

I scramble and fall, my back hitting the dirt once more. I grunt and amidst the bustling camp, my heart racing with both urgency and worry.

The realisation hits me like a punch to the gut— I've lost Ansel in the portal's chaotic transition. My fingers reach for the space where my bag should hang, and a sense of frustration wells up within me.

Ansel, hopefully, still has it.

Without the bag, I'm left without my healing herbs, without my tools, and without the means to tend to Ansel's injury.

My eyes scan the surroundings for any sign of his distinctive white hair or his tall figure. The camp is a whirlwind of activity, faeries moving in all directions, exhaustion set on their faces as they return to their tents. Panic threatens to consume me as I push my way through the crowd, calling out his name in vain, hoping that he'll hear me and respond.

"Ansel!" I call out again, my voice filled with a mixture of desperation. But there's no response, no glimpse of him in the sea of faces. I grit my teeth, frustration mounting as I consider my options.

Don't lose focus now; I need to find him.

But my shades rise, whispering delicately in my ear, and my back straightens.

What am I doing?

Calling out his name in a *panic* when there are so many eyes and ears around to notice.

Inhaling deeply, I calm the storm inside me, even as my mind races and I try to come up with a plan. If Ansel is injured, he'll need help, and I don't know if he has anyone else who can provide it.

I search for Jill, the faerie who had been providing me with the healing herbs. Eventually, I find her with a bag of supplies, helping a wood nymph deep in the Seelie's half of camp. I approach her with a determined stride, catching her attention.

"Jill, I need more healing herbs," I say in a rush, my voice earnest as I meet her gaze. "Someone's hurt."

She sighs, her expression softening a fraction. "Child. Everyone coming back is hurt. And I told you, I can't *spare* any more. But I might have something that can help." With a quick motion, she reaches into a pouch at her side and hands me a vial filled with a sparkling liquid. "Potion made from moonflower petals. It won't heal completely, but it'll ease the pain whilst you treat whatever wound it is."

I nod my thanks, clutching the vial tightly in my hand.

"I owe you," I tell her.

She grins. "I know."

The potion is better than nothing, and I'm relieved that Jill is willing to help in whatever way she can. With the vial secure, I turn my attention back to the task at hand—finding Ansel.

I continue to navigate the camp, my senses on high alert, looking for any clue that might lead me to him. My heart pounds in my chest, and a sense of determination fuels my steps.

As I weave through the sea of faeries, I don't allow my thoughts to drift to why I care so much.

I tell myself rationally that it must be because he helped me, and not because I now consider him a friend.

I search for a couple of hours, my determination unwavering, but despite my efforts, Ansel remains elusive. He wasn't in his tent, and I waited there for an hour. It also doesn't help my nerves that I could not spot Beinon with the returning faeries.

The camp bustles around me as faeries go about their activities, their faces a blur. Frustration and fatigue settle into my bones, and I finally admit to myself that I need to let go of this search for now.

With a heavy sigh, I concede defeat, my shoulders slumping as I turn away. The weight of exhaustion pulls at me, tugging me toward the familiar comfort of my tent. My steps are slow, each one a struggle against the disappointment that lingers in my chest.

Inside the confines of my tent, I collapse onto my bedroll; the weariness engulfing me. My body aches from the trials, from the relentless searching, and from the anxiety that has gripped me since Ansel's disappearance. I close my eyes, hoping that sleep will provide a temporary escape from the uncertainty that plagues my thoughts.

As I drift into slumber, the sounds of the camp fade into the background, replaced by the soothing embrace of darkness. It takes a while for my mind to temporarily let go of its worries, allowing me to sink deeper into the realm of dreams, where the trial loses its grip on my consciousness.

"Can't... do it... anymore. It hurts too much. I refuse... I'm lost."
RECOVERED JOURNAL FROM PRINCE BEINON

CHAPTER EIGHTEEN

I find myself abruptly roused from my slumber in the dead of night—having slept a full day, only waking to bathe—a harsh and angry whisper echoing through the darkness. Reacting on instinct, I snatch a sword and sit up, my eyes locking onto the figure that my shades have ensnared near the entrance of my tent.

"Beinon?" I mumble, my voice tinged with sleep, and I rub my eyes, allowing the shadows to recede at my command. The hushed murmurs of the shadows linger in my ear, reluctant to dissipate entirely. Beinon takes in a sharp breath as they release him, his fingers rising to massage his neck. I squint at him and smile.

"You're all right," I say, but then I realise the time of day. "What's wrong? What's happened?"

His reply is slow to come, his gaze skimming over me before he averts his eyes, a flush colouring his cheeks. Glancing down, I realise the thin straps of my camisole have slipped, baring more than I intended.

"I just came to make sure you were safe," he explains, his voice carrying a hint of embarrassment.

"At this hour?" I retort dryly.

"I know your father's watchful eye is upon you," he counters. "I thought it best not to arouse suspicion by visiting during the day. I didn't want his spies to see me."

"So, you opted for the *less* suspicious option of having his spies see you sneaking around at night?" I raise an eyebrow, a small smile tugging at the corners of my lips as realisation dawns upon him. Tapping the furs beside me, I invite him to sit. He hesitates for a moment before approaching, settling onto the pallet next to me.

"Beinon, we've known each other for how long?" I ask, my tone laced with amusement.

"Too long?" he responds, a playful glint in his eyes.

"Exactly." I laugh softly, but concern creases my brow. "I know you. What is it?"

His fingers rake through his tousled golden hair, a frustrated exhale escaping his lips. His gaze flickers to my arm, the bandages now removed, leaving only a faint red line as evidence of the wound. Soon, even that will be gone, thanks to Ansel's actions.

Beinon fidgets.

He never fidgets.

After only a brief moment, determination settles in his expression, and he turns fully toward me, reaching down to take my hand in his.

"Efia," he says, his eyes alight with a mixture of anticipation and nerves, causing my stomach to flutter. "I can't stop thinking about how close I came to killing you."

I gave him a wry smile. "'Killing' might be an exaggeration."

"Please, just hear me out."

I nod in agreement, my curiosity piqued.

"It felt like I'd been hit with a boulder, once I realised it was you. I've never felt such fear. It made me realise how serious this whole contest is."

"Oh, *that* made you realise?" I quip.

"Be serious," he scolds. "I know your father is pressuring you to win. My mother on my back… and that makes me your enemy."

I bite my tongue to tell him he isn't. Not really.

"If that means my life is in your hands when we reach that final test, then so be it."

"Beinon—"

"Because I will not be the one to end your life, Efia. I promise you that. I… I cannot, I will not." He stares at the floor for a moment, as if speaking the words to someone else. "You mean more to me than some crown."

"Beinon, you're not seriously saying you'd let me win, even if it means risking your own life?" I shoot back. His words might have been spoken with a touch of earnestness, but their weight lingers like a fog, casting a shadow over the levity of our usual banter. It's hard to ignore the unsettling feeling they've ignited within me.

"I would," he says with finality.

"You might want to keep those sentiments away

from your mother, Beinon."

"I don't give a fuck what my mother hears," he growls. His response cutting through the tension like a blade. His eyes bear into my own, and it makes me nervous.

"Why are you telling me this Beinon? What do you want?" I ask him.

But I realise. This isn't just about the contest. It's about that kiss in the maze.

"You know what I want, Efia," he says, his hand tightening on mine as his eyes drop to my lips.

My lips that part in shock.

Not shock at his attraction—I have always known we were attracted to each other. I'm shocked that he is openly discussing it with me. That he is being so brazen about it. We have always toed this line with our flirting, but have never dared cross over it, not before the kiss.

"Beinon."

His free hand cups my cheek and I inhale. I don't know what to do in this situation. Outward affection has never been something freely given to me, besides the very few moments I would have with my uncle and my friendship with Wen. This intimate softness is unfamiliar to me, and I don't know how to respond.

"Efia," he breathes out, and I realise he has leaned closer.

"Beinon, we shouldn't—"

"But do you want to?" he asks, and I do not answer. His nostrils flare as my shades whisper. "Do not think about what other people want for you, Efia. Tell me I am wrong in thinking this is reciprocated, and I will leave. But if you want this as much as I do, please… tell me."

I consider lying. I consider telling him I have never wanted him. But then he would leave, and the gentleness would too. I consider our friendship, and what this could do to it. But the stress of the trial and what is to come weighs heavily upon my soul.

And I never realised how much I wanted this physical intimacy.

"I want this," I almost whisper, but he hears it and his lips crash to mine.

His kiss is fierce, almost urgent, a raw need emanating from every touch of our lips. It's as if the weight of unspoken desires has finally burst through the dam, flooding my senses with a hunger that matches his own. My stomach clenches as I realise we've crossed a threshold, and he pulls himself under the furs, as we move beyond the confines of friendship and into uncharted territory. His presence under the covers with me feels both forbidden and overwhelmed.

As he settles between my thighs, my back presses into the furs beneath me, sending a shiver of anticipation down my spine. His hand traces the curve of my hip, leaving a trail of sensation that sets my skin ablaze. A guttural groan escapes him as his lips leave mine, realising that my legs are exposed, clad only in lacy underwear. I can't help but react to the fervent caress of his tongue against my lower lip, our mouths melding together in a dance of need and exploration.

Desire pulses through me as I wrap my legs around his waist, drawing him closer. The pressure of his hips against mine sends shock waves of pleasure radiating through my core.

"Fuck." He exhales as he pulls away, burying his face against the curve of my throat. I arch, a soft sigh escaping me as his lips trail a path of open-mouthed kisses along my skin. He finds a spot behind my ear and I move away, too ticklish. He kisses it again and I growl.

He can't help but respond with a breathless laugh, the tension and longing of the moment mingling with a playful edge. "You're going to regret this tomorrow," I whisper, my voice laced with both teasing and genuine concern, a plea that our shared desires won't cast shadows on what we have.

"I could never regret this, Efia." He kisses along the edge of my jaw, up until he runs his tongue along the outer shell of my ear, finding a spot I do like. "I could never regret you."

My fingers run through his soft hair as my breathing turns ragged, burning at the lascivious throb in my core.

"I have wanted this for such a long time, Efia," he says, his kisses moving further south. "Wanted to taste your delicious skin upon my tongue, see if you taste as good as you look."

I whimper as his tongue runs along the edge of

my camisole, gasping as he pulls it down and takes a nipple in his hot mouth. My back arches into it, needing more. He sucks and nips at the sensitive peak, and I pull him closer, my hands sliding up under his loose shirt and along his ribs. His mouth moves to my other breast, his free hand raising to squeeze the one he has just left. His eyes are so bright as he watches me hungrily.

"Touch me," I whisper into the air around us, hating being watched but too consumed to say anything else.

I want more.

"I am touching you." His smile is devilish. "You're beautiful," he breathes out against my skin, his hand moving lower until he firmly grips my arse, squeezing until I hiss.

His fingertips brush along the outside of my thighs, as if mapping my skin as he goes. He grips the fabric of my underwear, his brow raising.

"May I?" he asks, and I nod.

I sit up awkwardly, removing my camisole as he removes my underwear, and soon I am naked before him.

He sucks in a breath and is quiet. His eyes blaze a path over my naked flesh, making me squirm. But there is only hunger in his eyes—the hunger of a man who has craved for something for so long and finally has it in front of him.

"You are…" he breathes out in what sounds like awe. "You are my water after a thousand years of drought. You are… you are better than I shall ever be,

Efia." He flashes me a rueful smile.

"Less talk, more touch," I tell him, surprised by the sudden emotion that is showing in his eyes. It almost gives me pause. I reach out to him, and he returns to me, his mouth on mine immediately. His hands are on my breasts, my waist, brushing up my inner thigh. My legs open of their own accord and his touch wanders higher, my breath coming in pants between our kisses as my heart thunders against my ribs. I groan with relief when his fingers brush against the wetness between my legs, and his eyes close.

"I cannot deny how many times I have dreamed about this." His gaze falls to where we are joined, where his fingers are rubbing against the most sensitive part of me, working me into a frenzy and causing an intense pressure in my lower belly. "How many times I have thought about your taste upon my fingers."

He kneels once more, pushing my thigh gently as if to see more of me, and by the heat in his bright eyes as he pushes a finger inside me, he is enjoying this very much.

"There." I gasp when his finger curls and catches a highly sensitive spot inside. He does it again.

My breathing is rapid and reckless as he pushes me towards that edge. My hands curl in my hair in need of something to hold on to. He groans and my eyes open, and it's when I see his own hand wrapped around himself and pumping in time with his talented fingers inside me that I fall.

Everything shatters as I ride out my orgasm on his hand.

My senses return to me quickly, my gaze going to Beinon as my body fights to take in more air. Abruptly, he removes his fingers causing me to gasp, and I watch as he brings them to his mouth, sucking on them like he is starved as his eyes roll back.

"Efia," is all he says as his darkened eyes meet mine.

But there is an odd feeling creeping through and tarnishing the release. It's not something I have felt before, but it rises quickly, my knees raising as I sit up. A fierce pull in my chest distracts me momentarily until I ignore it, and my fingers brush against my lips as doubt slips in.

The feeling that perhaps… this means more to Beinon than I thought.

That all our playful banter and his flirting mask true feelings.

Beinon's expression flashes for a moment, but he rolls to the side of me, pulling the fur up over my legs. Without a word, I lay by his side.

Silence lingers between us, broken only by the quiet rhythm of our breathing. He draws me in closer, guiding me to rest against his chest, and I nestle there. His fingers brush along my arm in a tender caress, the gesture soothing and filled with a tenderness I hadn't anticipated.

"I am yours, Efia." His words, soft and earnest,

tickle my ear, and his lips press against my hair. The statement, though whispered, reverberates in the air, hanging between us with a weight that I struggle to fully comprehend.

I still, my shades returning to float gently around me as they whisper soothing sounds. A tremor of unease dances along my spine, a nagging tug of uncertainty that I can't shake. One that leaves me with an unfamiliar feeling in my chest. My hand comes up to cover it, and it feels like... hurt. I feel the tension in my body, a coiled spring of conflicting emotions I dare not give voice to.

He seems oblivious to my inner turmoil, his touch and words communicating a depth of feeling that is both overwhelming and perplexing. The boundary between us has been irrevocably crossed, and I'm left grappling with the implications of what this could mean for us.

A disquieting realisation dawns upon me like a sudden storm. This wasn't just lust for him, a simple act of desire. It does mean more.

I've allowed myself to be swept away by something I wasn't prepared for. And as his hand continues its gentle caress, I'm left with a gnawing ache in my chest, the growing awareness that what was meant to bring us closer has instead driven an irreparable wedge between us.

And that there is a tug in my chest that is pulling me in a different direction...

This was a mistake.

In faerie courtship, partners claim each other through distinct scents. Faeries emit unique fragrances, a mix of floral notes and their magic. When drawn to each other, their scents blend, signalling a union in the realm of faerie courtship.

PAGE 46, THE BOOK OF FAIR FAMILIES

CHAPTER NINETEEN

I stand beneath the dense canopy of the ancient forest surrounding the Seelie court. Light shadows wrap around me like a protective cloak, trying to camouflage me as I lean against a sturdy oak tree. It's daylight, so they are like a thin mist, but I've started to master control over my shades. My eyes drift up to the elaborate tree house perched high in the branches above.

I'm in the heart of the Seelie court for one reason—Wen. She and I have been friends for years, defying the boundaries of our respective courts. Today, I'm here to see her. It doesn't take much skill to sneak into the Seelie court—perhaps I could play it up and make father proud of me.

No. He would punish me for putting myself in harm's way.

The surroundings do make me wary, if anyone spotted me, they'd know exactly who I was due to my shadows. The fact I am in the Seelie court would alarm them—they could even tell the queen.

I know my friendship with Wen can't protect me from the watchful eyes of the Seelie. They don't take kindly to intruders from *the Unseelie court.*

As I wait, a soft rustling in the foliage alerts me. A figure emerges from the bushes, and I straighten, allowing my shades to dissipate and hide, though they whisper in my ears from behind me. It's a light fae, and he doesn't appear to be a guard.

My hand hovers over my thigh, where a dagger rests. His eyes narrow slightly as he spots me.

Bright. Blue.

He's very handsome.

"Who are you, and what are you doing here?" he asks, his tone curious but not unkind.

I tighten my grip on the hilt of the small dagger concealed at my side. I'm prepared to fight or flee if necessary. "I'm here to see Branwen. We're friends. Who are you?"

"Beinon," he replies.

Just then, the tree house's door creaks open, and Branwen drops down gracefully. Her eyes widen when she spots Beinon, and she immediately bows. "Your Highness."

My heart races as I realise the significance of the situation. Beinon is the prince of the Seelie court, the son of Queen Lilah. I remain still, not bowing, and I don't turn my back on him.

"Branwen." He nods. His gaze shifts from Branwen to me, a glint of curiosity in his eyes. "And who is this?"

"Efia," I say curtly, my shadows flickering behind me as a sign of my readiness.

Beinon takes a step closer, studying me with a discerning look.

My shades dash from behind me without my control, whipping about his face as if to distract him so I can escape. I curse, but I don't move. I don't know if I can leave Wen alone with him.

It takes effort to pull them back from his still form. Once they clear his face and return behind me, whispering furiously, he is still standing where he was. He has paled but is unharmed.

My jaw tightens. "I apologise."

He is silent for a moment, blinking at me. His eyes dart over my shoulder and he clears his throat. I'm expecting guards to appear at any moment. To take me to his mother's palace and punish me. They wouldn't do much, my uncle would be furious. It's the thought of Father finding out that worries me…

But his smile returns, and he offers a nod. "Well, you certainly know how to make an impression, Efia."

I can't help but feel a mixture of surprise and wariness. Beinon may be a prince, but he's not like the other Seelie I've encountered. His seemingly unafraid open-mindedness is unexpected, so as I smile lightly back I think, perhaps I can be open-minded too.

As the first rays of sunlight pierce through the entrance of my tent, rousing me from my slumber, I find myself alone. The space beside me is vacant, and the absence doesn't stir any sense of disappointment within me. Instead, there's a peculiar sense of relief that washes over me.

While some may be dismayed at the loss of such

pleasurable nightly company, I bear no such resentment over Beinon's departure. In fact, all I can feel is a profound sense of respite. The idea of engaging in conversations about what happened and how we proceed is a treacherous road I'm hesitant to traverse—not without deep thought first.

Regret lingers beneath the surface, an undeniable ache that courses through me. I'm grateful that Beinon isn't here to witness the turmoil I'm experiencing. It is not only Beinon's heartbreak I worry about. I panic about the dire consequences that could unfold if our indiscretion were ever brought to light before my father's unforgiving eyes.

The truth is, we cannot be more to each other, other than comforting flesh in the shadow of night. The risks are too great, the dangers too imminent. And…

Even if I were inclined to entertain the thought, a deep-seated feeling restrains me—a whisper in my chest that goes beyond the soothing voices of my shades. It's a call that is unfamiliar, urging me to acknowledge a reality more potent and intricate than the urges we succumbed to last night.

That I do not love Beinon in the way he needs.

I had felt it momentarily whilst we were being intimate, and it had ensured I didn't lose myself completely to the pleasurable feeling of what we were doing—it had been a distraction. An unwanted one. Because I do not know what it means.

I bathe and dress, determined to find Wen and see

if she has an idea. Lunar faeries usually have a sense about these things, and I wonder if she'll be able to tell me what's wrong with me.

The rustling of canvas interrupts my thoughts, but I do not turn towards the entrance of my tent, knowing if I do, Beinon will see the emotions on my face. I lace up my shirt and I address him without facing him, hoping my reluctance doesn't betray my words.

"I'm going to see Wen, if you want to come?" I extend the invitation, though secretly wishing he won't take me up on it.

He doesn't answer.

"Bei—" I turn, the word cutting off as I notice who is stood in front of me.

"Ansel," I breathe out his name in surprise, a wide smile naturally spreading across my lips. He looks weary but grins at me, evidence of his recent struggles etched on his face. Claw marks and blood near his shoulder, remnants of the owl's attack, are a stark reminder of what happened.

Why hasn't he healed it and changed? Surely, he hasn't only just got back?

He holds up my sack. *"Thought I'd bring this back."*

"Thank you," I say earnestly, taking a step forward. "How is your shoulder?"

His smile fades slightly. *"It's all right. Almost fully healed. I, uh… I hope you don't mind, but I've borrowed a few of your herbs to help heal it."*

"Of course I don't mind." I shake my head. "You

helped me during the trial. More than once. What's mine is yours."

His eyes widen in surprise, before he schools his expression into one of gratitude.

"I'm glad you're all right—" he takes a step forward before his whole demeanour changes. His eyes harden, his nostrils flare, and he looks away, his lips thinning.

"Ansel?" I ask, wary of his sudden change, and I take a step forward. He holds up a hand.

"I… I must leave. I'll speak to you later." Without another word he turns, dropping my bag and leaving the tent, almost knocking poor Wen over as she enters.

"Careful!" She turns and looks at me, bewildered. "What was that all about?"

"I have no idea." I shake my head and put it to the back of my mind for now.

Wen shrugs, walking closer to me and wrapping me in a comforting embrace. I rest my chin on top of her head, sighing. Far too soon, she pulls away, her nose wrinkling. "I think I'll leave you to have a bath."

"I just had one. Why?" I ask, my head tilting in confusion.

"Because you smell like Beinon has marked his territory so badly, no faerie male would dare to come near you. Is there something you want to tell me?"

Well, shit.

In the faerie realm, where shadows and light coexist, seers play a crucial role as guardians of the unseen. Their visions influence the possibilities that shape the faerie world, making them integral to the intricate cosmic dance of fate.

PAGE 93, FAERIE FOLK AND THE MAGIC OF SIGHT

CHAPTER TWENTY

Wen and I find a secluded clearing within the trees to talk. She seems anxious to hear about Beinon, and why I had Ansel in my tent this morning.

I settle down on a fallen log beside her, taking a deep breath to steady my nerves.

Wen raises an eyebrow, her interest piqued. "First, Beinon. What happened?"

I hesitate, searching for the right words. "We… were intimate."

A slow smile creeps onto her face as she tucks a dark curl behind her ear. "I guessed that. But I will admit it's unexpected. Not on his part, poor boys been trying for years. I'm surprised you gave in."

I can't meet her gaze, a mix of guilt and regret swirling within me. "I regret it, Wen. It was a mistake. I shouldn't have let it happen. And I feel like I may have ruined my friendship with him."

Wen is silent for a full minute, assessing me in that eerie, knowing way she does—even though she can't explain it. "That's not just it," she replies. "Your heart doesn't want anything with Beinon."

How she always knows these things I'll never know.

"I…" I pause, wondering how best to explain it. "It was a pleasant night. It meant more than just a one-night thing, because I do have feelings for him, but… I don't know. I felt like there was something still missing. Like my head and my heart were being pulled in different directions. Do you know what I mean?"

She hums. Her brilliant eyes narrowing as she takes in my response—faerie is too bloody clever for her own good.

"There is something different about you. But it is not from your night of sin with Beinon."

"What do you mean?" I ask her seriously, despite her joking. Her senses have always told Wen things. An instinct almost.

"I'm not sure." She shakes her head. "But my gut tells me you are right about Beinon. He is not the one to give it all to." I snort at her choice of words, and she rolls her eyes at me. After a moment her expression softens, her concern evident. "Don't be too hard on yourself. Sometimes things don't go as planned, but that doesn't mean it's the end of the world."

I sigh, my gaze fixed on a distant point in the

woods. "It's not just that, Wen. It's Ansel."

Wen's brow furrows in confusion. "What about him?"

I finally look at her and know I can trust her enough to share information. My tongue seems to move of its own accord, telling her everything that happened in the maze. Her eyes grow wider and wider as she listens patiently, never interrupting.

When I finish, I think I take the biggest breath of my life, and Wen purses her lips in thought for a moment.

"Do you have any idea of who his parents are? I've never heard of Seelie and Unseelie faeries creating a child together."

I shake my head. "No idea. I don't think he gets on with them."

She hums in thought.

"I don't know what to think of it all. But something's been bothering me ever since the trial. It's like there's this nagging feeling that I've overlooked something important."

Wen leans in, her concern deepening. "Are you saying that… you have feelings for Ansel?"

My fingers trace absent patterns on the grass. "I can't explain it properly. But it's like... my gut knows I can trust him. I mean, even my shades seem to trust him. And when I realized he knew about Beinon, I… I felt *guilty*."

Wen studies me intently. "You know, Ef,

sometimes our hearts sense things before our minds catch up. Maybe there's a reason you're feeling this way. But have you talked to Beinon about any of this?"

I shake my head. "No, I haven't. I don't even know where to start."

Wen offers me a supportive smile. "Maybe it's worth having an open conversation with him. Who knows, maybe he's been grappling with similar thoughts since last night."

I let out a sigh, my mind a whirlwind of emotions and uncertainties. "I don't know, Wen. All I know is that I need to sort things out."

Wen gives my arm a reassuring squeeze. "You'll figure it out, Efia. Just know that I'm here for you, no matter what."

"Thanks, Wen."

Wen's sudden laughter tinkles beside me. "Well, at least Beinon isn't your *mate*," she teases, a playful glint in her eyes. "Imagine your father's reaction."

I snort at her comment, shaking my head at the preposterous notion. Paired mates are a rarity among us faeries. It's not like the romantic stories Gwydion brought me from the human realm. The ones that talk about soulmates. Our bonds are more complex, often forged for strategic alliances, destiny or to strengthen bloodlines. Love rarely factors into it—even if *every* paired mating I read about in Uncle's castle depicted those couples as madly in love.

I am grateful Beinon is not my mate. Love is a

luxury neither of us could afford right now. The weight of my responsibilities presses on me, reminding me of the impending trial and the crown that awaits the victor. Love and personal desires must take a back seat to the demands of our roles.

And anyone tied to me is potential leverage.

I don't have to wait for long to speak with Beinon.

He finds me in my tent, later that afternoon.

He takes a deep breath, his eyes never leaving mine as he smiles. "I can't stop thinking about what happened."

I press my lips together, my heart sinking. This is the conversation I dreaded, the one where he'd lay bare his feelings once more. I had hope perhaps I had read too much into his words the night before. That his feelings didn't run much deeper than just physical urges.

"Beinon—"

He comes forward and takes my hands within his own. "It wasn't just a distraction, Ef."

"Beinon, stop."

"I care about you, more than I've cared about anyone. And—"

I remove my hands from his and take a step back. "Beinon, stop!"

"Efia, what... what's going on?"

"It was a mistake, Beinon. Last night should never have happened."

His lips part slightly, his brows furrowing over his bright eyes. After a moment it seems he thinks I am joking, and huffs.

"Efia, you don't mean that. If this is about your father finding out, don't worry—"

"It's an impossible scenario, Beinon. And not just because of my father." My voice echoes with frustration, a mix of exasperation and a desire to knock some sense into him. The recklessness, the vulnerability—it all makes me want to shake him senseless. "It would never work."

"Because of your refusal to fight for it." Beinon straightens, his words sharp. "Because you're choosing to be someone you're not, instead of being true to yourself."

"I may have been raised by a tyrant," I snap at him, a fury tightening my chest. "By someone who cares about nothing more than what I can do to bring glory to his house. But I am who I am because I *choose* to be—"

"And you're choosing wrong," he interjects, his tone edged with urgency. "Together, we could achieve so much if only you—"

"I won't carve pieces of myself to fit into a mould you've designed." My voice raises, and his startled step shows he's taken aback—as if my words struck him physically. "Not you. I've been shaped and manipulated by many others... Please, allow me this. Don't become another architect of who I am."

I groan, rubbing my hands over my face, weary and frustrated. He recovers from my verbal blow, shaking his head.

"I... I'm sorry, Efia. I didn't mean I wanted you to completely change who you are."

"But that's exactly what you're asking." My exhale quivers. "This is why we should've never crossed that boundary."

"Please don't say that," he whispers, his voice barely audible. "Never that. I don't regret it."

"I regret that it led us here," I confess, genuine remorse weighing heavy within me. Our friendship was a refuge from the blinding glare of the outside world. And my chest tightens, now knowing how Beinon feels… because the truth is, I don't feel the same.

"Beinon, I love you, but... I'm not *in* love with you."

His weak nod suggests he already suspected as much. "I... I thought being friends would be enough. I never meant to fall for you."

I narrow my eyes at this, confused.

"It was never supposed to—" He runs a hand through his hair, frustration radiating from him. "I understand what you're saying, I really do. But my heart doesn't seem to get the memo."

Guilt swirls within me as I watch him unravel, exposed and wounded—all because of me. Deliberate or not, I inflicted this pain in his eyes.

"I'm so sorry, Beinon. Sorry for my blindness, for

not seeing how you felt," I admit, my voice heavy with regret. "But it doesn't matter now. What does is that I hurt you, and for that, I beg your forgiveness. I just... I can't be the one for you. Someone else will love you, Beinon, just not me."

He takes a step closer, gripping my hand tightly. "There's no need to apologise, Ef. I could've been honest about my feelings long before this. I gave no indication that our night meant more to me, until after... but I should have. This mess is my creation, not yours. Never yours."

A heavy silence descends between us before I muster the courage to voice my concern.

"Can we still be friends?" I ask, cringing inwardly at the question's selfish undertones. It's an unreasonable request.

He nods, a glimmer of hope kindling within me.

"I... I need time," he admits, vulnerability etched across his features. "But I could never bear a life without you, Efia." His expression falters. "In whatever capacity you'll allow me.

Hope, fragile yet tangible, blooms within me as he clasps my hand. A heavy silence settles between us, and I search his eyes, seeking some glimmer of assurance, a hint that this mess won't sever our connection entirely.

"Time is all I can ask for," Beinon's voice is gentle. A bittersweet smile tugs at the corner of my lips as I squeeze his hand, acknowledging his words without uttering a sound.

"Take all the time you need," I reply, my voice holding a mixture of understanding and empathy. "And if you ever need to talk, you know where I am."

His gratitude is evident in the warmth of his gaze, the sincerity that flows from his eyes and wraps around me like a comforting embrace. There's something else hidden in his gaze, and—knowing how stubborn Beinon is—I briefly wonder why he has not fought this more.

"Goodnight, Beinon," I murmur, feeling the heaviness in my chest grow as the reality of our conversation sinks in.

"Goodnight, Efia," he replies softly, his thumb brushing over the back of my hand before releasing it with a reluctant hesitation.

As the flap closes behind him, the quiet settles around me like a heavy shroud. The emotions I've held back during our conversation rush forward, overwhelming me with a mix of regret, longing, and sadness. It's as if the path we've walked for so long has suddenly diverged, and I stand at a crossroads with no clear direction.

I remove my shirt and breeches, sliding beneath the furs that once held a different kind of warmth. Closing my eyes, I let out a shaky breath, my head heavy. Sleep evades me as my shades swirl around me, brushing over my skin with what comfort they can offer. The memory of our shared laughter and conversations tangle with the realisation that things might never be the same again.

I bury my face in my pillow, my fingers clutching at the fabric. As the night stretches on, I find myself adrift in a sea of conflicting feelings, each one vying for dominance. But buried beneath them all is the truth—I made the right decision.

Join us, faerie folk, for a grand ball beneath the glow of the Rose moon. Let's revel in the victories of our competitors and anticipate the imminent final trial. Your presence is requested at Castell Narbeth for a night of celebration.

A reminder that any faeries found breaching the peace of the Betwixt will be executed on sight.

DECREE OF QUEEN LILAH AND KING LEW, RULERS OF THE FAERIE COURTS

CHAPTER TWENTY-ONE

Last night I dreamt.

The images drifting away from me like a fine mist, and I don't recall the last time I hadn't slept soundly. I'm usually comforted by the darkness. By the shadows and quiet of night.

But last night was different.

And I've woken again with a dull guilt churning in my stomach. I haven't seen Beinon for seven sunrises, and the weight of our conversation lingers... but somehow, the raw edges of my emotions feel smoother, less jagged.

So why am I dreaming?

After a few moments of collecting my thoughts, I push aside the furs and rise from my makeshift bed. The early morning air is crisp for summer, and I shiver slightly as I pull on my breeches and a white shirt, securing my belt around my waist. The familiar routine of dressing feels grounding, helping to calm my frayed nerves from the unsettled sleep.

With my attire sorted, I push open the flap of my tent and step outside. My eyes nearly immediately land on Arawn, who is approaching with a determined stride. He holds a small parcel wrapped in brown paper in his hand and a brown sack in the other. As he draws nearer, a faint smile tugs at the corners of his lips.

"Morning, Efia," he greets, his voice carrying a cheerful note, and he hands me the sack. I open it to find new clothes and leathers that one of my father's maids no doubt packed for me. The two guards accompanying him stop a short distance behind. Several faeries walking throughout the tents around me give us a cautious eye.

"Morning, Arawn," I reply, returning his smile with a small one of my own.

He extends the bundle of fabric toward me. "I've got something else for you."

I raise my brow, curiosity piqued. "Oh?"

"A dress," he replies, his tone carrying a hint of amusement.

My nose wrinkles, and I take the bundle from him and unwrap it to reveal a beautiful gown in a dark shade of green. The long sleeves are made from thin lace, the delicate fabric seems to shimmer in the morning light, and intricate embroidery adorns the bodice. It's an exquisite piece.

"Is this my reward for surviving the trials so far?" I ask with suspicion. My father never gives me anything without motive.

Arawn chuckles. "Consider it a gesture of goodwill from your father."

I hold the dress up, admiring its craftsmanship. "It's quite lovely. But you do realise I prefer breeches."

He raises an eyebrow, a playful glint in his eyes. "A future queen must embrace her feminine side."

I scoff, shaking my head. "I'll consider it, but only if you promise not to laugh if I trip over the hem."

"Deal," he says with a mock-serious nod. "Which reminds me, there are shoes to match."

A guard hands over another package.

Arawn laughs at my groan. "The king and queen are hosting a ball. At the Rose moon, the night before the final trial. Your father wishes for you to attend and has told me to remind you of your *duties* to the guild."

There it is.

Of course, my father would never do anything out of the kindness of his heart—there's no kindness to be given.

Arawn's words hold a subtle edge, a reminder that my actions carry consequences beyond personal preference. The realisation tempers my playful mood.

"I understand," I reply, a note of bitterness entering my tone. "I won't forget the *importance* of my responsibilities."

"Good," he says, with a frown. "I'd hate to think of you disappointing my lord."

I roll my eyes, feigning exasperation. "Oh, how

could I ever bear the weight of such expectations?"

He laughs now, the sound genuine and warm. "I have no doubt you'll rise to the occasion, Efia."

As he turns to leave, his words hang in the air—a reminder of the game I'm part of, the balance I must maintain. The dress in my hands seems to symbolise not just a change of attire, but a reminder of the many roles I'm required to play. With a sigh, I fold the dress back into its bundle and head back into my tent.

When I leave again, a wood nymph strolls past, hesitates on her step and *nods* in my direction… as if in greeting. I almost glance behind me, but I know there is nothing there, so I gawk at her as she continues to walk.

How odd.

I find Wen by the edge of the camp, her attention fixed on the intricate patterns the breeze makes as it rustles through the leaves. I feel a sense of relief wash over me as I approach her.

"Morning, Wen," I greet her.

She turns toward me, her expression brightening. "Morning, Ef. How did you sleep?"

"Hmmm," I reply, forgetting about the nymph as I join her by the trees, a weight lifting from me in her presence.

Wen quirks an eyebrow, her gaze searching mine. "Oh?"

I chuckle, nodding. "Perhaps. But there's something you should know."

Like a moon bunny, popping their head out of

long grass, her curiosity is piqued. "Go on."

"There's going to be a ball."

"A ball?" Her silver eyes widen, a delighted grin spreading across her face. "Oh, Ef, you know how much I love to dance! When is it?"

"On the night of the Rose moon," I explain, and I can see her anticipation growing at the prospect of a night filled with festivities.

Wen's eyes practically sparkle. A ball during the full moon has her practically vibrating in her spot. Her fellow lunar faeries will be just as excited. "I can't wait! It'll be so much fun."

I can't help but share a bit of her excitement, despite the lingering worries that persist beneath the surface. "I'm glad you're looking forward to it. You deserve a night of joy."

As we chat about the upcoming event, I feel a pang of curiosity tugging at me—a question that has weighed on my mind. Taking a deep breath, I decide to voice it.

"Wen," I begin, my tone hesitant. "Have you seen or spoken to Beinon lately?"

She looks at me with a knowing glint in her eyes. "You're worried about him, aren't you?"

I sigh, unable to deny it. "I just haven't seen him around, and… well, I think our conversation ruined everything."

Wen places a comforting hand on my arm. "Ef, I'm sure he's just taking some time to process. These things can be complicated."

"I know," I reply, a mixture of frustration and concern knotting in my chest. "I just wish I could talk to him. Make sure he's all right."

"He's a big boy," Wen reassures me. "He's just sore because he's not used to rejection."

I wince at that.

"And he knows that he's lucky to have you as a friend. I'm sure he'll come around. This distance is just because his pride is a bit bruised."

I offer her a small smile, grateful for her unwavering support. "Thanks, Wen."

"Of course," she says, squeezing my arm gently. "Now, let's focus on the ball and all the dancing we're going to do. Oh, I'm so excited! I wonder if I have time to make a new dress. Oh! I wonder if— "

Her voice dims as I watch her chatter. Her enthusiasm is contagious, and for a moment, I'm able to set aside my worries and immerse myself in the excitement of the upcoming event. We continue to talk and plan, and I have a glimmer of hope that the Rose moon ball might just be the distraction we all need—even if it's just for a night.

After spending the rest of the morning with Wen, I eventually return to my tent alone, the weight of my recent conversations pressing on my chest. I purposely miss the announcement from the king and queen's guards, informing all the contenders of the Rose moon ball. It felt redundant after Arawn's visit.

Lost in my thoughts, I push aside the entrance to my tent, stepping inside without a second thought. The space is dim, the afternoon sunlight filtering through the canvas.

My shadows whisper harshly in my ear, but their warning is lost in the chaos of my mind. I walk further in, my thoughts wandering, and I unfasten the ties of my shirt, my skin slightly sticky from the heat of the day.

They whisper louder.

"What is it?" I wave a hand by my face, as if that could deter them.

It's only when a chill runs down my spine that I notice the presence behind me.

Someone else skipped the announcement.

I whirl around, my heart skipping as I see her—dark green, earthy skin that camouflages her against the fabric of the tent, raven hair, and eyes that hold a predatory gleam. The wood nymph from earlier, standing mere feet away, her features twisted in a menacing grin.

She lunges at me with unnatural speed, her sharp teeth bared in a feral snarl. Instinct takes over, and I bring up my forearm just in time to block her attack, but not in time to prevent her sharp, jagged teeth from embedding into my arm. The force of her impact sends me stumbling back, my heart racing.

Pain sears through me, both physical and a surge of anger. I lash out with my free hand, striking her across the face. She releases me with a growl, stumbling back. Blood drips from the wound on my arm, staining my white shirt, which is now torn.

Adrenaline courses through my veins, sharpening my senses. I quickly assess the situation—the confined space of the tent working against my advantage. I dodge her next strike, feeling the rush of wind as her clawed fingers brush past my skin. Her movements are swift and erratic, and I know that I can't afford to underestimate her.

With a swift kick, I knock her off balance, giving me the opportunity to counterattack. My fist connects with her side, and she lets out a hiss of pain. But she's not deterred—she lunges again.

I don't hesitate.

I wrench my dim shades up, blinding her for a second. But a second is enough to change everything. Ignoring the pain, I push forward, channelling every ounce of strength into my movements. My fists fly, pummeling her and forcing her back. Her resistance weakens with every blow, until finally, she collapses to the ground, unconscious.

My chest heaves as I stand over her, bloodied and bruised, but victorious. The shadows that surround me murmur their approval; their whispers now laced with some calm. I take a deep breath, wincing at the pain in my arm, and quickly gather what I need to secure her.

Tying her hands and feet, I ensure she won't escape before seeking help. Jill will need to examine the bite, and I can't afford for anyone to tell my father I'm injured.

Jill cleans and wraps my wound discreetly, and I summon Arawn by firesprite once I get back to my tent, hiding my wound from him whilst my father's guards take the wood nymph. She is awake and her eyes blown wide with fear by the time they arrive, and for a split second, something deep within me feels sorry for her… until I remember my arm.

After they've left, the reality of the attack settles in. I have become complacent in the illusion of peace here. I have forgotten my place.

Emotion has clouded my mind and judgements.

It's gone too far, and I can't allow it to happen again.

The Daeva Guild stands as one of the oldest and most esteemed factions within the Unseelie court, second only to the ancient Umbra Guild. Renowned for their bloodthirsty cunning and mastery of manipulation, Daeva members are some of the most feared in both the faerie and human realm.

PAGE 237, THE BOOK OF FAIR FAMILIES

CHAPTER TWENTY-TWO

"**E**fia." My father smiles, but it carries a weight of accusation. "You took your time."

I bow my head, feigning submission. "I apologise, Father."

I've been summoned to the manor, anticipating another target.

My gut churns.

Each time, it gets harder to stomach.

"Who is it this time?" I inquire, perhaps a bit prematurely. My father glares, but thankfully, he lets it slide.

"I've heard a rumour that Andric has been... associating with someone from the Luz Guild."

Andric, a lamia from the Daeva Guild in the Unseelie court. If he's involved with someone from the Seelie court, it can't be for anything good.

I narrow my eyes at my father. "Do you think the

queen is trying to interfere in the trials?"

His eyes flicker. "Of course she is. But involving the Unseelie Guilds is a step too far."

"Should we inform King Lew?" I suggest, wondering if we should keep the king informed of the queen's actions.

He shakes his head with a dismissive smirk. "No need. We'll handle it. And it'll send a warning to the rest of the Unseelie court. This meddling won't go unanswered."

I lift a brow, considering king Lew could take offense to not being alerted of these matters. "Won't the queen just seek out other traitors in the court?"

Father smirks, a calculated glint in his eyes. "Let her try. If they're foolish enough to do so, they deserve whatever punishment deems fit."

I nod, keeping my internal reservations hidden. Shielding the court is crucial, but if the queen is attempting to disrupt the trials, she must be more desperate for the crown than I thought. I'd rather unravel those reasons than merely fulfill my father's role as an assassin.

But I can't say that to him.

"As you wish, Father."

Turning to leave the study, my mind races with the implications of my father's order.

"Efia."

My steps falter as his threatening tone sends a shiver up my spine, and I swear I feel the scars on my back tighten.

"When I say make an example, I mean make an *example*."

Feeling a wave of nausea, I force myself to respond. "Of course, Father. Consider it done."

Tension is thick in the air as I approach Andric's dwelling, a cavernous burrow skilfully carved into the side of a hill. There's no doubt dozens of tunnels run underneath, where he could use to escape.

The moonlight filtering through the trees plays tricks on the edges of my vision, and I pull my cloak tighter around me.

I had to interrogate a kappa for Andric's location, and luckily the kappa's information proved reliable.

My steps are silent on the soft earth as I slip into the shadows, my senses alert to any hint of movement. The entrance yawns before me like a gaping maw. I press on; the darkness embracing me like an old ally.

Within the burrow, I navigate through a maze of dimly lit tunnels. The air grows colder, and the scent of damp earth permeates the atmosphere.

Finally, I reach a chamber, where the faint glow of phosphorescent mushrooms reveals Andric.

The lamia lounges on a makeshift bed, his serpent-like

lower body coiled beneath him. He doesn't look surprised to see me at all, his slitted pupils narrow.

Turn it off.

"Andric." I pull down my mask and greet him, my voice an icy whisper, shadows rising to dancing menacingly around me. "I hear you've been involved in dealings with the Seelie."

His forked tongue flickers. "I don't know what you're talking about."

I raise an eyebrow, my shades materialising and solidifying behind me like silent sentinels. The kappa had been quite forthcoming in detailing Andric's meetings with Seelie contacts.

"Let's not lie to each other," I smile, watching carefully as his body unwinds beneath him and he rises slightly. "Perhaps if you give me the information Bron wants, he'll let me go easy on you."

Andric hisses a laugh. "Don't pretend he hasn't sent you here to kill me."

I shrug, and Andric's words hang in the air, a challenge laced with venom. "You'd be nothing without those shadows of yours."

I chuckle, the sound echoing through the cavern. I wave a hand, allowing the shadows, once a protective shroud around me, to dissipate, leaving only the dim glow of the luminescent fungi that cling to the cavern walls.

"Let's find out," I say, the amusement in my voice belying the seething anger beneath the surface.

Andric lunges forward, his predatory instincts kicking

in. His movements are swift, but he underestimates me, blinded by arrogance. I dart to the side, avoiding his outstretched claws, and jump when he swings his tail around, attempting to whip me.

The absence of shadows doesn't diminish my skill; it only sharpens my focus, especially as the need to survive pumps through my body. My hand moves like lightning, ripping a blade from its sheath at my side. I parry his attacks with calculated precision, grinning as he hisses when I cut across his arm.

As Andric falters, his head jerking around, I seize the opportunity. His tail coils behind him, readying to swing for my legs once more. But I unsheathe my other blade, throwing it and relishing the cry of pain from his mouth as it cuts through its flesh.

"You'll pay, Mathonwy! I swear it!" Andric spits at me through his teeth, whilst he scrambles for the sword.

I ignore his poisonous words, darting forward and bringing the blade down through his chest. There is a second, a split second, as I stare into his reptilian eyes… that I feel guilty. But I quash it down and rip out my blade.

His body crumples to the ground.

The next morning, when I am safely back at camp, I hear the whispers around me as faeries discuss the gruesome discovery in the Unseelie realm. How the carved body of Andric had appeared in the centre of the Daeva's Guild, strung up as a warning to all around.

Betraying your guild or your court will only end one

way…

Even though sharks can be scary, we need them to keep the oceans healthy. Unfortunately, due to overfishing, many shark species are in danger of extinction, and that can cause big problems in the oceans and even on land.

IF SHARKS DISAPPEARED, BY LILY WILLIAMS

CHAPTER TWENTY-THREE

*I*n the quiet corner of the library, I stand beside my uncle Gwydion,
who's utterly engrossed in a small, brightly coloured book. Its pages are filled with vivid illustrations of creatures from the human realm, and Gwydion's eyes shine with a childlike fascination.

"Uncle," I say, trying to contain my amusement. "What has captured your interest?"

Gwydion looks up, his black eyes crinkling at the corners and a wide smile spreads across his face. "Ah, my dear Efia, I know many would look down upon it. But the human realm and all its wonders have always fascinated me. Look at this!" He points to an image of a terrifying but sleek, powerful creature with rows of sharp teeth. "Sharks! They are truly remarkable."

I gaze at the illustration of the strange animal, its form both elegant and menacing. Gwydion's enthusiasm is infectious.

"Their teeth look like vampires," I comment.

"I know!" he exclaims. "Amazing, aren't they?" He leans

closer to the book, his eyes alight with excitement. "They are creatures of the deep. They roam the vast oceans, and I've always found their existence utterly captivating."

As he continues to flip through the pages, showing me images of various marine life, I can't help but chuckle at his boundless curiosity. Gwydion's enthusiasm for the human realm is endearing.

"Uncle," I say, my voice tinged with affection. "Your love of the human realm is bordering on obsession. But I must admit, I do enjoy the treasures you bring back. It's as if you've stolen a piece of their world."

He grins at me, his eyes still fixed on the book. "In a way, that's precisely what I've done, Efia. There is beauty and diversity that exists beyond our own realm, a source of endless wonder and inspiration. I want you to remember that. Even with our own courts. I know we are dark fae, but there is beauty in both courts. In all faeries."

I smile and nod. "I'll remember."

The evening of the Rose moon descends upon us far too quickly, the atmosphere charged with excitement. I no longer resent the time spent getting ready, allowing Wen to stain my face with coloured powders and black kohl, because the result is far beyond anything I could have done.

With her minimal water magic, Wen creates a surface where I can check my reflection in. The dark green dress clings to me like a glove, accentuating my curves and flowing gracefully with every step I take. Its deep hue complements my complexion. Even in the subtle ripples of the water, I can see that I'm glowing, my eyes bright, lips a cherry red, only a shade brighter than my hair.

Wen stands before me, her fingers delicately smoothing over the fabric of her flowing, light lavender dress. The gown drapes elegantly around her, the intricate lacework and subtle shimmer catching the light in a mesmerising dance. With a contented smile, she adjusts a loose strand of dark hair, her eyes sparkling.

I can't help but roll my eyes at Wen's preening, her excitement practically tangible in the air. "You'd think you were going to meet your true love, not just attending a ball," I tease, smirking as she sends a playful swat in my direction.

"Well, Efia," Wen retorts with a sly grin. "You never know who might be waiting for me at that ball." She twirls slightly, causing the lavender fabric of her dress to swirl around her like a delicate cloud. "Besides, it's not every day we get to attend such an extravagant event."

I chuckle and shake my head, a fond exasperation tugging at my lips. "Well then, Wen. I promise to hold a monthly ball in your honour if I win this contest."

"*When* you win this contest," she corrects me.

I laugh lightly. "Let's not keep fate waiting, then."

With that, we make our way out of the tent, and toward the line of royal guards at the bottom of the field, conjuring portals to Castell Narbeth. I follow Wen through a shimmering doorway, allowing the magic to trickle over my skin, the anticipation of the evening's festivities tingling in the air.

Faeries from both courts converge upon the castle, draped in their most exquisite attire, as portals open in a dazzling array around me. The anxious atmosphere is palpable, not just for the imminent final trial but also for the enchanting festivities that this night promises. Yet, my stride falters as I approach the castle, a surge of emotion washing over me. The castle, built into the mountainside, stands before me with an eerie familiarity. Its appearance remains unchanged, except for the excessive display of blossom pink silk that adorns the entrance—Queen Lilah's unmistakable touch, I presume.

So many years I spent wandering its halls. It's gardens. It feels surreal that it looks the same when so much has changed. When Uncle Gwydion isn't there with his booming laughter.

It feels… wrong, that the king and queen have been able to *bless* it with their touch for the night, even if this is what he would have wanted. Unity.

Gwydion's ideals were not just spoken words; they were threads of hope woven into the very fabric of his rule. His belief in unity went beyond political alliances and temporary treaties. He sought to mend the deep-rooted divisions between Seelie and Unseelie, to dissolve the barriers that kept us apart. I can still hear his voice, soft yet unwavering, as he addressed both courts, always urging us to embrace our shared heritage and transcend the bitterness that had festered for centuries.

He would have loved having the courts mingle on a night like this.

Would have loved seeing them trying to unravel the castle's secrets.

But now only I know its magic. What it hides in its dark halls.

The king and queen are fortunate the ancient building allows them in.

I force the melancholy to drift away as we continue. The ascent to the castle is lined with grand braziers emitting the scent of burning sage and juniper, their flickering flames casting a warm glow upon the steps. Wen wraps a slender arm through mine, squeezing me tightly for a moment as if she knows where my thoughts have gone.

We continue, and with a tight knot in my stomach, I pass through the entrance, half-expecting to feel the lingering magic of Uncle Gwydion.

But it's not there.

The castle's magic now stands on its own, distinct from the enchantment that once intertwined with my uncle's presence.

We step into the cavernous entryway, hewn from solid rock, and the castle's magic washes over me like a bittersweet caress. Before Gwydion's passing, the protective wards would have permitted entry only to those granted permission. Now, despite the old guards stationed attentively, the threshold to the great hall is open, allowing anyone to pass through until a new ruler takes their rightful place and keys the wards.

They wouldn't be able to explore the rest of the castle, the wings would have closed themselves off when Uncle died. But it still feels strange as faeries can enter with ease.

The High Castle guards are neither Unseelie nor Seelie. They are as ancient as the castle itself, created from carved stone, brought to life by magic and forever duty bound to protect the ruler of the realms. They cannot be manipulated or controlled by anyone other than the rightful ruler.

I jerk slightly as I enter, and they stand to attention, the sound of the metal armour that encases their stone forms ringing out loudly. They tip their blank heads towards me, which I take as a mark of respect for my late uncle. It fills me with a sense of belonging. These guards, their allegiance unswayed by the politics of courts, are devoted to the high crown above all else.

The grandeur of the event is already in full swing. Trows, shifters, pixies, nymphs, and fae whirl and twirl to the melodies of the faerie band positioned at the back of the hall. The irresistible music weaves its enchantment, coaxing guests to join hands and lose themselves in the timeless circle dances. In the alcoves on either side of the room, faeries are entwined in passionate embraces, their voices merging with the music in sighs of delight. Some wander aimlessly through the opulent halls, their eyes wide with wonder as they take in the castle's magnificence.

The sweet fragrance of fresh berries teases my senses, and I catch sight of the sumptuous feast laid out before us. Piles of summer berries, cherries, and delectable pastries grace the tables, while carafes of candlewine flow freely, ensuring no goblet remains empty.

I wander through the bustling ballroom. The flickering lights and lively sounds stir memories of another ball held in this very castle. I was young then, barely more than a child, but the vivid recollections still dance through my mind. Amidst the vibrant festivities, I caught sight of my uncle Gwydion and my father, their voices low and heated as they disappeared into a hidden alcove. Curiosity tugged at me, but I had been too small to understand the significance of their argument. I tried to get closer, to glimpse their expressions, but a passing group of dark faeries swept me away, their laughter and merry chatter drowning out the strained voices behind me.

Even now, I wonder what had driven that heated exchange between them. The memory lingers like a puzzle piece, a fragment of my past that has never quite fit into the larger picture.

The grand chandeliers overhead cast ethereal light, creating an enchanting atmosphere for the mingling guests. I'm awed by the unity between Seelie and Unseelie, as if the division doesn't exist. I know it's fleeting, and I can't help but feel a pang of bittersweet nostalgia.

Amidst the glittering gowns and laughter, I see potential in my uncle's legacy.

Tomorrow's trial will bring chaos once again. For this moment, harmony envelops the ballroom, offering a glimpse of the coexistence that *could be*—if only they would try.

Wen and I find a momentary respite from the crowding faeries and pause at the edge of the ballroom. She tosses a playful grin my way, her eyes sparkling. "So, Ef, any handsome suitors caught your eye yet?"

I snort, rolling my eyes at her jest. "Oh, absolutely. You know me, Wen. I can't resist a faerie in a fancy suit."

A fae approaches Wen, interrupting us, and bows gracefully before extending his hand. "Care to join me for a dance, my lady?"

Wen glances at me, mouthing *'my lady'* with widened eyes. "Mind if I steal him away for a dance, Ef?"

I shake my head with a small smile. "Go ahead, enjoy yourself. I'll be fine."

Wen twirls away into the dance, and I watch her for a moment before my gaze drifts across the room, landing on my father. My heart quickens, and tension coils within me as he approaches. Arawn is not too far behind, my father's ever vigilant man. I straighten my posture, preparing for whatever conversation or expectations he might bring my way. The weight of my responsibilities and his watchful eyes make the air feel heavier around me, and I take a steadying breath.

But then I spot Celeste.

The vampire elder wears a form-fitting dress in a deep purple, her hair coiled tightly on her head. She smiles to the faeries she passes as she approaches us, but here is hate in her eyes.

"*Celeste is approaching behind you,*" I murmur into my father's mind, a subtle exertion of my lesser magic sending a faint shiver down my spine. My father, in response, only grins maliciously as he ends up by my side.

"Celeste, how lovely to see you," he greets the vampire with feigned warmth.

Her eyes narrow, and she forces a tight smile. The moment her gaze lands on me, they ignite with fury.

"Bron, I know you had your abomination do it."

"Do what?" Father feigns innocence, a subtle tilt of his head.

"I know!" Celeste hisses, closing the distance between us. My hand drops to my thigh, and she catches the movement. A shade slithers from a nearby alcove, swirling over my shoulder, its tip darkening and pointing straight at her. A threatening reminder of who she speaks to.

A faint pallor washes over her features. "I know your little bitch killed Darick, and I will make sure you pay for it."

Father's amusement deepens, and he regards Celeste's accusatory stance. "My dear, I have no idea what you're talking about. Perhaps you're letting paranoia cloud your judgment."

Celeste's nostrils flare, and her gaze flickers between my father and me. The tension in the air is so brittle it feels like it could snap at any moment, and the shade beside me seems to dance with anticipation.

"Bron, if your pet assassin thinks she can meddle in vampire affairs without consequences, she's sorely mistaken," Celeste warns, her voice carrying a venomous edge.

"Meddle?" Father chuckles, the sound dripping with mockery. "You give Efia too much credit. She merely executes the tasks *assigned* to her."

Celeste's eyes narrow further. "This won't end well for you, Bron. There are rules, even for you."

He leans in. "Power speaks louder than rules, you know that, Celeste. But perhaps we should take this to King Lew, inform him about the little Rixin operation you have running in several of the districts?"

Celeste's fangs snap out, and she bares her teeth.

"No please, go on." Father's eyes shine with glee, hoping and daring her to cause a scene. King Lew and Queen Lilah would punish her dearly for doing so.

Without further words and a final disdainful glance, Celeste retreats, her anger obvious in the way she storms away. The tension in the air lessens, and I feel my father's gaze fix on me.

I remain silent, my mask concealing any hint of emotion. The shadows that cling to me seem to mirror my inner turmoil, and I can't shake the feeling that the consequences of my latest assignment are far from over.

But there is no time to discuss it, and the tension escalates when I catch sight of Queen Lilah walking over towards us.

"Your Majesty." I incline my head respectfully. The subtle curl of the queen's lips is not lost on me.

"Your Majesty." Father's words are curt, his sharp gaze sweeping over the faeries gathered in the hall, ever watchful for potential threats, even when the most significant one stands beside him.

"Efia, I must say," the queen's melodious voice chimes in, "I was thoroughly impressed by your performance in the maze. Word has it you emerged *unscathed* from a confrontation with both Aisling *and* my Beinon."

My father's lips twitch, an almost imperceptible smirk.

"I did," I admit, "but luck wasn't the deciding factor."

My father emits a subtle, humour-laden huff, while Queen Lilah takes a step closer, tilting her head to meet my gaze. Though physically smaller, her demeanour exudes confidence, as if she doesn't perceive me or my father as a threat.

"I *also* heard." Her smile turns cruel, and my muscles tense. "That you not only spared the life of a water nymph… but actually *saved* her."

From the corner of my eye, I see my father's head turn ever so slowly in my direction, feeling his eyes burn holes into the side of my face.

Fuck.

The Rose moon, reaching its full brightness in June, is hailed as the most beautiful and romantic among lunar phases. Legend has it that love kindled under the Rose moon's gentle light is destined to endure a lifetime.
PAGE 739, THE BOOK OF FAIR FAMILIES

CHAPTER TWENTY-FOUR

I knew my involvement in that altercation would come back to haunt me.

Father's attention is only ever on me when he gives instructions… or when he's furious.

Neither is wanted.

But his icy and wrathful gaze burns. My resolve almost wavers under the intensity of his stare, but I force myself to hold his gaze.

Swallowing the unease that threatens to surface, I respond coolly, "In this competition, it's wise to cultivate potential allies, Your Majesty. Elimination can always come later if necessary."

My words ring hollow, and my shadows gather like wisps around my arms; I sense that both the queen and my father see through the facade.

Queen Lilah's knowing grin and slight nod of acknowledgement speak volumes as she turns and departs without another word, the rustling of her gown fading into the murmurs of the crowd.

I wrestle to steady my breathing and quell the surge of fear and anxiety that threatens to overwhelm me in the wake of my father's stern expression.

Turn it off.

It takes a moment; this situation was unexpected. But I do it. The mask comes into place, and I am still under his scrutiny, not giving anything away.

He scans the room again, and my apprehension lessens somewhat. I wisely hold my tongue, knowing that silence is the better part of valour in this moment.

"Enjoy your evening, Efia," is all he says as he turns and walks away.

I'm left utterly stupefied, incapable of forming a response.

Arawn looks at me regretfully for a split second before following. His departure leaves me in a state of astonishment, the absence of his usual scolding or even a veiled threat of retribution catching me off guard.

I decide to revel in the moment. Approaching a passing member of staff, I procure a flute of candlewine, and swiftly empty it before placing the glass back onto the tray. I slip discreetly behind a stone pillar, and I take the chance to truly breathe.

A hand clamps onto my arm just below the elbow, my shadows quiet. With a forceful tug, I'm pulled into a shadowy alcove towards the back of the room.

Taken by surprise but not unprepared, my small knife is unsheathed from under the hidden slit by my thigh and placed against the faerie's throat. In the dim seclusion of the alcove, I tip my chin up and smother a gasp when I see who towers over me—Ansel.

A rush of happiness quickly takes over my surprise at the sight of him. I haven't seen him since the day he ran from my tent, often wandering past his own, but never finding him. I started to feel like he was avoiding me.

"Ansel," I say without second thought, and throw my arms around him, embracing him tightly.

His initial surprise melts, and his arms wrap around me in return. The warmth of his body against mine is comforting, and his scent—sweet and familiar—envelopes me in a cocoon of solace.

What are you doing?

My mind questions where the instinct to embrace him came from. I pull away, clearing my throat and sheath my knife, a smile tugging at the corners of my lips.

"*Hello, vicious one.*" Ansel's mental voice enters my mind, a gentle greeting accompanied by a small, heartwarming smile on his lips.

I pull back slightly to take in Ansel's appearance— the all-black suit that fits him so well, the air of elegance he carries effortlessly, as if he was brought up in this world of royal etiquette. A teasing grin forms on my lips as I playfully remark, "Well, well, Ansel. Look at you, all dressed up. I almost didn't recognise you."

He raises an eyebrow with a sly smirk, his gaze leisurely roaming over me in a way that sends a shiver down my spine. I feel a flush creep up my cheeks at the intensity of his gaze. I clear my throat, suddenly aware of how close we are in the intimate alcove.

"*You, on the other hand, Mathonwy,*" he says, low and seductive. "*I noticed straight away. I could hardly take my eyes off you when you entered the room.*"

The words hit me like a delightful jolt, and pleasure dances in my chest. Our playful banter has taken a slightly more charged turn, and I'm not entirely sure how to respond.

Feeling a little self-conscious under his gaze, I decide to shift the conversation. "How have you been? It's been a while since we last saw each other."

He lets out a quiet sigh, his expression momentarily distant and guarded before he offers a vague smile. "*Busy. Preparing. You know how it is.*"

The music swells in the background before I can respond, and Ansel looks at me with a smile that holds a hint of mischief. "*Indulge me in a dance?*"

His request is sincere, and I catch a softness in his eyes that I haven't seen before. The formal tone surprises me, and I nod, unable to resist the intrigue in his gaze. I sigh dramatically, as though he is imposing. "I suppose I could make an exception for you."

He offers me his hand, and I place mine in his with a mix of anticipation and curiosity. We step onto the dance floor, the world fading as the rhythm of the music envelops us. He places his hand on my waist, and we begin to move, a shiver running down my spine at the gentle touch.

Ansel's lead is confident and sure, guiding me effortlessly through the steps. As we twirl and sway, I catch glimpses of the wide smile he's wearing. The mask of guardedness momentarily lifted.

It doesn't last long.

"*I saw you talking with your father. Everything all right?*"

My stomach clenches.

"I believe so," I tell him with a tight smile. "We'll find out after tomorrow." I joke, looking towards my feet, though there's truly no humour there.

"*You are stronger than him, Mathonwy.*"

My eyes find his again at his words. I know I'm stronger than Bron. It's a cause of his jealousy and bitterness that I, instead of him, inherited the Nüwch abilities. But to hear someone else—someone new—tell me so, after years of being made to feel weak.

I appreciate it far more than I will ever let on.

I nod but can't find the words to reply. So, we dance.

The ballroom seems to transform into a world of its own, where it's just the two of us lost in the dance. My heart beats in time with the music, and I'm taken aback by the warmth of Ansel's hand on my waist. The way his touch ignites a spark within me. It's a sensation I've never experienced before, unfamiliar and yet strangely comforting. And as the music sways and the night continues, I fight those unfamiliar feelings taking root, trying not to allow myself to be swept away in this dance.

It ends far too soon.

The dance felt like a fleeting dream, a momentary escape. As the music gradually fades, the piercing thrum of magic washes over me as a guard uses their staff against the marble floor.

We turn, spotting King Lew and Queen Lilah stood atop the stairs. Their regal garments seemed to absorb the light, casting an ominous radiance as they stepped forward. Ansel's hand moves to my lower back, my stomach clenching as the skin there warms under his touch.

"Faerie kin of both courts," Queen Lilah's voice, silky yet commanding, permeates the hall. "As the roses bloom and our hearts revel, we declare the commencement of the final trial of the Gwenhwyvar contest."

A subtle hush falls over the courtiers, the air thick with anticipation. The once-celebratory music now lingers in a haunting undertone.

"With the descent of the sun tomorrow, the final trial shall unfurl in the Gwenhwyvar fields," Queen Lilah continues, her eyes gleaming with an unsettling intensity. "To reach the heart of the arena is to claim not only victory but the throne that oversees the entire realm—the throne of the High King… or Queen."

Another maze, perhaps?

"This is the final test," King Lew, his harpy claws gleaming, says, "Your *final* chance. To claim victory and honour for your Guild. For your court. I do not say it lightly when I tell you to leave it *all* in the arena. Weakness will only result in your death. Fight well. Die well."

The courtiers exchange uneasy glances, and the rulers' words hang in the air like a foreboding mist. The festive melody had transformed into an eerie cadence, mirroring the gravity of the moment.

Queen Lilah's eyes bore into the assembly, her smile anything but sweet.

"May the trial unfold, and the strongest claim their destiny," King Lew declares, and as they withdraw to two identical thrones erected at the top of the stairs, the once-joyous ballroom now echoes with a chilling uncertainty.

"Continue," Queen Lilah's high voice calls out. "And may Gwydion bless you all."

No one moves, even as the instruments start back up—the merry atmosphere of the ball having been ruined by the reminder that we'll all be killing each this time tomorrow.

Ansel raises his brows as we turn and face each other, but a throat clearing behind me draws our attention.

Arawn's interruption is unexpected, and I reluctantly step away from Ansel's embrace.

"Arawn?" I ask.

"Your father needs to see you urgently," he says, narrowed gaze travelling over Ansel.

I don't want to question Arawn in front of Ansel, so I offer the latter an apologetic smile. "Duty calls. I'll come find you after?"

He nods, though his eyes still hold a hint of disappointment. *"Of course, Mathonwy. We can talk later."*

Wen's concerned gaze catches mine as I walk away, and I give her a reassuring smile, silently conveying that there's nothing to worry about.

"Who is the fae?" Arawn asks, and there is a hint of bitterness in his tone.

"Just someone who asked me to dance," I tell him. If he believes Ansel to mean anything more to me, he will tell father.

"A *light* fae?" he responds with a sneer.

"Well, if I'm going to rule over everyone, I best make some acquaintances in what will be one of my courts, don't you think Arawn?" I smile with teeth, playing off the nervousness that has settled in my gut.

He says no more, seemingly buying my words, and I follow him out of the castle, the cool night air hitting me as we step into the private gardens. His silence is unnerving, and I can't help but feel a sense of unease settle over me.

"Arawn, what's going on?" I finally break the brief silence, my tone a mixture of curiosity and concern. Arawn doesn't respond, but he guides me toward a secluded corner of the gardens, where my father's imposing figure stands in waiting.

"Father," I address him, alerting him to my presence. "You wish to speak with me?"

Behind me, Arawn opens a portal without

warning, leaving me momentarily bewildered.

Father shifts his attention slowly, and an icy shiver races down my spine, a stark contrast to the cooling air around us. His eyes betray no emotion, only a chilling disdain that twists his lip into a sneer. A nod from him signals to Arawn, whose brows knit, his face full of regret.

Not today.

With a swift pivot on my heel, I press my back foot and break into a sprint, my determination propelling me away from their looming presence.

Two of my father's men emerge from the shadows, reaching out to intercept me despite the fear in their eyes. The first guard chokes, his hands grappling at his throat after my fingers jab and swiftly find their mark. As the second guard seizes my arm from behind, a shadow detaches from my form, slamming into him with a forceful blow. I whirl around, my leg arcing in a satisfying strike that lands squarely on his face, the sound of impact echoing through the air.

A sharp gasp rips from my throat and searing pain erupts in my shoulder. My eyes dart to the source, my father's silver throwing knife buried to its hilt.

The fight within me fades, and I cease my struggles, knowing if I kill his guards or fight any more, my punishment will be worse. Knowing he will only threaten Wen.

Two more guards emerge from the portal to seize me. My shades whisper harshly in my ear, thickening as if willing me to make them protect me—fighting my control. As we pass, I land a kick on one of the fallen guards, my defiance dwindling before we go through the portal.

"Brave," Father's voice drips with spite as he follows us through and wrenches the blade free from my shoulder. His guards hold me tightly, and I hiss through gritted teeth, feeling my fangs elongate slightly in my boiling rage. "Stupid, but brave."

A bitter retort forms on my lips, but I swallow it down, my gaze hardening, and I meet his eyes. "You'd wound me before the final trial?"

He offers a callous smile. "Your body will heal. You will forget."

I will never forget. The memory will forever remain etched in my mind. Just like every other time.

"But *everyone* will remember your weakness!" The back of his hand strikes me across the face with sudden force, wrenching my neck to the side. He hands the knife to another guard, the fae averting his eyes as he hands my father a short signal whip—a favoured tool of torture of my father's.

But he's correct.

Providing the injuries tonight doesn't cause me to lose consciousness, and I can get back to my herbs quickly. I should be able to mostly heal them by tomorrow's trial. However, the pain that lingers isn't just physical.

I choose not to resist. I remain silent, and the

guards turn me around, holding my arms outstretched. They don't bother stripping me, the dress low enough to expose the skin of my back. Arawn is fortunately, stood by father, so I can't see his face, and I breathe in and out quickly, expecting the whip.

The bite of the first one arches my back, and I focus on breathing so I can prepare myself to get used to the sting of it.

Then the blows rain down upon me, their impact relentless.

My knees buckle under the onslaught.

The guards release their grip on my arms, and I curl into a protective ball as the strikes continue, each one marking me, both physically and mentally. I hear my dress rip as the whip strikes the skin of my back. I will endure his punishment, as I have countless times before—always the disappointing daughter.

Turn it off.

My mind drifts away from the torment, seeking solace in images of Wen, Beinon, and even Ansel. Anything to stave off the consuming darkness that threatens to engulf me. Eventually, it subsides. Strangely, relief washes over me despite the agony that now courses through my body. The relief is strange because many would assume the worst is over. It isn't. The healing and treating of the wounds are the worst. The burning sting that comes after the shock has worn off.

Without a single word, Father departs through a portal of his own making, leaving me broken and bleeding amidst the woods until I can muster the strength to move. Before he leaves, Arawn at least has the decency to open a portal back to the entrance of the camp.

I do not look at him; I do not speak to him as I crawl through it. Getting back to my tent becomes a gruelling effort, my body battered and bloodied. I disregard the hushed murmurs of nearby faeries and suppress the urge to cry out.

Their pity makes me furious. They feel sorry enough for me, that no one makes an attempt on my life. It would be seen as dishonourable whilst I am in this state.

Father will relish in this spectacle, in the sight of me brought low.

A statement to all that not even his daughter escapes his wrath.

If he can do this to his own daughter, what could he do to them?

But he will expect me to heal. To make myself better. To show everyone tomorrow how quick the *mighty* Nüwch rises to end them all.

Because if I don't, I will be punished ten times worse.

Only moments after collapsing onto the furs of my bed, the tent flap rustles open. My body tenses, and I twist onto my back, a knife from under my pillow clutched in my trembling hand. Despite my wretched state, I'm ready to defend myself, prepared to fight back if any faerie has chosen this vulnerable moment to strike me down.

A group of four water nymphs enter cautiously, their movements respectful as they bow their heads upon spotting me. Buckets sway in their grasp, and one by one, they pour the steaming liquid and other things into the waiting tub.

They're preparing a bath… for *me*.

They are… taking *care*… of me?

Silently, they go about their task, their radiant eyes darting to me intermittently as I steadfastly maintain my defensive stance. Their glances reveal their sympathy, their perception of the glassiness that has overcome my eyes. Their departure mirrors their arrival—quietly. The last nymph pauses before closing the canvas flap, and I recognise her.

The nymph from the second trial.

"For your mercy," she murmurs, offering me a nod before she leaves, and I am suddenly reminded of words spoken to me years ago, by my uncle.

Where mercy is shown, mercy is given.

Water nymphs, mystical beings dwelling in lakes and rivers, are known for their unyielding loyalty and strong sense of honor. According to folklore, when someone aids or befriends a water nymph, they incur a debt that the nymph is compelled to repay.
FAERIE CREATURES AND KNOWN WEAKNESSES BY TOMAS CEREDWEN

CHAPTER TWENTY-FIVE

The strain in my arm is a persistent ache, and I finally let the blade fall, a shaky exhale escaping me. Gathering an unwanted yet familiar reserve of strength, I rise, albeit with a limp, and use the wooden pole in the centre of the tent to get up. My steps carry me toward the inviting tub, and I suppress a sob that threatens to surface as I peer within.

It is not just a bath. It is a healing bath.

Steam tendrils rise delicately from the frothy liquid, its surface adorned with a symphony of curative herbs, salts, vibrant lavender petals, and citrus slices—each element meticulously chosen to cleanse my wounds and soothe my pain.

The nymphs' kindness warms my guarded heart; they've provided a reprieve that feels like a gift. I contemplate embracing them in gratitude, but I know better—their perceptions could misconstrue my intentions.

My back throbs as I gingerly peel off the remnants of the dress, letting the tattered fabric cascade to the floor beside the tub. I carefully rest my knife beside it on a little wooden table. Dealing with my undergarments poses a different challenge. Perched on the warm edge of the tub, hissing through my teeth as I drag them down, I use my feet to gently ease them off, unable to bend down fully and stretch the muscles of my back.

Once my attire is cast aside, I extend myself carefully, releasing the tension from my muscles before I pivot to step into the bath with caution. I navigate the transition meticulously, wary of making my injuries worse.

The liquid embraces me as I sink in, cocooning every inch of my submerged skin, and I thank all the Gods and Goddesses for the warmth. The fragrant blend of healing herbs fills my senses, acting as a calming elixir for both my weary body and battered spirit.

Sat in silence, I feel a growing ache in my chest, intensifying the longer I linger in this moment of introspection. My thoughts march through my mind like the heavy footfalls of a fae horde, denying me any respite. My teeth clench as memories surge behind my closed eyelids. The stabbing pains that sear my skin. The intrusion shatters my peace, memories that never let me be at ease, reminders that I'll never escape.

For years, I've harboured the desire to unleash my shades upon him. But there is no greater crime in our realms than patricide. I would be exiled, banished to the human realm if I ever were to raise my hand against my father. It is an old rule, one put in place to prevent killing parents for their wealth, power, or position. It is a rule which has stayed my hands for all my life.

I summon my shades to me, and relish in their comforting darkness and loving whispers. Tears slip down my cheeks, unbidden, cooled by a breeze that flows in through the opened tent flap as a shade swipes them away.

I don't have to look to know who it is—a calm awareness brushes over me.

The darkness recedes from around me, and I tense, refusing to glance his way as the shadows whisper against my ear before brushing against my cheek. They allow him to approach, surprising me, considering my condition. When I first became friends with Wen, they used to force her away.

They would not hurt her, but they would refuse to let her near when I was in such a vulnerable position, and they have never allowed Beinon within twenty feet of me after one of my father's attacks.

"*Mathonwy,*" his voice whispers into my thoughts, a mixture of softness and horror that I can't bring myself to face. He skirts around the side of the tub, coming into my line of sight, and he kneels, despite my resolute refusal to meet his eye directly. I feel his gaze, fiery and gentle, assess the scarred expanse of my back, the new wounds on my back, arms, and face.

My knees draw close, a tight embrace that guards against the chill that courses through my body. I hug them to my chest tightly, a few tears escaping my eyes and running down my cheeks. And I hate it. I hate the vulnerability... but I am too tired. I'm not ashamed of the scars he sees, nor the expanse of my exposed body. Instead, it's the rawness of my emotions that fills me with a sense of disgrace, and I can still hear my father in my head as he makes his marks upon my body.

"*What happened?*" Ansel asks, his voice taut and dangerous, his fingers tracing gentle pathways across my already healing—albeit slowly—wounds, sending shivers through me.

"My father," I say, my voice a hushed confession.

I can feel that they are deeper than usual. Father's anger worse than it has been for a long time. I can only pray the bath and herbs will be enough.

Ansel's hand pulls back and his fingers curl, the lengths of them turning a golden-black hue as feathers crawl up his arm, a sharp talon extending from each digit. There's a wicked fury in his face as he tries to control his urge to shift, to become more predator than fae. I don't flinch when a golden claw raises, the brush of it so sweet when he swipes the tear from my cheek.

My heart skips.

His eyes shutter closed, his inhalation deep and deliberate, causing the harpy-like manifestation on his arms to recede until it vanishes entirely. When he reopens his eyes, his vulnerability is palpable, an uneasy flush on his cheeks. He scrutinises me for several seconds, as if wrestling with some internal decision.

In a swift motion, he rises, and crosses to the small table on the opposite side of the bath and retrieves the soap bar.

My gaze tracks his every movement. "What are you doing?"

"*What does it look like I'm doing?*" He arches a brow, a faint smile threatening to crack his otherwise solemn demeanour. I sense it's a fleeting gesture, offered for my sake, judging by the way his throat bobs uneasily when his attention returns to my back. Nevertheless, I'm thankful for it.

I don't reply as he kneels behind me, nor as he drops his hands into the water, rubbing the soap bar between them and gathering bubbles. When his hands come out of the water, I tense and he hesitates, before raising them and running them over my head.

This is a lot.

This is…

I can't explain it. I have never turned my back to another faerie, let alone someone who from the other court, even if he straddles the line of both.

My mind tells me not to trust this… But something in me reassures me I'm safe.

It takes a few moments for my body to realise he won't wrap his hands around my neck. When it does, my shoulders relax, my head tilts back to give him more access to my scalp, and he lathers the soap, scrubbing at my head.

I am grateful he remains silent; the feeling is indescribable, and I can't remember the last time anyone washed my hair for me. I suck in a shaky breath, my eyes closing at the unbelievable feeling as the warm water seeps into my skin, easing my anxiety.

My dark thoughts have scattered. The only thing my mind can concentrate on is what Ansel is doing. His hands pause for a second when I sigh in contentment before he continues his ministrations. I let the scent of lavender and citrus fill my nostrils, soothing my body and mind.

Much too soon, he cups water in his hands to wash away the bubbles, the warm water running over my shoulder and back, causing me to tense, though I soon get used to it. My pointer finger draws random patterns across the top of the water once he settles back, humming in satisfaction with his work—the wet strands of my poppy-red sticking to my skin.

"*What would you be doing if you weren't in this contest?*" he asks, settling back at my side and resting his elbows on his knees.

I huff without humour. "Unfortunately, probably something very similar to this."

He flinches.

"*All right,*" he drawls, "*in another realm, perhaps… What would you be doing?*"

I think about his question. *Really* think. And my stomach gutters when I can't answer it. His brow furrows, and his gaze makes me realise I can trust him with this answer.

"I don't know." I rest my chin on my knee. "My whole life has been spent training or educating myself on everything my father deemed was important for me to know. This time away from him, away from his tight control… it has taught me I don't know who I am. The monster Efia Mathonwy, the unfeeling warrior daughter of Bron, Nüwch niece of Gwydion…"

My eyes fall to the water, my voice a whisper as soft as my shadows. "But I do not know who Efia is."

Ansel's hand stretches out, his fingers cupping my cheek, gently tilting my face to meet his gaze. His touch is tender, and he leans in, his chin resting on the edge of the tub. There's an unexpected intimacy at the moment.

And in that instant, my body flushes for an entirely different reason.

Because he is looking at me.

He *sees* me.

"*I know who you are,*" he says with complete certainty. "*I've watched and seen the love you have for your friends, even if you try your best to hide it. Even though your father would sooner have you kill them in their sleep than befriend them. I've heard of your kind heart, from the multitude of faeries around camp who talk about how you saved that water nymph. How you saved* my *life.*"

I swallow hard as a niggle of guilt swirls in my stomach. He can tell from my expression.

"*I know you considered using that poison in your pack in*

the first trial."

My mouth opens, but he holds a hand up. *"It was like your father to think of it, but it was* you *that decided to spare me. To help me. You have no idea how much I wish you could see yourself the way others see you. The way I see you."*

A fresh tear makes its way down my face.

"You see yourself through the eyes of your father." His teeth bare slightly. *"A monster or a tool to be used. But you need to understand the strength you have. To be someone with so much power and* not *use it… but be so kind, so merciful. That doesn't sound like a monster to me."*

The intensity of his golden gaze makes my stomach flip as it roams over my features, dropping once to my lips before returning to my eyes. His words have frozen me in place. Have sliced through my defences and exposed my raw nerves for him to see.

To really see.

And before I can think myself out of it, or tell myself what a terrible idea it is, I lean forward, closing the distance between us by pressing my lips to his.

A faerie bargain isn't something to take lightly. It's a powerful currency in our world, capable of shaping destinies and stirring up conflicts. More than just an agreement, it's a force that can impact lives and entire realms. Caution is advised, for the effects of a faerie bargain can extend well beyond the initial transaction.

PAGE 229, THE BOOK OF FAIR FAMILIES

CHAPTER TWENTY-SIX

Ansel is frozen for a moment, his lips unmoving against mine. As if he is allowing me this, believing it to merely be a comfort in my emotional distress.

It isn't. And I want more. I want to please him.

I take his plump lower lip between my teeth and bite him gently.

My kiss was a gentle press of my lips against his— a giving kiss.

But Ansel takes.

Almost as if my action shattered a spell, he responds. His hands cup my face, fingers tangling in the strands of my wet hair, as his lips soften against mine. The kiss starts gentle, a tentative exploration of each other. But as the seconds pass, the intensity deepens. His lips press more firmly, igniting a spark within me. I can't help the whimper that escapes me, or the shudder that causes goosebumps to rise along my flesh when his fangs lengthen, brushing against my lips.

Our mouths move in sync, a wordless conversation of desire and vulnerability. His thumb brushes against my cheek, his touch as tender as his words earlier. It's like he's tracing the outline of my heart, soothing the fears and doubts that have plagued me for so long.

As our kiss deepens, the sound of my breath mixing with his becomes the only rhythm that matters. His lips part slightly, inviting me to explore further.

I lose myself in the taste of him, the way he cradles my face, the warmth that radiates from his body.

We pull away, our breaths coming in soft, ragged gasps. Ansel's gaze is filled with a mix of surprise, longing, and a touch of mischief.

"*I didn't see that coming*," he says, a hint of a smile playing on his lips.

I manage a breathless chuckle. "I don't think I did either."

He leans in, his forehead resting against mine. "*That was…*"

"Yes," I breathe out with a smile.

"*We should stop though, before this turns into more.*"

"Should we?" I ask, my mind lust hazed and voice like velvet—a tone I've never heard.

"*Yes.*" Ansel takes in my expression and growls, as if in pain. "*Because you are naked before me, soaking wet and surrounded by healing water… and if we do not stop, I'm going to be inside you, surrounded by that soaking wetness between your deliciously thick thighs. And I think we both know that you're not up for that in your current condition."*

I could be. Dear moon above, I tell myself I could be.

I gulp hard, my fingers gripping the edges of the tub as I slowly rise to my feet. The ache between my legs intensifies, a relentless throb that matches the pulse of desire in Ansel's eyes.

His heated gaze traces the path of a single droplet of water down my skin, a sensation so intoxicating my breath hitches. I've never felt self-conscious before, and under his intense scrutiny, I feel like the most exquisite work of art.

His eyes, a molten gold, reflect a tumultuous storm of desire as he looks up and locks onto my gaze. *"Not helping."* His voice is practically a snarl in my mind.

I refuse to apologise, my voice strong despite my trembling body. "I'm not sorry."

I step out of the tub with a shaky sigh. But my legs betray me by wobbling, and his presence is immediate, his strong hand at the bend of my elbow. He guides me, righting me on unsteady feet as I take a deep, shuddering breath.

He momentarily leaves my side, retrieving my bag and a towel from the table. When he returns, he drapes the towel around me, cocooning me in its warmth. My lips remain sealed as he guides me to the bed, sitting down first before easing me down to sit between his legs.

The fabric of the towel is gentle against my skin, and he runs his hands soothingly up and down my arms. I turn my head, unable to tear my gaze away from him, watching the concentration etched across his features as his hands work their magic. His beauty is breathtaking, from the depths of his captivating eyes to the flawless expanse of his ebony skin. If his physical allure wasn't enough to leave me in awe, the way his touch resonates deep within me certainly does.

"Ansel," I murmur, my voice a soft confession amidst the intimate atmosphere.

"*Yes, vicious one?*" He responds with a teasing tone, his words laced with playful affection.

My gaze holds his, unwavering, my gratitude a sincere offering. "Thank you."

Ansel's lips curve into a tender smile, his eyes holding mine with a warmth that seeps into my bones. "*You shouldn't thank me,*" he replies softly. "*But… taking care of you feels like the most natural thing in the world.*"

The air between us becomes charged, a palpable tension that pulls us together. With an almost imperceptible movement, his hand reaches out to gently lift my chin, tilting it until our gazes meet once more. His thumb brushes against my lower lip, sending a shiver down my spine.

In that moment, I feel a gentle brush of cool shadows against my skin, an affectionate caress from my shades. It's a reassurance that they also see the sincerity in his eyes, the tenderness in his touch. His lips draw closer to mine, a magnetic pull that I am powerless to resist. And then, with a whisper of a sigh, his lips finally meet mine again. It's a tender kiss, a promise woven in each brush of his lips against mine.

The fragile moment shatters as the tent flap rustles, and I turn to see Wen standing there, still in her lavender gown, her eyes wide and her expression a mixture of surprise, hurt, and disbelief. Ansel and I quickly untangle ourselves, my heart pounding as my shades rise once more, swirling around in the air protectively.

"Wen, I..."

Ansel rises from the bed, meeting Wen's eye. He looks over at her for a moment with a calculating eye, and I know he is assessing if she is a threat.

The action makes me want to cry as much as it makes me want to laugh.

"*I… I should go,*" he says, his voice soft yet tinged with regret. He leans down and presses a gentle kiss to my forehead before heading towards the tent flap.

Wen's eyes follow him as he leaves, but her gaze quickly shifts back to me. I can see the turmoil in her expression, the unspoken hurt that she's carrying. My heart aches, knowing that her pain is from the trauma my father inflicted on me.

"Efia," she says, her voice trembling as she takes a step closer. "I can't believe he did that to you so close to the final trial."

"I can," I whisper. Tears well up in my eyes as I

see the mix of anger and sadness in Wen's gaze. "I didn't want you to find out like this," I can't help the cracking of my voice; I hoped to have mostly healed myself by the time I next saw her.

Wen rushes to my side and clings to me, her tears soaking into the towel at my shoulder. "I'm so sorry, Efia. I'm sorry for not protecting you, for not stopping him."

My heart aches for the pain she's carrying, and I hold her tighter. "Wen, none of this is your fault. You wouldn't have been able to do anything. He would have found some way to hurt you, too."

The only reason Father hasn't hurt her or Beinon himself yet was because they were part of the Seelie court. But he was clever, he would find a way if he deemed it necessary.

Wen lifts her head, sniffing and wiping her cheeks with the back of her hand. She takes a deep breath and manages a small smile, her eyes still holding a mix of sadness and determination. "Okay, let's get you cleaned up."

Wen moves over to my bag and starts unpacking the contents, searching for the herbs and salves she knows I keep for situations like this. I feel a mixture of gratitude and guilt; gratitude for her unwavering support, and guilt for burdening her with my pain.

"Drop the towel," Wen instructs gently, her voice warm and reassuring. I do as she says, letting the towel fall to the ground. I can feel her eyes on me, but there's no judgement in her gaze, only empathy.

She takes the herbs and works them into a salve, her skilled fingers mixing the ingredients with care. As Wen applies it to my cuts and bruises, her touch is soothing.

I hiss softly as the cool salve meets my damaged skin, but the pain is quickly replaced by a numbing sensation. I close my eyes, allowing myself to relax into her touch, trusting her to take care of me.

Wen clears her throat, breaking the tense atmosphere hanging in the air. "You know, walking in and seeing that was a surprise," she says, her voice lightening a little. "You and Ansel."

I open my eyes, meeting her gaze, and a small smile tugs at the corner of my lips. "Why?"

Wen chuckles softly, her fingers still working the salve into my skin. "You're usually so guarded, and then there you were, just following your heart."

I let out a soft laugh, feeling a warmth spread through me. "I guess even warriors have their vulnerable moments."

Wen gives me a playful grin. "Well, I'm just upset I didn't wait a little longer. Get a better look at all those muscles."

I roll my eyes, but the tension in the air has eased, and for the first time in a while, I feel a glimmer of lightness. "You're impossible, Wen."

She winks at me. "And you're lucky to have me."

I can't help but agree as she works, her hands

steady and caring, the salve a testament to the healing touch she brings not just to my wounds, but to my heart as well.

As Wen finishes applying the salve, the mood in the tent shifts again.

"These are really deep, Ef."

She's concerned. Of course she is. If they don't heal, it's a disadvantage in tomorrow's trial. Wen may not enjoy the killing the more ferocious faeries commit, but she would rather I win than anyone else... even Beinon.

She's like the little sister I never had, her love and unwavering care for me—I've probably never appreciated it enough. Probably never deserved it.

"I know," is all I reply.

She looks at me, her gaze searching, and I know what's coming next. "Are you ready?" she asks, her voice soft and full of concern.

I am tired. Is what floats through my thoughts.

I sigh, my eyes dropping to my hands in my lap. "I don't really have a choice."

I don't want it, is what I really want to say.

Wen's hand rests on my shoulder, offering comfort. "You've come this far, Efia. You're stronger than you know."

I nod, grateful for her words, but a heavy feeling settles in my chest. The final trial will demand everything from me, pushing me to my limits. It's not just the physical challenges, but the emotional ones as well. The possibility of facing Beinon or even Ansel on the battlefield makes me sick to my stomach. The idea of having to fight and kill more of my kind, perhaps even someone I care about, tears at my insides.

The weight of the crown and the title of High Queen looms over me, a heavy burden that I'm not entirely sure I want. But the bitter irony is that winning this contest might be my only chance at escaping my father's control, even if it means trading one kind of captivity for another.

But is it?

Is it the *only* way to escape his control? That dark voice whispers in the quiet of my mind, the voice that I only hear when I'm at my lowest. Now is the most dangerous time to hear it, just before I enter a deadly trial.

Because what would stop me from giving up? Allowing myself to become a victim to the other hungry faeries vying for the crown? Absolutely nothing.

It would be so easy…

"Whatever happens, Ef, you have me. I've got your back, no matter what." Wen's voice breaks through my thoughts.

Her words anchor me, reminding me I have allies, people who believe in me and support me. I meet her gaze, gratitude filling my heart. "Thank you, Wen. I'm lucky to have you."

She smiles, her eyes warm. "And don't forget, you're not just fighting for yourself. You're fighting for change, for a better future for all faeries."

I smile tightly, trying hard to remind myself of that. After a moment, the tent opens and Jill walks in; she spots us and curses, spitting on the ground before entering.

"Jill?" I ask, my eyes fluttering in exhaustion.

"Move, moon faerie," she orders Wen, forcing her to move over as she settles behind me. She hisses at the sight of my back. "He has cleaved you to muscle and bone, child. It will take more than healing herbs to close these."

"It will have to do—"

"The final trial is tomorrow at sunset," Wen tells her desperately.

Jill exhales deeply. "I can heal you, Efia. But at a price. I'll require a bargain."

Wen's eyes widen. "Efia, don't—"

"If I wasn't sacrificing an awful lot of my own magic, I'd do it for free, moon girl. But for this… I require a bargain," she repeats.

A bargain is more than my word.

Bargains come with a price.

I wonder what piece of me I'll be giving up for Jill's help…

But I have no choice.

"What do you want, Jill?" I inquire, my gaze steady.

"When you win, I wish for your protection from harm and a place in the castle." Her response comes without hesitation, and it's not an "if" but a "when" that she uses.

I narrow my eyes slightly, recognising the importance of asking for specifics when it comes to magical bargains. "A place for what?"

"In the kitchens," she replies earnestly. "I wish to be your personal potioneer, healer—whatever you wish of me. But please, grant me a place in your court, and I will serve you."

I turn slightly to study her, my shadows fluttering around her without causing her to flinch or retreat. Her bright eyes hold no deception, and her sincerity is evident. She is willing to align her fate with mine, and the shadows whisper their approval.

With a decisive nod, I extend my hand toward her. "We have an accord."

What's the harm in it? If I die tomorrow, the bargain will be off anyway.

A smile graces Jill's face as she reaches out with her own small hand, clasping mine. The moment our hands meet, we both wince at the surge of magic that flows between us. My head tilts back slightly as I absorb the power, feeling it course through my veins until it eases from my skin.

We pull our hands apart, and I glance down at mine, where a small rune for 'promise' has appeared below the second knuckle on my middle finger. It glows briefly before fading away, sealing our magical bargain.

"Now," Jill says, flexing her hands, "this may hurt."

I nod, swiping the vial of moon petals from my emptied sack, swallowing it in one. It should help with the pain. But I brace myself for whatever she's about to do. With a potioneer's expertise and a healer's touch, she begins her work, and the pain surges through me, feeling as though my skin is being pulled and sewn together.

Jill's light magic, pure and healing, courses its way through my broken skin and damaged tissues, stitching them together with a bitter agony. The pain is excruciating, but I grit my teeth and bear it, knowing that each moment of suffering brings me closer to the strength and healing I'll need for the trial ahead.

As Jill gets closer to the open wounds near my spine, the pain becomes unbearable, and I give in, screaming out in agony. The world around me blurs, and I swear I see a raven's wings as the darkness of unconsciousness fights to claim me, surrendering to the healing magic and the pain that accompanies it as my father's voice screams inside my head, reminding me never to offer my back to another faerie…

There is a belief, amongst some, that the shades the Nüwch can manipulate are more than what they appear. More than just shadow. No one has dared approach a Nüwch to ask, but from watching them interact, it's clear they appear to have *thought* of their own. As if they are sentient.

DARK FAE AND DEATH GODS, BY UNSEELIE KING BENEDICT

CHAPTER TWENTY-SEVEN

I'm in the pretty garden of my uncle's castle. My shadows are like fluttery butterflies, their presence fills me with joy, and I chase after them, giggling in the soft, warm sunlight.

But out of nowhere, I collide with someone, and we both fall to the ground. When I get up, I see a small light faerie with bouncy brown curls and wide silver eyes.

Her cheeks darken, but she smiles so widely at me.

"Hello, I'm Branwen," she says, her voice as sweet and melodious as a songbird. And she's so pretty. Her eyes remind me of the moon.

I smile. "I'm Efia."

"I'm sorry to be in the gardens," she tells me, looking scared. I wonder what she's scared of. "I was just chasing moonflies."

I can't help but laugh, my heart feeling warm. I link my arm with hers, pulling her deeper into the gardens and I say, "I *think I'll call you Wen."*

When I wake, Wen is lying beside me, still in her
ballgown. I smile at her peaceful form, so grateful for her.
The memory repeats in my head and I can't help but miss
those simpler times. Scared then since she trespassed on
the High King's land. That she strayed too far to his
young niece, someone who recently presented as a
Nüwch, just like her uncle.

But the dream was so magical, and I made
memories with Wen that I would never forget. Memories
and light and laughter that had helped me continue after
my sixth birthday. Memories I held onto once my
training started. Her friendship kept me going.

It still did.

I tucked a strand of her hair behind her ear.

The trial will not start until sunset, so I slip out
from her slender arms, changing into something more
comfortable after stretching out my muscles. Jill has done
a swell job at healing my back, the skin only red and
slightly sore. My body aches as it does after a heavy
training session, but that should ease by the time the trial
comes around.

I step outside, deciding to visit one of my
favourite places. The early morning sun paints the sky

with hues of pink and gold, casting a warm and gentle light over the whispering wood. I sit in the fields of Ffawydd, past the vast forest surrounding camp.

The seeds of the tall, white-puffed flowers that decorate the field breaking free and floating away on the soft breeze. The sight brings me peace and the world around me seems to hold its breath, as if nature itself recognises the gravity of the day's events.

Closing my eyes, I focus on the sounds of the forest: the rustling leaves, the distant calls of birds, and the soft murmurs of the light breeze through the trees. It's a moment of solitude, a stolen respite before the storm. The final trial looms ahead, and every nerve in my body is coiled with anticipation and apprehension.

"Can I join you?"

His voice interrupts the stillness, and my eyes snap open to find Ansel approaching. His footsteps are soft, deliberate, as if he knows not to disturb the fragile peace that envelops me. I narrow my eyes at the wispy dark blue shadowy ether that is swirling around me—keeping silent at Ansel's approach.

The shades I have pulled towards me are dancing around, the slight breeze of them lifting strands of my hair as they rejoice in the freedom of their movement, their whispers calm—limited in their power during the day.

I shake my head, a small smile tugging at the corner of my lips. "Of course, you don't need an invitation."

He settles beside me, his presence a comforting weight against my side. Together, we sit in silence, sharing the quiet moment as the sun continues its ascent.

"*How are you?*" he finally asks.

"I am…"

Tired. My mind finishes.

"All right," I tell him.

He tilts his head in a way that shows he is completely sceptical of that answer, and he has every right to. He saw me immediately after. Saw my vulnerability.

But his gaze reverts to my shades as they continue to dance, tendrils of darkness that twirl like playful mist. They're visible, ethereal, as if the boundary between the corporeal and the mystical has blurred.

"*They seem to like you,*" Ansel comments, his gaze fixed on the shadows that brush against my skin.

"They're a part of me," I reply softly, feeling their gentle caresses against my arms and face. "They've always been with me, really."

"*What* are *they, exactly?*" Ansel's voice tiptoes into the edges of my mind like a gentle air, so delicate that it's almost as if he wishes not to startle them, even though I don't know if they can hear him.

"I'm not entirely sure. Though I have my theories."

They sway and twinkle around me. The ones I've beckoned are particularly exuberant today.

His casual smile gleams, his gaze fixed on the

dancing shades. *"Can't you just ask them?"*

I chuckle. "It's not exactly a verbal exchange. I can't quite decipher their whispers like words. It's more like a sensation, an understanding on an instinctual level. Like knowing if someone's sneaking up on me."

He raises an eyebrow playfully. *"Did they clue you in about my arrival?"*

I grin. "No, actually. They were surprisingly quiet about that."

His head tilts. *"What if I were a threat?"*

His curiosity about my abilities is refreshing, a deviation from the typical veiled fear. I shrug, pondering his question. "I suppose it's that instinct again. They seem to sense intentions, as if they can differentiate between those who mean harm and those who don't. Almost like they're gauging a person's character."

His brow falls for a second. *"What do you* think *they are?"*

His next question hangs in the air, and I mull it over before responding. "My theory? They might be echoes of both memories and magic, fragments of those who've walked these paths before us."

Ansel's eyes linger on the shades, and a thoughtful silence envelops us, the whispering wood around us serving as a backdrop to our conversation. In this quiet moment, as the sun begins its afternoon ascent, I find myself grateful for his company and his genuine curiosity. The shades continue their dance, their enigmatic presence a testament to the mysteries of the world we inhabit.

Ansel's fingers brush against my hand, his touch warm and grounding. "*Are you really all right?*" he asks, his concern evident in his gaze.

My eyes trail over my middle finger, where the rune for promise had shone, a secret I choose not to share with him. "I am," I reply with a nod. "Jill showed up and healed me. I'm practically good as new."

His lips thin, and I can tell he still doesn't entirely believe my words. It's as if he knows, from his own experiences, that these wounds run deeper than the physical scars.

His expression falls, and he seems to think twice over what he's going to say. He shakes his head.

"What?" I ask.

"*You're just… different from what I expected, Mathonwy.*"

A wistful smile tugs at my lips. "Is that a good thing?"

He turns his head to look at me, his golden eyes searching. "*Yes, it is.*"

The shadows seem to respond to our proximity, their movements becoming more animated, like playful spirits. I can feel their presence intertwining with mine.

"*Are you scared?*" Ansel's question cuts through the tranquillity, his voice low and sincere.

I let out a slow breath, the weight of the impending trial settling on my shoulders. For the first time, I don't feel scared about admitting my vulnerability to someone.

"Terrified, if I'm being honest. But I can't let fear dictate my actions."

He nods, his expression thoughtful. "*You're stronger than you realise. And no matter what happens today, you won't be alone.*"

His words stir something within me, and I turn to him, meeting his gaze head-on. "I know that now, Ansel."

As we hold each other's gaze, the shadows seem to pulse, a soft luminescence emanating from their depths.

He is so, so close. And it doesn't take long for me to lean forward, relieved when he closes the last few inches between us, so our lips come together. It's a collision of not just lips, but of yearning and raw, unbridled want.

Our mouths mould together, and Ansel clutches my face like his life depends on it, his touch setting my skin ablaze, every brush of his fingers a lightning bolt of sensation. His lips taste of both sweet anticipation and smouldering need, a blend that leaves me dizzy with wanting more.

"Ansel," I gasp into his mouth as he pulls away.

"*I don't deserve this. I don't deserve you.*" His words sweep through my mind as he pants, his breath ragged against my skin.

It sends shivers through me, mingling with the involuntary moan that escapes my lips when he playfully nips at my lower lip.

He pulls back slightly, a mischievous grin playing on his lips before he returns, trailing searing kisses along my jaw and the curve of my neck. "*I should stop… should go.* He sighs, his voice a blend of desire and regret.

"You're absolutely right. You should definitely go." I breathe out, knowing this will only hurt us more later, even as his fingers brush over my cheek.

The dark chuckle that leaves him causes his warm breath to brush against my neck. "*Here?*" he asks, his hot mouth travelling over my pulse and biting down gently. "*Or here?*" His lips find my shoulder as he moves my shirt to the side, and I gasp as his touch electrifies my senses.

"*I think I'm addicted to the taste of your skin against my lips,*" he admits, his eyes radiating an intensity that matches the sun's brilliance. "*Do you want me to stop?*"

The question lingers, hanging between us, suspended in the charged air that crackles with longing and a hunger that we both know can't be fully sated.

"Quite the opposite, please."

His smile widens just before his lips claim mine, a languid and deliberate kiss that causes my eyelids to flutter closed in response. He tastes like sunshine. He tastes like warmth and power. My fingertips trace the rough texture of his jawline, a sensation that sends tingles down my spine. My touch ventures further, brushing over gently through the locs of hair, and as my nails graze lightly against the shaved back of his head, a low, guttural sound escapes him, muffled by the connection of our lips. The resonance of that groan reverberates between us, and all I can think about is his lips where I feel that noise the most.

The blood rushing in my ears is so loud as we remove each other's clothes, too needy for each other to allow ourselves to separate. I've never felt hunger like it.

The words that whisper into my mind as his mouth is busy moving over my skin feel like magic. My hands roam freely over his skin, a mixture of smooth and rough from the scars, but every inch is perfect.

There is no foreplay, only an urgent need for each other—as if we have all the time in the world to explore each other later… which we know we don't.

My head tips back, giving him more access as he peppers kisses along my collarbone, across the top of my breasts—my hands gripping onto his hard shoulders. He groans when I move to sit on his lap, wrapping my legs around him. His arms around me tighten as the wetness between my legs rubs up against his hardness. Bracing one hand on his shoulder, I lift myself and align him with my entrance before he drives up into me with a powerful thrust. The sensation of it all is too much, and I feel out of control.

My teeth find my lower lip, biting hard as I get used to the stretch of him.

"*Vicious one,*" he pants.

I lean forward and nip at his ear, tilting my hips. He chokes, holding my hips still.

"*Wait, just a second. You feel too good,*" he pleads.

"Daylight is passing, Ansel. I need you to fuck me

now. I may not get another chance to feel you inside me," I say, almost ruining the mood, an odd expression passing over his face.

But I grind down on him, seizing his mouth for another kiss. A whimper escapes my throat as he pulls back and thrusts up again.

"More," I tell him.

"*I don't want to hurt you,*" his voice is raspy in my mind and heightens everything.

I roll my eyes a second before he releases a growled curse, his eye darkening as he takes in the view of me on top of him. I grind my hips, whimpering at the feel of him and take my pleasure. He holds my waist, groaning as he helps me rise and fall through each stroke. It doesn't take long for him to lose composure.

His thrusts become deeper and harder, the force of them enough to take my breath away as he chases me to the precipice. Incoherent words escape my throat. My fingers dig into his shoulders as I muffle my moans with his kiss, until he pulls back, his hand coming up to hold my face.

"*I want to hear every word from you. I want to see every moment of pleasure on your face, my vicious one.*"

Warmth rises in me, but I don't want this to end.

I never want this to end, I think as I press down, meeting him thrust for thrust—the delicious glide of his length in and out of me, a needed friction.

Our hips move together, and I moan with abandon, desperately seeking release as he leans down and captures a nipple with his hot mouth. He releases it, and I can feel him throbbing inside me as he approaches his orgasm, can tell from the way his movements increase.

"*Come for me,*" he begs. "*I want to feel your legs shake and your beautiful pussy squeeze me.*"

His words are all it takes to throw me over the edge. My head falls back as I cry out, but he grips the back of my neck and swallows the moans with a kiss, his tongue fucking my mouth like his hard cock fucks me.

His free hands brushes against my clit and I jerk, but he holds me still as he rubs small circles on my most sensitive area.

"I-I can't," I whimper.

"*You can.*" He purrs the words as his hand moves and tightens deliciously on the back of my neck. "*You can take it.*"

Hearing him speak in my mind as his tongue swirls in my mouth is too much. But I do take it.

I practically scream as he drives me to another orgasm. He grunts loudly as warmth fills me and I ride out the final waves of my climax.

My chest is warm, my heart fluttering as my shades dance around us in a display of contentment.

But dread settles in my stomach like a stone in deep water, and the reminder of what will happen later today makes me feel sick. The idea of coming up against Ansel is suddenly something I cannot bear.

I can tell he feels the same. Can see the conflicted

emotions flashing across his gaze.

And I realise I can't do it.

I won't be able to do it.

I have failed my father.

Because I have allowed my emotions to cloud my mind. I tuned out of being the unfeeling monster he wants me to be.

But when I look at Ansel, I know. I have always known. Since the moment I met him…

That if it comes down to him and me… I'll choose him.

I have no idea why. But because in the middle of all this chaos was him. He has given me moments of peace during a life of pain.

And perhaps that's my way out.

His head jerks as if realisation has dawned on him. As if, under all the hungry gazes and soft expressions, his mind has entered mine and uncovered my most hidden thoughts.

He picks me up gently and sets me down before standing. I watch as he pulls up his breeches, lacing them up slowly before handing me my own clothes without looking at me.

I dress in silence, watching his back rise and fall with heavy breaths. Once I have finished, I reach out, gently brushing my fingers over his shoulder.

"*Don't,*" he says horrified, his eyes furious as he looks at me. "*Don't look at me like that.*"

"Like what?"

"*Like you won't be able to do what you must.*"

"And what must I do?"

"*Kill me.*"

I scoff. "You'd just let me?"

"*Undoubtedly.*"

I rear back, my teeth baring. "Don't *ever* say that."

"*Why?*" He demands, not shocked by my harsh reaction. As if he understands it. "*It's true. If it comes down to me and you, there is no choice. There hasn't been a choice since I met you.*"

"Ansel—"

"*I know what it will mean for you if you spare me, vicious one. Because I won't kill you. But neither will your father. He'll take you to that very edge and then heal you before starting again. He may even kill Wen, or even Beinon.*"

I flinch because he's right. But he can see my reluctance on my face.

"*You are stronger than your father. Stronger than anyone I know. So please do this for me. I will gladly go to my end, knowing that I at least got to have you before it. Knowing that I met you and knew you. So don't give in. Why wouldn't you fight?*"

"Because I'm tired of fighting, Ansel. And I…"

I stumble over my words. Because it's admitting a vulnerability. It's giving someone power. But it's me. My words are all me.

"I don't think I can hurt you."

He comes forward and grasps my hands.

"*But you will. You* must. *Because I don't want it. Not at the sacrifice of you. And you could do so much, you could make an enormous change across the faerie realms. Just like Gwydion tried to. Don't throw your life away in the final trial because you're scared of hurting me."*

"Ansel, you don't understand—"

"No, you don't understand! So you've had an extremely difficult life with your father? Guess what, not many of us are blessed with loving parents. My mother found me laying with a faerie from the Unseelie court when I was a young naïve *boy. She used her magic on me, cursing me to be mute until I found my* mate," he spits, his lips curling into a sneer as I gasp.

To find your mate was considered to be the defining moment of a faerie's life. All-consuming and ever-changing. But the cruelty in his mother's actions was that finding one's mate was incredibly rare. Only several mated pairs have been recorded in our entire history, many of those couples being instruments in great change throughout the realms. It was as if the magic knew that two faeries with compatible energies could do great things together and bonded them for life.

It was a cruel punishment.

An unjust punishment.

"I'm sor—"

"For years," Ansel continues, *"I struggled with my magic, keeping up the connection to ensure I could communicate with others as easily as breathing. Now I can project my thoughts to multiple faeries at a time. But all the while, I was dealing with her beatings and her cruelty. But I never gave up. And this is me taking control of my life. Choosing for me, for once. So, I want you to do the same. Choose to make a change. To take control. But*

don't give up. You're giving up if you don't finish this contest."

"I'm—" I swallow the thick ball of emotion that builds in my throat, my eyes feeling warm as I blink away the layer of tears building there. He's right. "I'm just so tired, Ansel." The honest admission slips out as a whisper. "What do I do?"

Ansel takes a step forward, his warm, brown hand taking hold of my own and giving it a comforting squeeze. "*You fight. You* always *keep fighting. You know how to do it. I know you don't want to, but you do it anyway. This battle isn't lost, so don't you dare give up. Why are you letting them win? Get angry!*"

"I am angry!" I shout at him, my shades whipping around the space. "I'm so angry! All the time! Because if I win, who will be there to look out for *me*? Who will be there to take care of *me*? I can't put this burden on Wen. Not when my father or the queen could easily use our friendship against me. I trust Wen with my life but even I have to be careful with what I share with her. There has been no one, *no one*, that I have been able to be my true self with… until you."

And I could only guess at why.

Maybe it's because I believed him strong enough to withstand the might of my father, or the wickedness of the king and queen. Maybe it was because I didn't feel for him like I did for Wen and wanted to protect her more.

Should he die, any of my secrets would die with him. And who would believe the heartless Nüwch would share her secrets with an unfamiliar fae?

Ansel's expression is heartbreaking. Because even he can't guarantee he will be there for me after all this.

"Don't let them win," is all he says.

"And if *I* win?"

"When *you win. Because it's you. It's* meant *to be you, vicious one. So, when you win, you will win for you. And you will make this realm great."*

He sounds so sure as he rubs soothing circles into the skin of my hand. So confident that I am destined to rule and to do great things, and my chest warms at the thought of someone having that faith in me. Someone other than Wen and Beinon.

But it's time to go, and Ansel has given me much to think about.

He seems to realise at the same time I do that our time is up.

He presses a final kiss to my forehead. *"I'll see you later."*

I can't reply. I can't do anything.

So I watch him leave.

As Nüwch, there are many who would fear us, Efia. This is a good thing. As Nüwch, we cannot trust many, but the shades will help protect you. Remember my dear child, our kind must run with the shadows, in order to walk in the light.

PERSONAL CORRESPONDENCE FROM HIGH KING GWYDION TO EFIA MATHONWY

CHAPTER TWENTY-EIGHT

Only monsters such as the king and queen would think of a trial like this.

Sunset came around far too quickly, and I wonder why the king and queen would choose the trial to start at this point, knowing my gifts are stronger at nightfall.

We have been returned to the Gwenhwyvar fields, where the second trial had happened.

I've been portalled to a hill overlooking the old labyrinth. Other portals pop up around the outside, dropping off more faeries.

Stands are erected all around us, the noise from the faeries watching is deafening.

I can't see Beinon or Ansel. But either side of me is a pixie and a vampire, both eyeing me with hunger as they realise who I am.

But I focus on what's in front of me.

The outer four walls of the labyrinth remain from the second trial, but they have been altered. Now—being half their size—I can see inside the large structure; the hedges have shrunk.

Inside, instead of pathways that lead to dead ends and to the centre of a labyrinth, there are now sixteen equal square areas of space within the hedges, a pedestal in a corner. In the centre of the structure, cutting some space out of four of the squares, is a large dais—that's where I need to head.

I quickly scan over the sections but can see no discernible route through it.

The hedges are too high to climb, and too thick to cut through.

A clang from one of the royal guards sounds out, the sun's last rays sinking below the horizon, and I breathe a sigh as I feel my powers run through my veins.

Run with the shadows, Efia.

Uncle Gwydion's words run through my head as my mind begins wanders, dreading the number of lives that will be lost this night.

It's not needed. It's unnecessary.

A fresh wave of disgust rises for the king and queen. And I think… perhaps it will be worth it if I win. Perhaps I can make a change.

I turn it off.

I bring up my mask as the hedge in front of us opens, my fingers uncurling as we walk into our section, the trees knitting together to seal us in. I pull the shadow from beneath the pedestal, allowing it to flutter around me like a gentle butterfly, and my companions eye it with concern.

The moon rises in the sky, allowing my shadows to swirl around me in strength.

I scan my surroundings, seeing if there is any hint at what direction I should go in. It is obvious the pedestal will open to a hedge on either side of it. But which direction should I go in from the next area? I need to make my way to the centre to win, and that will not be easy.

And how do we open it?

The pixie walks towards it, avoiding straying too close.

I take a step, seeing the small bowl shape in the centre.

Our eyes meet, and we realise at the same time…

The only way to move forward is to spill blood onto the pedestal.

And the way the two faeries are now staring at me makes me realise whose blood they most urgently want to spill.

This is where unlikely alliances will be made. Where faeries of all kinds would come together to eliminate the strongest competition.

But no one will make alliances with me.

For a moment I think of Ansel, of Beinon, and I hope they are safe.

But more than that, I hope I do not come up

against them.

"*Move, Efia*" his voice bites into my mind and I can feel the eyes of my father burning into my skin from the huge stands around us. I refuse to glance up at him, clearing my mind and allowing the calm to take over. Instead, I look for Wen amongst the lunar faeries, unsure if I feel relief or concern when I cannot find her.

A loud bell rings once more, and immediately the whole area is full of cries of pain and the desperate sounds of battle.

The vampire lunges forward, and I barely move, a shade taking firm hold of the silver sword at my side and ripping forward to embed it into his chest. His red eyes bulge as he looks down, and the pixie screeches at me, her harsh cry ringing in my ears.

I duck under her sharp nails as she swings for me, her wings beating furiously behind her. I throw a hard punch to her ribs, smiling at the sickening crunch as she chokes on her breath.

Wanting to end this quickly, and not draw out her suffering, my shades encircle her wrists, holding her steady as I unsheathe my other blade and swing it through her neck.

I can hear the crowd express their joy at the chaos and death, and it makes me sick.

Holding the blade over the pedestal, I allow the pixie's blue blood to drop onto it, hearing the snapping of twigs as the hedge in front of me recedes.

The faeries in this next section have already dealt

with their contenders—five dryads stand over a goblin, its own life force spilling across the ground beneath it.

Their beady little eyes spin to land on me, as they haven't opened the hedge for them to continue yet—perhaps did not realise it was the way to do so.

Their hands clench around crudely carved wooden knives, and I revel in the cruel smile that graces my lips, their snarls revealing the twisted satisfaction of preying upon a fellow faerie. In response, I unleash my shades, and with a mere thought, they coalesce into solid forms. Like vengeful spirits, two of them seize a dryad by its gnarled limbs, tearing with relentless force until its appendages are gruesomely wrenched from its body.

Effortlessly, I glide across the rough sand and my swords become an extension of my will, slashing through the air with a lethal grace. In a swift, calculated motion, I carve a precise arc across the abdomen of another faerie, leaving a trail of crimson in my wake. Snarls and screams harmonise with the slicing of my blades, creating an ear-piercing symphony of chaos.

The skirmish is short-lived. My shades and I dispatch the faeries, leaving their fallen forms scattered across the sandy battlefield.

As the last echoes of struggle fade away, I turn my attention to the pedestal that guards the entrance to the next section of the arena. With a deft movement and a drop of blood, I open it, the shadows dancing at my command.

I find myself in a new section filled with eerie, bioluminescent mushrooms casting an otherworldly glow on the surroundings.

The next group of faerie creatures awaits me, and they are unlike any I've encountered so far. These ethereal beings resemble will-o'-the-wisps, their bodies glowing with an eerie, blue-green light. They are golwyl, creatures with a barely corporeal form—until they decide to sink their teeth or claws into you.

Their eyes shimmer like distant stars, and their graceful, elongated forms seem almost translucent. There's a group of six of them, their beautiful bodies turning when they hear the hedge open.

One of the wisps floats forward, her delicate features twisted into an unsettling grin. Her companions follow, circling around me, their movements fluid and mesmerising. Humans used to be lured by these creatures, following their naturally beautiful appearance, until the golwyl found a secluded place to devour them.

But I am no human.

I'm not fooled.

I've learned not to underestimate even the most beautiful faeries. I ready my weapons, gripping them tightly in my hands. The first wisp darts toward me, her fingers elongated into sharp, needle-like points. I sidestep her attack, feeling the rush of air as she narrowly misses me.

With a powerful thrust of my blade, I cut through the air, slashing across the chest of her ethereal form. She lets out a high-pitched, haunting shriek as the silver connects with her. Her body shatters like fragile glass, and her glowing essence scatters into a thousand tiny sparks, drips of what looks like pure starlight falling to the ground.

The remaining wisps hiss and converge on me, trying to use their elusive movements to confuse and disorient me. I summon my shades to encircle them, trapping each of them within a pulsating, shadowy sphere—it's difficult to hold in place, but I plunge my blades, piercing the heart of each wisp, one by one.

The area is filled with the sound of ethereal wails as the wisps shatter. Their eerie glow dims and fades, leaving behind only a haunting memory.

It's haunting.

But as their essence dissolves, I catch a few shards and drop them onto the pedestal. The hedge in front of me recedes, granting me passage to the next section.

Ah.

This is a bit more of a challenge.

The transition from the ethereal wisps to the hulking ogre is stark and jarring. The air in this new section of the structure feels heavier, and the atmosphere more oppressive. There are splatters of blood across the leaves, blood covering the ogre's hands, but I see no trace of whatever poor creature came up against it. The towering ogre before me grins with a menacing glee, revealing a mouthful of yellowed, rotting teeth.

The ogre is massive, easily twice my size, and its muscles ripple with a grotesque strength. Thick, mottled skin covers its bulky frame, and its beady eyes fixate on me.

My shades encircle me, swirling viciously as they form a protective barrier, and I ready my blades, bracing myself for the impending clash.

The ogre roars with a thunderous sound, charging forward with a massive club in hand, determined to crush me with a single blow.

I sidestep and avoid the bone-shattering impact. A shade sharpens and cuts across its exposed forearm, eliciting a bellow of pain. Dark, oozing blood spills from the wound, but the ogre's rage only intensifies.

The ogre swings again, this time with a horizontal sweep aimed at my head. I drop to the ground, narrowly avoiding the attack.

The ogre shouts with rage, swinging round a large arm that takes me by surprise and smashes against my ribs. I cry out, flying back until my back collides with the hedge. My shadows stall for a split second, and I grit my teeth, commanding my shades to hold its feet steady as I recover.

I suck in a breath.

Something is broken.

But I have suffered worse.

I suppress the pain, darting in and out, striking the ogre's massive legs and arms. With each hit, I create shallow wounds, causing it to bleed profusely and weakening its movements. It furiously swings its arms about before swiping at my shades, which dissipate when it hits, reforming instantly and holding him steady.

They push on, with the ogre's swings becoming slower and less precise as it weakens. My spare shades maintain their protective barrier, shielding me from more harm as I continue my relentless assault. Finally, I see my opening as the ogre raises its club for one final, desperate attack.

With a burst of energy, I leap forward, my blades slicing through the air. They find their mark, sinking deep into the ogre's chest, piercing its heart. The massive creature's eyes widen in shock, and its roar turns into a pitiful gurgle as it crumples to the ground.

I watch as the ogre's life force seeps out, staining the ground with dark, viscous blood. With a triumphant feeling, I release some onto the waiting pedestal.

I press forward and as I step through the receding hedge; the air is thick with the scent of damp earth and moss-covered stones. In the dim light, I spot a figure, small and deceptively delicate-looking, standing amidst a ring of standing stones. There is no evidence of another faerie creature being here with her, and my spine tingles.

It's a changeling. Her long, auburn hair cascades like a waterfall, and her black eyes hold an unnerving glint. The Changeling tilts her head, her lips curving into a sly smile as she regards me. Without warning, she unleashes her earth magic, causing the very stones around us to come to life, forming into towering stone guardians. These stone monstrosities lumber forward, their massive fists poised to crush me.

I'm quick to react, but the stone guardians have taken me by surprise. I grunt under the effort of avoiding them, my arms aching as I parry what small swings I can.

This changeling has powerful magic, her attacks unpredictable.

A stone fist crashes into my side—my injured side—sending me tumbling across the uneven ground. My shades swarm around me in a vicious vortex, enduring the attacks as I grit my teeth, the pain searing through my ribs.

I see blood as I spit on the ground and regain my footing, rubbing the bodily fluid into the ground with my foot. Anger runs through me, and I dart through the shadows, launching an assault on the guardians. My blades clash against their solid forms, each blow resonating through my body.

I dismantle one of the stone guardians, sending it crumbling to the ground in a cascade of rubble. The changeling's smile falters for a moment, but she doesn't waver. Instead, she weaves a new enchantment, summoning vines from the earth that snake their way toward me, seeking to entangle me and sap my strength.

My shades help as I slash and cut at the writhing vines, but they keep coming, their thorny tendrils leaving painful scratches and lacerations on my skin. It seems relentless, and my strength wanes.

Despite the pain and exhaustion, I refuse to give in. With a final, desperate effort, I launch myself at the changeling, my blades poised to strike. She tries to evade, but I land a deep gash on her arm. The changeling shrieks in agony, her enchantments unravelling as she loses focus.

Her hold on the stone guardians and the vines weakens, and I seize the opportunity to finish the battle. My shades dart out to dismantle the remaining stone guardians and cut down the vines. The changeling, now weakened and vulnerable, offers no further resistance as I catch a hold of her throat and drive my sword in, pushing her back until she hovers over the pedestal.

She shrieks as blood leaves the wound, dripping generously into the bowl until I hold nothing but a lifeless corpse.

The new section is empty, the hedge to the right already open as I hear fighting and take a moment to catch my breath, feeling the pain of my injury.

Hours have passed, and the moon is no longer in sight. Soon, sunlight will appear over the horizon and my shades will lose most of their power.

I understand now.

The king and queen knew these battles could take a while. They guessed by the time I reached the centre, it could be almost daylight. Meaning that whatever opponent I face will have the upper hand.

I need to get to the centre as soon as possible.

I hiss as I touch my ribs. The injury is not lethal, thankfully, but I rip a long bit off the changeling's gossamer gown and wrap my ribs tightly over my leather armour.

Stepping into the next segment, I'm taken aback by the size of my newfound enemy. Its iridescent wings shimmer with a captivating palette of colours, and its eyes glint with an unsettling fury, a characteristic trait of its kind. The creature before me is a phooka, renowned for its cunning and trickster nature. The air shines brightly, multiple versions of the creature appear in the section—all so lifelike.

Without a moment's pause, I jump forward, blades poised for a strike. The phooka's movements are erratic as it avoids my swipes.

But I have read countless books from my uncle's libraries about the creature. I know what to look for.

Knowledge is power.

Faced with its illusions and attempts to mimic my own shadows, I concentrate, unwavering in my focus.

As my shades dart forward, trying to grasp the elusive creature, they clutch at nothing but air. The phooka's illusions make it difficult for them to find a solid form to latch onto. Undeterred, I press on, using the subtle shimmer of magic along the edges to guide my strikes. Feigning an attack at another duplicate, I pivot at the last possible moment, anticipating the creature's presence at my back. The magic dissipates as my blade punctures its neck before it can impale the back of my neck with its claws.

The phooka's eyes widen, blinking before its head lulls in defeat. I withdraw my blade, leaving it to hover momentarily over the pedestal as I stand before the hedge, ready for the next area—hoping I am close.

As I step through the hedge and into the new area, my heart skips a beat.

I am in the centre.

But the hedges on the other sides open simultaneously.

And before me stands Ansel and Beinon.

Their eyes widen as they find me, the hedges behind us closing, and the only obstacle between us is the short stone pillar in the middle—the final one between the winner and the crown.

"*Vicious one,*" Ansel says calmly in my mind. Ansel's arm is shining with blood, a gash travelling across his bicep. He pants with exertion, his brow lined with sweat.

Beinon hasn't fared better. There is a cut from his hairline, slicing through his eyebrow and ending on his cheek. He has narrowly missed losing an eye, and he looks tired.

"Ef?" he says, as if shocked to see me. As if he had forgotten I was a part of the contest.

My shades whisper frantically, feeling the safety of night disappearing below the horizon as the sun peaks her head.

They notice the other. Beinon's hand tightens on his sword, and I a muscle clenches in Ansel's jaw.

Beinon takes a step towards me. "Ef, you can't go through that portal."

Ansel's sword slashes through the air, pointing

towards him.

"She *may not raise a blade against you, princeling. But I swear to you, take another step towards her and I'll remove your head from your shoulders.*"

There's such promise there—such familiarity—that I frown and look between them.

Ansel's teeth are bared, his eyes ablaze, and Beinon's expression is just as vicious.

"Efia always knew there was a possibility of us coming up against each other," he spits. "She knew the stakes. But who do you think she'll feel more betrayed by?"

Beinon raises a brow and Ansel flinches.

I continue to look between them—but I don't know what to do.

"Ansel?" I ask him, wondering what Beinon is talking about, but he is silent.

The crowd around is almost deafening, the faeries thirsty for blood—to know who their new king or queen will be.

I can almost hear my father shouting from the stands somewhere for me to finish this. But my eyes dart from Beinon to Ansel, knowing that there is nothing I can do in this impossible situation.

I don't get a moment to decide.

As the first rays of light enter the sky, Aisling emerges from a hedge opening, jabbing their spear toward my gut, and it all happens in a whirlwind as I try to avoid being gutted. Both Ansel and Beinon shout in unison as they join the fray, pushing to *protect* me.

Ansel's blade moves with calculated precision, knocking the spear down and sending the tip into the ground at my feet. Beinon, with a fierce determination, engages Aisling in a duel, sword and spear clashing with an ear-piercing noise.

I watch in awe and disbelief as Beinon and Ansel now rally to shield me from harm. Beinon, on a mission to kill Aisling—but Ansel seems to pull his attacks.

Aisling is unfazed by how many foes they face. Their eyes furious, as is their determination to kill me.

I can hear the cheers and shouts of the onlookers, urging us on, but I can feel the furious eyes of my father, for not turning against my companions-turned-protectors.

As minutes turn into what feels like hours, Aisling struggles against our combined might. But *we* also tire.

It takes a second.

One second, as Beinon stumbles during a swing, allowing Aisling to use their harpy speed.

I hear tearing flesh before I feel it.

My breath leaves me in a gasp, and I look down to see Aisling's spear sticking in the right side of my gut.

"*No!*" Ansel's voice shouts in my mind.

Beinon turns, his mouth parting in shock as he sees what his slip up resulted in. Aisling smiles, their face sweaty with the effort of our fight.

They jerk the blade out and my hand covers the wound, trying to stem the loss of blood as my knees buckle.

Aisling raises the spear again, and Ansel jumps forward, swinging his blade with a new ferocity as he pushes Aisling back. Beinon shakes his head, joining the battle with anger written into the lines of his face.

I open my hand, staring at the blood there, as the action around me seems to slow.

I don't know if it is my injuries, or the blood loss making me dizzy.

All I know is that the only way to move forward is to spill blood on the pedestal...

But who said it couldn't be my blood?

I stagger to my feet, and Aisling's eyes narrow. Their attacks falter and they cry out as Ansel catches their arm with his sword. Ansel smiles, but both he and Beinon see something else has captured Aisling's attention. They turn, and I take in their expressions. But I pivot and jump forward, my eyes fixed on the pedestal before me.

"Efia, don't!" Beinon's urgent cry rings out. The sensation of their presence brushes against my senses like a fleeting breeze, fingertips barely grazing my shoulders in a desperate attempt to stop me. Their efforts arrive a fraction too late. The die is cast, the irrevocable step taken.

In the crucial moment, as my blood touches the bowl, a portal yawns open. A voracious maw that gobbles my form, dragging me inexorably through the void. The exit slams shut, sealing off any return, and we crash unceremoniously onto a carpet of emerald, green grass.

I have seen the bruises on her face, *brother*. We've discussed this matter once before, and I comprehend the necessity for Efia's training. However, I cannot stand idly by when the bounds of discipline are overstepped. Let this serve as a stern reminder that if I find Efia's grievances are justified, I will not hesitate to tear out your throat.

PERSONAL CORRESPONDENCE FROM HIGH KING GWYDION TO BRON MATHONWY

CHAPTER TWENTY-NINE

I shield my eyes from the blinding sun as I get to my feet, my brain still reeling from the quick portalling and my wound. We stand before Castell Narbeth, a small grassy dais erected before its entrance.

Beinon swings me around and shakes me lightly even though I can't hear what he's saying properly.

"You must go! Run, now!" he is telling me, though I know not why.

"*Vicious one, he is right. Go, now!*" Ansel calls loudly in my mind, and the surprise of them agreeing and what they are saying wrenches me from my stupor.

Behind them, two portals open.

The king and queen step through their respective portals, and I shrug off Beinon's hands, taking a step towards them, ready to accept my win.

Ready to make change.

Two guards each join them, stepping to the side of the raised grassy platform.

"Ahhh, daughter of Bron. I wondered if it would be you who would take the throne." King Lew's lip curls with a sneer. He looks absolutely outraged that his child has not beaten me, his eyes dropping to my abdomen for just a second. But with a quick, distrustful side eye to Queen Lilah, perhaps I am the lesser of two evils.

"Yes," Queen Lilah says. "Congratulations, child." The words are hard coming from her lips. A severe glance in Beinon's direction as he walks to stand next to his mother, besides the king, his bloody sword still in his trembling hand.

"What does the treaty dictate about what happens after the contest?" I ask, for I have never seen the treaty myself.

Queen Lilah laughs and looks at King Lew. "She is eager, isn't she?"

"Hmm," he responds. "Wouldn't you be?"

"Oh, I am." Her eyes flash and mine narrow.

I suddenly feel vulnerable, as Ansel steps to my side.

"*Mathonwy*," he whispers into my mind, just for me. "*Leave, now.*"

The king's voice draws my attention instead.

"The folk will be heading this way soon, ready to greet their new queen. We should prepare for the crowning."

"Not so quickly, Lew," the queen says in her singsong voice. "There are a couple more matters I would like to deal with."

My spine stiffens, Ansel's hand quickly grabs mine.

A grip tightens, a breath catches.

I shout an objection, but it is too late.

King Lew's head falls to the floor, rolling crudely before landing on the soft grass, his body crumpling immediately after. Beinon's grip is still tight on his outstretched sword, his chest heaving.

"Wh-what have you done?" I ask in a quiet voice.

"Only what I commanded him to do," Queen Lilah says, her voice cruel, as King Lew's guards rush forward, and end up being slaughtered by her own.

"Why?" I ask her, staring into those emotionless eyes.

"My dear, did you really think I would allow someone other than myself to take hold of the crown? I may not have been able to enter myself, but control of the realm will have always fallen to me."

This makes no sense.

I cannot take my eyes off Beinon.

But I am acutely aware of more of the queen's guards who have appeared from the borders of the trees around the castle. I am acutely aware of Ansel at my side, and the danger he is now in.

"You want Beinon to win? Take it. The throne is yours."

Her sweet laugh tinkles, and it offends my ears.

"Child, everyone in the crowd saw you win, rightfully. I couldn't take the throne without an uprising."

I take a step forward but her guards level their spears at me, two coming from behind to take hold of Ansel and move him away several steps in her direction as he groans in discomfort. And I hear that groan deep in my chest—the feeling unfamiliar as the breath is sucked from my lungs.

I gasp, my head swivelling to catch his golden gaze as my heart suddenly feels like it bursts in my chest.

Not him.

It hits my stomach like a battering ram. The shadows whisper urgently, though they cannot reach out, and the feeling running through me can only be described as divine magic. A thread pulls taut, straightening and solidifying so no blade could ever cut it. Ansel gasps as our gazes connect, the feeling of inner peace unlike anything I have ever felt. It goes beyond friendship and enemies. Eradicating the parasitic grasp my father has held over me for years. Eliminating the conflict I felt at having to fight him in the final trial.

I couldn't kill him even if I wanted to.

To kill him would be like ripping my heart from my chest.

I was wrong before—when I believed I could've ever been anything more with Beinon if I forced it. Because I didn't know what love was. And as my heart stutters, beating a new furious rhythm as it matches Ansel's, and I see the horrified realisation on his face,

only one word repeats itself in my head over and over.
   Mate. Mate. Mate.

Curses bind their victims in almost unbreakable chains of misfortune. Whether uttered by vengeful spirits or invoked by powerful fae, these curses are said to twist fate itself. If you find yourself with a condition to break one, I suggest you do everything in your power to make it happen.
PRIESTESS MWFANWY, 96bcr

CHAPTER THIRTY

I swallow hard, my hands shaking with the urge to go to Ansel as my chest tightens painfully. The closing of his eyes reveals he is feeling the same.

"Efia," he says.

He *says*.

I can't even deny what I feel. Because his curse is broken. The curse his *mother* put on him, meaning he would never speak unless he found his mate.

He *speaks*.

His voice is deeper than when he has spoken to my mind—a smoky whisper floating on the breeze between us.

I almost whimper at the sound of him, my nerves fraying at the distance between us.

The queen hasn't noticed our odd behaviour and the mate bond that has snapped between us. Fortunately, she is too busy laughing to have heard Ansel say my name. I hope she doesn't realise what has happened.

For Ansel's life could be used against me.

She continues laughing as she walks down the dais, running her hand in a loving caress over Ansel's locs.

A dark wickedness unfurls in my chest, rushing to the surface before I can stop it as the shadows whisper in my ear indecipherably.

"He is *mine*," I spit at her, my hand tightening on my sword and my fangs baring. "Touch him and I will rip you apart."

Beinon's head jerks slightly, suspicion written in his eyes.

"*Efia*," Ansel calls out my name in my mind now, like a prayer. Like a rueful plea, and I look at him in confusion.

Queen Lilah laughs. "That's some temper on you, girl. Do you think *I* will hurt him?"

I glance towards Beinon, confused at the rising tension in the air and looking for some indication of understanding of the queen's words. He looks crestfallen.

"Release him," I tell her.

"Girl," she huffs. "He was never captured." She snaps her fingers and the guards holding Ansel's arm release him, allowing him to stand as he turns to give the queen a pointed gaze. "Why would I hurt my *child* when he has delivered you to me so nicely?"

The thread slackens, and I can feel its distance as I focus on the words that left her mouth.

Ansel, who is unrestrained, standing mere feet from the queen, shakes his head with a heartbreaking expression on his face—but he denies nothing.

His mother… his *mother*.

"You are lying!" I shout at her. "Beinon, tell me this is a falsehood!" My head turns in his direction, pleading, wishing my *friend* would look at me.

Was he ever your friend?

"Beinon?" I ask, turning my gaze to him but he looks away.

Beinon, my supposed *friend*, avoids my gaze as the realisation hangs heavy in the air. Ansel, my companion, my…

He is the offspring of the very queen who wanted me dead. Betrayal grips my heart, a bitter taste of anguish. Queen Lilah smirks, enjoying the chaos she's unleashed.

Ansel's eyes meet mine, a silent plea for understanding, and my world unravels in the wake of his familial treachery.

"I would not lie, child," she smiles. "Ansel was my alternative plan. And by the look and smell of them, Beinon, my disappointing child, did a better job of capturing her affections than *you*." Queen Lilah laughs, and it sounds like a birdsong, but it grates along my nerves like a dull knife.

"What?" I ask, not understanding her meaning.

"Did you honestly think my son, the prince and future ruler, would choose you of his own accord?" Queen Lilah asks cruelly, looking gleeful.

I catch Beinon's eyes, my brows meeting in the middle, and he looks in pain.

The queen continues. "He has cultivated your friendship, your fondness over many years, under my instruction. I knew the day would come where you would be in our way—a steppingstone towards my quest for the throne once I got rid of the High King."

Got rid of… the High King?

"You… you killed Gwydion?" I ask.

I always knew there was more to his death, but there had never been any proof.

Queen Lilah tilts her head. "Years! Years it took me to find something that could get around those shadows of his. The human realm is an interesting place. Did you know they have an incredible water creature with spines, and the toxin from it is so deadly, it can make any living being appear to have died from a bad heart?" Her laugh is piercing, and several birds take flight from a nearby tree. "As if our kind could die from such a thing. But I was thrilled when the pixie told me, of course. And as she usually flicks in and out of the realm, I had her procure me some."

Pixie?

"Jill," I whisper.

"Precisely," the queen grins.

That's why Jill made a bargain with me. She wanted protection *from* me, since she knew I would find out.

I try not to choke on these truths.

The insane and gargantuan amount of hurt threatens to suffocate me. Like the boot of my father pressing down upon my chest has been replaced with a heavier one.

This probably hurts worse than Ansel's betrayal.

Because Uncle Gwydion was the only family I had that treated me like I was more than a weapon. He… showed me loved when I didn't receive it from my father.

He gave me a reprieve from the pain and torment.

How ironic that something from the very realm he was fascinated with would kill him.

I feel like my world crumbles around me, movements of those around me slow as my chest tightens, every nerve in my body electrifying and feeling more sharp than any knife.

Ansel and Beinon, pawns in her game, orchestrated relationships with me, showing me what kindness could be like.

But it was fake.

Gwydion's death, a fabrication—a cruel ruse.

Jill, the pixie, traded secrets for protection, ensnaring me in a bargain, so I am unable to punish her.

The weight of it all presses upon me, and the tapestry of my existence unravels, leaving me adrift in a sea of lies. The person I thought I was and the friends I thought I had—all shattered, leaving only the disorienting echo of years built on falsehoods.

On trust… I built on falsehoods.

Fuck, my father had been right.

My shades rise like mists, swirling around my arms as I feel a poisonous rage inside.

"*Mathonwy, I swear, it is not what it seems!*" His voice brushes against my mind and I can't bear it. "*Please, just—*"

I bare my teeth at him in a hiss and his words cut off.

I should just kill them all.

But it is daylight, and I'm losing blood, dizziness blurring the edges of my vision.

"The High King was growing old," the queen continues. "He no longer cared for the courts—"

"He cared more about peace between the courts than anyone!"

"We do not want peace!" The queen rages, her eyes enlarging slightly.

She does not want peace.

"Then why does it matter? Why go to all the effort of *forcing* my company upon your son?" Beinon flinches at that. "It was not guaranteed that I would win this contest!"

"You were always destined to win, you *stupid* child… you are the only one with a *rightful* claim," she spits out in my direction.

"I… Only a child can inherit the throne of their parents," I whisper.

Queen Lilah's lip curls in disgust. "Exactly."

Ansel sucks in a sharp breath, and I finally understand. Why the king and queen hated me so. The arguments between Uncle and my father. Why Bron had isolated me and trained me from such a young age—had not loved me, had not cared for me. But had honed me, ensuring I didn't need a weapon.

Because I was one.

Gwydion was my father.

I look up and catch Beinon's eye. "Why?" I ask him, and his expression looks devastated. Why did he go along with it?

Queen Lilah smiles again. "It dances and skips, it's read in the eyes, but it cheats with the hips," she calls out so eloquently, and I am reminded of the large maze owl. "If it meets its match, it's easily caught, but it's worth nothing if it is bought."

My breath hitches, Beinon's gaze falling to the ground as Ansel growls lowly.

"The heart," I whisper.

"Precisely," Queen Lilah whispers. "What better way to take care of an enemy than to own their heart?"

I suppress the angry disappointment as my faint shades brush against my cheeks, my hair... suppress the twisting in my chest as Beinon refuses to look at me. But it is the cracking and tightening of my heart that takes my breath away as Ansel approaches me.

The bond flares in my chest, wanting his touch. But I slap away his hands as he reaches out to me, Queen Lilah's face grinning behind him.

"I trusted you!" I shout at him, disgusted I have allowed someone in and been betrayed. Furious that fate has bonded me to my enemy. My father—no, Bron—was always right. Right to have treated me so cruelly and try to suppress those emotions rising in me. Because this is worse than any wound.

"Efia, I am so sorry—"

But the queen has seen his expression. She lets out a high, tinkling shriek of amusement. "Oh, my dear boy, don't tell me you have *fallen* for the girl?"

A muscle in Ansel's cheek twitches as he clenches his teeth.

The queen tuts at him before exhaling deeply through her upturned nose.

A portal suddenly opens beside them, and *Bron* steps through, with Arawn following closely.

Bron's expression is a cruel, satisfied smirk as he directs his gaze toward the queen. She acknowledges him with a nod.

She smiles, a cruel, twisted thing. "Ah, the final matter of business."

Bron's triumphant countenance falters as he notices the dismembered head of King Lew. Before he can utter a word of inquiry, a sickening squelch fills the air, and blood dribbles from the corner of his mouth.

His gaze drops, and he spots the silver blade protruding from his chest. Behind him, Arawn regards him with undisguised disgust.

"Arawn!" I exclaim, my voice filled with shock.

Bron's eyes meet mine for a split second, but they betray no emotion before Arawn rips the blade free and

Bron collapses to the floor.

      Unconscious… but not dead.

All I ever wanted was for Efia to be happy. To be more than what Bron had tried to make her. At the time, I didn't truly understand what had happened. But after everything that day, I saw the exact moment the darkness settled in her eyes. The exact moment I lost her.

RECOVERED JOURNAL FROM WEN SUKINO

CHAPTER THIRTY-ONE

"Arawn?" I repeat. My chest hurts from the broken rib, but also from the overwhelming abundance of everything that is happening. Everything changing so quickly.

The queen nods appreciatively. "Thank you, Arawn."

My fists clench, and I can feel my anger simmering beneath the surface. "You..." My voice is quiet but laced with disbelief. "You've been working for her this whole time?"

Arawn's gaze remains fixed on Bron's still form, his eyes clouded with a sense of resolve. "I did it for you, Efia," he says quietly, almost as if seeking my understanding.

My heart sinks at his words, a sick feeling settling in my stomach. "For me?" I whisper, my voice barely audible.

Arawn nods, his expression conflicted. "I believed this was the only way to set you free."

I scoff. "Do I look *free* to you? Do not use me to ease your guilt. What have you been promised for this?"

I don't need to ask, I can guess. I laugh with the realisation.

"Hail to the new king of the Unseelie court," I tip my head towards him in a mock bow, and he flinches.

I wish it was night. Wish we were under the cover of darkness so I could use my shades to rip them all apart. There's an unfamiliar surge of magic in my veins, dying to rip from my skin and tear through theirs. But I cannot. The strength has left me for now.

I can't find any other words to express my disgust. Arawn's misguided loyalty, his belief that he was protecting me from Bron's cruelty, fills me with a profound sense of unease. The truth is, Bron, my father, had been harsh and demanding, but I had never wanted Arawn to resort to such drastic measures.

Because since I had found out he wasn't my father. Since I had seen him walk through that portal… I had wanted to end Bron myself.

Knew that I could.

Arawn and the queen have stolen something from me.

Even in my hatred of him… Bron deserved better than a betrayal like that. Or maybe that was my internalised loyalty to a fae who had shown me nothing but disdain for my entire life. But at least now I understood why. I had never been his. I had been *his* niece.

Then why had Gwydion allowed him to treat me in such a way?

The queen watches our exchange with a calculating gaze, seemingly unperturbed by the turmoil in our midst. "Arawn, you have proven your loyalty to me," she states coldly. "You may leave us. Tell your Guild and the Unseelie court of King Lew's untimely demise. Guards, take Bron to the dungeons and get rid of the body before the others get here."

With a wave of a guard's hand, the earth below King Lew's body opens, swallowing his remains before closing around him, leaving no trace of what has happened. Two guards quickly take hold of Bron and take him through a portal.

I wonder what story the queen has come up with to cover up Lew's death. To prevent an Unseelie uprising.

Arawn walks away through a portal, leaving me with the queen and the gruesome aftermath of her revenge. Arawn's intentions may have been rooted in a twisted sense of protection, but the consequences are undeniable.

"Now come, dear. We really must be off," the queen says, her tone dripping with faux sweetness.

I take an unsteady step in her direction, prepared to end her even if it means my death, but with a casual wave of her hand, thick roots burst from the ground at my feet. They coil around my legs with a vice-like grip, rendering me immobile. I glare at her, understanding now where Ansel got his earthen magic from. Ansel storms towards me but his mother tuts, and he pulls up short.

"*Good* boy," I hiss in his direction, and he looks away.

Her eyes meet mine, and there's a cold amusement in her gaze. "Not so fast, Efia."

I struggle against the earthy restraints, but they hold me fast, leaving me with no choice but to listen. "Where are you taking me?" I demand, my voice laced with both defiance and fear.

The queen's lips curl into a sinister smile. "Why, home, of course? You are the winner, and therefore the rightful queen. You shall have your coronation."

Her words send shivers down my spine, and I can't afford to take them lightly.

"Why?"

Her teeth flash as she clenches them hard, her composure momentarily slipping before she takes a calming breath. "I needed contingencies in case my son lost to you in this contest. Let us not pretend you have not crawled your way under my son's skin. *Both* of them. Beinon is weak. He will not kill you."

My gaze shifts to Beinon, and the truth is written all over his face, a mixture of guilt and helplessness.

"You are to marry Beinon. And he will be your king," the Queen declares with a chilling finality.

My eyes drift to Ansel, who wears an expression of horror. Beside the queen, Beinon's jaw clenches tightly. It's clear that neither of them was aware of this plan.

"You are out of your mind," I laugh, and the widening of the queen's eyes does make her look quite insane.

She, however, remains composed. "I do not think so, Efia. You see, I always knew you would win this contest. And despite my efforts to ensure you fell for Beinon's charms, I could not guarantee that you would let him live during the last trial. So, I took measures to ensure your... cooperation."

Dread washes over me as I realise the depth of her manipulation. I clench my fists, willing them not to shake. "What did you do?"

But it's the sudden appearance of another portal beside Ansel, summoned by Beinon's fingers snapping together, that catches my eye. Through it comes a figure with thick brown curls, escorted by a royal guard.

"Wen." I whimper and try to take a step forward but prevented from doing so by the roots, my heart aching at the sight of my friend.

Ansel takes a step in her direction and a snarl breaks free from my throat, my fangs baring at him.

He may be my mate, and his death would destroy me. But if it came down to Wen and him, it was an easy choice. I would kill him to stop him from harming her. I would tear my own heart in two, but I would shove my sword through his chest if it meant saving her.

His steps falter, his expression torn between

concern and a sense of duty.

This is so much worse than I ever could have anticipated. I had a gut instinct there was more to the queen's interference over the past few months. But I never truly knew the depth of her desperation and greed.

If she could murder Gwydion, what would stop her from killing Wen?

I catch my friend's teary gaze. My sister by choice, not by blood. Her fate is woven into my very being. Our bond is sewn together by moonlight and shadow. Without her, there is no me.

I will do whatever it takes to protect her.

The queen's teeth flash. "Now, where were we?"

"*You don't have to do this, Efia,*" Ansel rushes out, his voice filled with desperation.

"Silence your tongue, child of mine," the queen snaps, her tone cold and unforgiving… and it all makes sense. The mother who *scarred* him. The mother who cursed him. Of course, it couldn't have been anyone other than Queen Lilah. A faerie who only sees her children as tools.

"*I'm not, nor shall I ever be a child of yours,*" Ansel bites back defiantly, still hiding his ability to actually speak now. But my attention is not on their argument; it's on my best friend, Wen, standing beside them.

I'm sorry, Wen mouths in my direction, before a sob escapes her lips. The sound feels like a crack in my chest, and I can't bear to see her like this. The queen's guard tightens his grip on her arm, his sword loose held in his other hand.

"Don't," I warn Queen Lilah, my voice trembling with anger and despair.

Beinon's throat bobs nervously, his expression torn between loyalty to his mother and his inner turmoil at having betrayed his friends.

"The choice is not mine, Efia. It is yours alone," Queen Lilah declares with a cruel smile. "Defy my wishes, and you'll see exactly how merciless I can be. *Or* marry my son, and your friend's life will be spared."

"No, Efia!" Wen cries out, struggling against the tight hold of the guard restraining her, but her efforts are in vain.

I fight hard not to tear up as I look at her, my heart aching with guilt and helplessness. I flash a hateful gaze at Beinon, unable to comprehend how he could have allowed this, how he could have taken Wen from her home and offered her to his mother as a bargaining chip.

His brow furrows with regret, but it's too little, too late.

Turn it off.

I inhale deeply, focusing to centre myself for what I must do.

This will hurt, but it will be for the best.

"The lunar faerie has been good company, but she means no more to me than Bron did." I force out in a drawl. Everyone's movement stops for a second.

I can't even look at Wen.

The queen narrows her eyes, but my gaze flicks to Beinon, who recovers and masks his expression.

I'm hoping with everything I have that Beinon has downplayed my friendship with Wen. Hoping to Corph that he has not completely sold me out.

She is probably my only weakness.

Bron couldn't act against it, not whilst she lived in the Seelie court. But Wen is not protected from the queen.

I must not show it, not if I am to keep some power in this situation.

"If it means I can stop *more* useless killing and avoiding the complete chaos of an all-out war between the courts… I'm assuming you wish to strike a bargain?" I ask, my voice hollow with resignation.

"No!" Wen's muffled voice calls out before the guard's hand rises to cover her mouth. I can see the apology in her eyes, and it tears at my soul. Wen will bear the guilt of feeling like I gave in for her. What she doesn't know is there never would have been another option. I will not allow her to come to harm if I can help it.

"Of course." The queen smiles, her excitement clouding her judgement for a second as she forgets her suspicion. If I break this bargain, it means my life—and possibly Wen's—will be forfeit.

My teeth worry the inside of my cheek as my brain ricochets from idea to idea, looking for a way out through this. I catch Ansel's eye, and he can see my mind has been made up. He shakes his head with horror written on his face.

"I accept," I tell her, and Beinon's face morphs into one of shock. "But I have conditions of my own."

Queen Lilah's brow raises in amused intrigue.

"I will marry your son," I say. "But we shall take residence in the High Castle. Gwydion's late home. We shall not reside with you in the Seelie court."

Queen Lilah's eyes roll as if this was obvious.

"Anything else?" she asked.

"I will not raise my swords against you—"

"Ah, ah. You shall not raise your swords, or *shadows* against me."

My teeth clench painfully.

"Fine," I say. "I shall not raise my swords or shades against you. And Branwen is to come with me. She is to remain *unharmed* by you or by your instruction, from your guards, your kin, or your subjects."

"I don't think her living—"

"We are striking a bargain," my voice rose. "So, what does it matter *where* she resides?"

"True." Queen Lilah's grin is vicious, ecstatic she is about to get exactly what she wants.

I swallow hard, catching Ansel's eye once more. His suspicious and contemplative gaze never wavers from my face.

"Finally," I say. "Ansel will accompany me as my own personal guard."

"Why—"

"Going once." I hold my hand in front of me for

her to clasp.

Her head jerks and eyes narrow. But I need to ensure she doesn't have time to think about it in detail.

"Going twice!"

She rushes down the few steps before her, coming to stand in front of me with her nostrils flaring.

"Deal," she hisses, grasping my hand.

There is a moment. A split second where I want to slice my sword forward, embed it into her black heart, and hear her cries of death. But it would also mean my death.

My death without protecting Wen first.

Instead, I let myself succumb to the bargain. My head falls forward with the magic that flows between our hands. My palm burns for a moment and then ceases. When we let go of each other, I glance at my hand, spotting the rune for promise upon my palm. My fingertip traces over it but I feel no change to the smoothness there.

My lips part as I exhale, looking at Wen. Her mouth is still covered but she looks between my sword and the queen. A silent instruction.

But I shake my head.

I would not dare put Wen's life in danger—not even to kill the monster before me.

Bron's furious voice screams at me in my head. I have allowed someone to become a weakness. To take my power.

Queen Lilah takes a step back, eyeing the rune

upon her own hand, before she looked up at me with such a gleeful expression—looking ten years younger as she allows the vines to retreat from my legs. I collapse to my knees, holding a hand up when Ansel comes forward.

I do not want him touching me.

"My son... Efia." I jerk at my name on her lips for the first time. She clasps her hands in front of her as she walks back up the dais. "We shall prepare for your wedding in two moons time."

My breaths are heavy. "Two moons—"

"Shall we make it one moon?" Queen Lilah asks smugly, and I hiss at her. She waits a moment before I nod, my chest cracking with the horror of leaving Bron's control, only to enter the queens.

Ansel's eyes widen, his head shaking imperceptibly as my sword escapes my grip, falling to the floor as tears prick my eyes.

"Get her," the queen calls out casually to her guards. "Take her to her new home and get her ready for her coronation."

Right now, I feel out of control. I feel weak. And as those strong hands take a hold of me, carrying me towards the castle, I do not fight them.

But I look closely at those I pass.

Wen, begging her to forgive me with my gaze.

Beinon. The heartbreak reflected in his eyes as he stares back at me.

I can barely look at Ansel, so my eyes pass over him quickly, landing on his mother.

The feeling of hatred that fills me is almost all-consuming, my fangs lengthening and resting against my bottom lip as I resist the powerful urge to throw the guards from me. Queen Lilah grins back with an expression of satisfaction—believing she has won.

I capture Beinon's gaze again.

And he *finally* sees.

He sees me for who I am. For what they have forced me to become.

Now, he *knows*.

He knows what will come for them.

Because Lilah's own expression lets me know as soon as her son has a crown, this will only end with my death... or her own.

The High King is dead.
His heir soon to take his place.
Let the games begin…

Art by Frankie Lupo

Acknowledgements

Thank YOU for taking the time to come on this ride with Efia. I hope you enjoyed the games.

This book came entirely out of nowhere. I was knee deep in writing book three of The Stag and Hollow Chronicles when Efia shattered her way into my mind and demanded to be written.

And I'm so glad she did.

I wrote this story whilst undergoing therapy for childhood trauma, and it has been incredibly healing for me doing both at the same time.

I can't thank Efia enough for this. And I know she will find peace in the next stage of her journey.

Now. Onto those who helped me with this little story!

Christana! The very first person who ever laid eyes on this tale! She has been one of my biggest supporters on my author journey and I trust her implicitly. Whether it's editing advice, character development or emotions, I know I can go to her for anything. Thank you, my dear friend!

My beautiful editor, Brittany Corley. You made my final draft infinitely better (and certainly more readable). I love seeing what you do with people's stories, and only wish you would hurry up and finish writing your own, knowing how beautiful you are able to express yourself and the emotions of the characters you create. You are insanely talented, compassionate and I am so grateful I met you online. P.S – When are you visiting Wales?

To my street team and those in my reader group, who always hype me up and make me feel better when I'm feeling burnt out with making content. You guys are so awesome, and I love every one of you.

My family at large – so many to name. I am so lucky to have a network who are incredibly supportive. As always, a big thank you to my rock – my Mammy. A special shout out to my Auntie Jill, who is named within this story! Hope you enjoyed being a pixie haha!

Lastly, to my gorgeous immediate family: Eleanor, Olivia, and hubby Caeron. You know I love you so much. My very own book boyfriend Cae. You have your moments, but I couldn't hope or wish for a bigger supporter of my dreams.

Now make me a cup of tea, time for book two!

Photo by Jack Harper

Amazon bestselling author of fantasy, Gem L Preston, comes from a small town in South Wales. It was there that she was influenced by the mythology and legends of her country and that, along with her love of video games, led to the creation of her debut series: The Stag & Hollow Chronicles.

Her characters are brave and outgoing, but in real life, Gem is scared of moths and loves nothing more than relaxing with a cup of tea. She wouldn't last one night without being able to charge her kindle!

When she is not writing (or trying to write whilst her two demon daughters run wild), Gem spends most of her time reading, gaming or spending time with her family and friends. A passionate member of perhaps too many fandoms, Gem loves nothing more than indulging in Marvel/Harry Potter/Star Wars theories—a passionate discussion is probably one of her favourite things.

Gem has been living with an incurable disease known as IIH for over a decade, something which she tries to raise awareness of often. She also has a heart condition and, knowing how these types of conditions can affect not just the physical health but mental health of a person, she loves speaking to others who deal with chronic illnesses.

Milton Keynes UK
Ingram Content Group UK Ltd.
UKHW040852030724
444933UK00004B/46